Danger Bearing Press

Credits:

Edited by Mollie Traver and Linda Ingmanson

Cover Design by Deranged Doctor Design

ALEX LIDELL

GREAT FALLS ROGUE

POWER OF FIVE BOOK 6

ALSO BY ALEX LIDELL

New Adult Fantasy Romance

POWER OF FIVE (Reverse Harem Fantasy)

POWER OF FIVE (Audiobook available)

MISTAKE OF MAGIC (Audiobook available)

TRIAL OF THREE (Audiobook available)

LERA OF LUNOS (Audiobook available)

GREAT FALLS CADET (Audiobook available)

GREAT FALLS ROGUE

GREAT FALLS PROTECTOR

IMMORTALS OF TALONSWOOD (Reverse Harem Paranormal Romance)

LAST CHANCE ACADEMY

Young Adult Fantasy Novels

TIDES

FIRST COMMAND (Audiobook available)

AIR AND ASH (Audiobook available)

WAR AND WIND (Audiobook available)

SEA AND SAND (Audiobook available)

SCOUT

TRACING SHADOWS (Audiobook available)

UNRAVELING DARKNESS (Audiobook available)

TILDOR

THE CADET OF TILDOR

~

SIGN UP FOR NEW RELEASE NOTIFICATIONS at https://links.alexlidell.com/News

CONTENTS

PART I: CLOCK STRIKES MIDNIGHT

1

LERA

My sword whistles as it cuts the night air, putting down a salivating sclice. I jump back, panting as the hog beast makes a final swipe at me before stilling. Sword high, I survey the forest over my weapon's tip, my heart drumming a strong steady beat against my chest. With my amulet off, everything inside me feels lighter. More alive. More tuned in to sound and touch and air.

More able to appreciate the dead sclice's stench.

I wrinkle my nose. This night's sclice is the third one I've put down this week—the tenth since I started these amulet-free nightly excursions a month ago. The spill of Mors's rodents and other magical refuse is increasing with the approach of the spring equinox—Ostera—the change no more pleasant for being expected. Like the other sclices I've seen here, this beast is distorted, its mottled skin revealing a pattern of warts, including one in that odd snowflake-like shape that Gavriel thinks serves as a crude rune of sorts, making the thing invisible to humans and veil-wearing fae.

My body's energy still singing from a good fight, I feel the forest come back into focus around me—the soft cracks of nocturnal animals, the heavy scent of damp pine. And with a deep breath, I force myself to get on with the true goal of today's outing: collecting another sample from a Yocklol tree to help Gavriel and Arisha develop something to neutralize the damn things. I know that we are but containing the damage, that more horrors will keep coming until I can find and mend the tear in the fabric keeping the mortal realms magic-free, but that makes the Yocklols no less of a problem.

Despite appearing to have a trunk and vine-like branches, Yocklols aren't true trees but rather mixes of creature and vegetation—just the latest delight leaking in from the dark realms. Yocklols also breed. And move. I've marked five since that young guardsman lost his arm to one last month.

On the bright side, the increased number makes them easier to find. Leaving the sclice, I follow the trail uphill to where I last saw one of the yellow blights and find the thing tucked between a cluster of aspen trees. Piercing the night's darkness with my fae vision, I can see the yellow slime covering the Yocklol limbs. It shimmers slightly but calls little attention to itself otherwise. Unfortunately for anything that likes staying alive, one touch of the slime to flesh, and there is no stopping the resulting pus-ridden corruption.

"Let's get this over with," I mutter, glaring at the Yocklol, with its one eye—closed for now—and shivering deadly branches. Drawing a glass vial out of my satchel, I slide the wide mouth slowly onto a tentacle-like tip. Slowly lifting my blade, I do a quick final survey of my gear. Leather gloves. Soft leather padded suit. Boots well tied and ready to run. Good. Taking a deep breath, I bring the edge of the blade down on the sleeping limb, scraping the tiniest bit of yellow bark into my vial.

The Yocklol's eye snaps open, the tentacled branches shifting like snakes.

Fighting the urge to bolt, which carries too great a tripping risk, I retreat one step at a time. My pulse quickens, my blood coursing through my tingling legs. It's odd how something that so wishes to kill you can also make you feel alive. Around me, the forest's night sounds are a familiar backdrop, the shifting branches and insistently hooting owl seeming to cheer me on. Another step, my foot checking the ground before taking weight, my gaze trained on the swaying tentacle-like limbs. Yocklol trees aren't fast, but with the damage a single tentacle touch does, they don't need to be.

Feeling a root beneath my foot, I adjust my balance. Three tentacles now slither along the ground, leaving no place to fall safely. My breath stills. *Step. Step. Step*. Inside me, Tye's fire-calling magic flails against its mortal shackles. Before I became fae, my weaver gift required proximity to my males to tap into magic. I echoed their power but had none of my own. Now, although being beside the males magnifies our strength manyfold, the cords of magic coiling inside me are my own. Shadows of Tye's fire, and River's earth, and Shade's healing, and Coal's strange inward-turned magic, all quiver within my blood.

Each day, I think a fraction of my power might break free. But not today. Not now.

A yellow tentacle suddenly whips toward me, fast as a striking snake.

My arm moves on reflex, the sword's honed edge severing the vine in midair. Falling to the ground with a soft thunk, the pace-long tip continues thrashing.

I curse. Separated from the trunk, the severed tentacle will continue flailing about, killing anything that might touch it. Forever. I'll have to come back and clean up before we have blight-struck animals running about with boils, making the humans realize the extent to which things are going wrong.

Step. Step. Step. Reaching back with my foot, I take the final stride to escape the Yocklol's reach. The thing continues stretching toward me, but the trunk moves much more slowly than the tentacles. In other words, I'm finally safe to run like hell.

Corking the sample vial, I tuck it securely into my satchel and lope through the now-familiar forest, my immortal eyes seeing the dirt trail and shivering pine branches plainly under the starlit sky. With the tall stone wall looming before me, I locate the covered exit of the escape passage leading back into the Academy and lower myself inside. A pool of ink-black darkness greets me, the ground invisible even in daylight. Hanging off the ledge with my feet dangling over the blackness, I take a breath, brace myself, and let go.

~

"You look feral." Arisha's voice greets me as I climb out of the passage amidst a thick cluster of trees and hedges lining the inside of the Academy walls. The fresh scent of evergreens and budding oaks fills my lungs, washing away the mold and stench.

"Is that a compliment?" I brace my hands on my thighs, looking at the brilliant girl whose frizzy brown hair and inability to braid it would no doubt make a scarecrow jealous. Behind her, torches on the tops of the towering Academy walls cast strange shadows on the silent stone, a stern reminder of where we should be right now.

"It's a fact." She taps her ears, then sneezes into her sleeve.

"Oh, right." Suppressing a groan, I snap my veil amulet quickly around my neck. A tightness settles over my skin at once, the pressure of the veil amulet's magic battling against my body's desire for freedom. Each time, it seems to become a little more difficult to make the transition, the veil's magic fighting harder for control against my body's rebellion. The pendant heats against my skin, insisting that I'm human, an Academy cadet, nothing more.

"Stars," Arisha mutters. "I know you've not moved, but I swear I saw a fae female leave and a human Lera walk over. It's unsettling every damn time. Do you have my new toy?"

"And you called me feral?" Surrendering the sample vial, I retrieve a cloak I stashed beneath the bushes and throw it over my leathers. If I'm caught now, I'm just a student breaking curfew with a stroll through the woods, not a renegade ready to bring down River's wrath. "I took down another sclice, by the way."

"That isn't a *by the way*, Lera." Arisha blocks my path. Planting her hands on her hips, she glares like a schoolmarm—her puffy red eyes and nose somewhat spoiling the image. She wears an all-black outfit similar to mine—because "black is the color of espionage"—that makes her pale face seem to float in the moonlight. "This is getting out of hand—and don't you tell me that you ran into the thing by sheer accident, because you lie as well as I do handstands. What if there had been more of them? You can't be romping about by your—"

"Gavriel thinks I can," I say quickly.

"Good try, but Uncle Gavriel thinks the sun will change direction if a book says so." Arisha adjusts her glasses, her voice stuffy as it has been ever since the flowers began to bloom. "I'm not saying stop fighting. I'm saying stop doing it alone. Moving the dead sclice to where River's patrols are likely to find it is a simple enough thing and will get the other fae involved."

"No."

"River wouldn't know it's you who put the beast down, but he'll certainly go out with Coal and Shade to do some cleanup," Arisha continues as if I'd not spoken, acting more like her uncle than she would care to admit. "It would take the pressure off. And eventually, you can work up to going out together without needing to say anything that would trigger their veil magic."

"No," I repeat. "First, the sclices have wart patterns that make them near invisible to humans—I can take off my amulet and see the rodents, but the males can't. They shouldn't be fighting what they can't see. And second…" I adjust my cloak, buying a heartbeat to gather myself. "Second, you were right when you said I should accept them as the personas they are now—and the personas they are now don't know me. Might not even like me if they did. When I go out, I need to take off my amulet and be myself, not some pretense of a noble lady I'm not."

"What happened to team, and quint, and mates?"

"A cracked rune tablet." After a month, the words have almost stopped stinging. Even after I laid out the virtues of joining forces against magic's threat so plainly that even Princess Katita bent the knee, the males still see me as nothing but a first-year cadet. River cares for little beyond my obeying rules and curfew; Coal goes out of his way to avoid physical contact with me even during training; Shade is too busy with all the girls lining up for sick call to even notice my existence; and Tye… Tye wants to talk. To reconcile the intensity of our unintended coupling against his Prowess training commitment. I've nothing to say to that. After serving in Zake's stable, one would think I'd have learned the dangers of relying on men—but apparently, I'd needed a sharp reminder.

"I've my hands full enough trying to stanch magic bleeding into the mortal world without also chasing cocks, Arisha." I give her a smile. "Besides, I've you and Gavriel and, err, Ruffle. And I did get you that beautiful snot-yellow Yocklol sample to play with, didn't I?"

Arisha sighs—not in acquiescence, but in a *we'll talk about this later* way. "You are exhausted. I took the liberty of writing up your essay on Ckridel's role in the Continental Alliance."

My shoulders tense. "Arisha—"

"If someone told me a year ago that my role in helping keep the mortal realm from doom would be through doing extra homework, I would have sent the messenger to the asylum. But reality is that there is no physical way you can fight evil by night, attend classes, muck stalls for three hours, *and* do homework. Once your stall duties finally finish tomorrow, the work is all yours." She pats my shoulder. "But for tonight—copy the paper before bed. Neatly. It doesn't do anyone any good if my brilliant words are all lost beneath smudges that make it seem like Rabbit wrote them. And truly, don't worry. With Ostera holidays coming up, we'll all be able to catch up on rest and studying soon enough. A week of liberty is going to feel like the stars' own gift by then."

I force a smile, thanking the stars Arisha can't hear my heart's sudden thundering. My friend still thinks it's only the lack of time that's keeping me back in class, and I can't bear to tell my genius friend—who thinks the *teachers* slow of mind—that I can barely read.

Slipping inside the room, I shed my leathers, stashing them beneath the bed, and fall into my cot. The cot groans, sharp lupine claws expressing their dissatisfaction with having their space encroached upon by some interloper. No wonder Arisha was so eager to sneak out of the room to meet me. I poke Shade. Push him. Brace against his sizable bulk and shove with all my might. The wolf twitches one ear, his eyes piously closed. Feigning deep sleep, the bastard. Fine. Carving out a spot against Shade's side, I curl up against his fur and capture the last few hours of sleep.

2

LERA

"Leralynn of Osprey proposes that Ckridel's role in the Continental Alliance was defined by self-preservation." Master Daniel's voice from the front of the room breaks through my haze of fatigue.

A moment later, Arisha's foot hits my shin. Hard. Then she sneezes.

Blinking my eyes open, I force my mind into a rapid survey of the battlefield. The individual wooden desks, each with a well for ink, stand in a semicircle of rows around a high-ceilinged classroom. The scent of someone too fond of rose perfume fills the thick air, mixing with the dust on the thick red curtains. Despite the pleasantly cool weather outside, the room is as stuffy as the bald master at the front of it—tall stained-glass windows let in streams of tinted light, but no air to speak of. The formal court attire we wear to academic classes little helps the cause either. Sitting at the back of the classroom, I've the protection of three dozen heads separating me from the instructor's dais—usually enough to guard against extra attention. Today, however, that fortune seems to have run out.

At the front of the room, Daniel is now pacing in front of a large chalk slate. "Princess Katita, on the other hand, asserts that Ckridel's role came from benevolence. Leralynn, could you summarize your thoughts for the class?"

Heads turn toward me as I rise to my feet, my face blazing. Despite what Arisha thinks, I can't even *understand* most of what she writes for me.

"This should be entertaining," Katita whispers to the girl beside her, my immortal hearing picking up the snicker without fail. Her silky sheaf of white-blond hair is clipped back behind her ears, an innocent look that clashes with the shrewdness in her turquoise eyes.

I clear my throat, my gaze darting to the window to check the sun's position. At least half an hour of the class still left.

"We are all here, Lady Leralynn," Daniel prompts.

Chuckles echo through the room. Even the two girls who were busy sketching outfit ideas for the upcoming Ostera ball put aside their side whispers to enjoy the new entertainment. Bloody Ostera. While the Academy readies to celebrate spring and fertility, all I can think of is the surge of magic the moon will bring that night.

"Could you repeat the question, please, sir?" I ask.

Daniel's lips press together, the sun's rays reflecting off his polished head. "Please tell us why you believe self-preservation was the driving force behind Grendel's actions in the establishment of the Continental Alliance."

On my left, I can feel Arisha's expectant stare. Here goes nothing. "Because, self-preservation is the force behind all decisions," I say. Nice and philosophical and—most importantly—can be argued based on common sense instead of the reading.

Daniel rocks back on his heels. I think he is waiting for me to continue.

I go to sit down instead.

"What about moral high ground, benevolence, love?" Daniel prompts, his glare enough to keep me on my feet.

"What about them, sir?"

Flashes of smirks and smiles ripple through the room, the public support swaying momentarily to my side.

Arisha covers her eyes. I'm sure she wrote something painstakingly brilliant on the topic and expects me to share it instead of antagonizing the teacher. Which I'd love to be doing as well, if not for reality getting in the way.

"I'm not finding your word games amusing, Lady Leralynn." Daniel's face colors, splotches of red nearly as bright as the trim on his black robes creeping up his bald scalp. When he speaks again, his words seem forced, as if he's battling for self-control. "Please explain to us how you believe these factors influence decisions and actions."

I spread my palms. "Unpredictably."

This time, a wave of outright chuckling races through the room, turning Daniel's face a new shade of red altogether.

Behind me, a small familiar creak of the floorboards sends a sudden hush over the room, the shift in atmosphere leaving no doubt as to the newcomer's identity.

Sure enough, a heartbeat later, I mark River striding along the side wall, his hands clasped behind his back. Observing the class. Or checking on me. Ever since I took a stand against Katita last month, I've felt River's eyes on me from across the dining hall or library or courtyard. He never comes anywhere near me—as if impulsive, reckless behavior might be catching—but he watches. Worried lest I do something to help the world without his permission, I suppose.

Dressed in a simple red silk shirt and flowing black pants that contour his muscular thighs and taper to a taut waist, River's strong lines are impossible to ignore.

The girls who'd been sketching dresses quickly cover their work, the male cadets sitting up straighter. Three steps, and River has morphed a chamber full of self-important lordlings into nervous cubs. Even the air in the chamber shifts, gaining a spicy tinge of anxiety.

Stars. No wonder Daniel is so bloody furious to be caught off-balance. In my defense, calling on me to speak while the deputy headmaster was in the room wasn't my idea.

Reaching back for my chair, I try a second attempt at disappearing.

"Come up here, if you please, Lady Leralynn," Daniel snaps, spittle flying from his lips as he points to a spot before him.

River stops walking, his perfect face unreadable.

"Now, Leralynn." Daniel jabs with his finger.

Stomach tight, I force myself to walk forward with a feigned confidence that seems to ratchet up Daniel's choler while not fooling River for a heartbeat. When I walk past the male, I can't help noting the tight set of his strong jaw, his woodsy scent waking my body to his presence—as if any more such reminder was needed.

"Do you imagine yourself funny?" Daniel demands over the class's greedy silence as I stop before him. His pale aquiline features are tight with anger.

"No, sir." A trickle of sweat snakes down my nape. *Think calming thoughts. Like… Killing sclices.*

"That's good, because I don't find you funny either," Daniel tells me.

"I'm glad they have that settled," someone murmurs, and I swear I can feel the heat blazing from Daniel spike in reply.

"Hold out your hands," Daniel tells me, his own reaching for a ruler.

My gaze darts about. I've been in an exhausted haze most of the month, but I'd have noticed if this had happened before.

"Your *palm*, Lady Leralynn," Daniel says, a dark glint in his pale eyes. "If you insist on imitating a ten-year-old lordling who can't be bothered to pay attention, then I shall treat you as such."

Over a smattering of snorts, the burn of River's unreadable eyes is a new humiliation. The twin blows of being punished before the class and the secret truth of my ignorance tighten my throat. Not even in Lunos did I let River suspect the extent of my illiteracy, my basic reading skills having carried me well enough through understanding letters and reports.

Resisting the urge to wipe my damp palms on my dress, I present the palm as ordered. And then, because it's better to be thought impertinent than stupid, I raise my chin and meet Daniel's beady eyes. "Does that mean I can be excused afterward, Master Daniel?"

"WHAT WAS THAT NONSENSE, if I might inquire?" River's deep voice cuts between me and Arisha as I try to scurry out at the end of class.

I jump, the books nearly slipping from my hands. We've just made it to the edge of the central courtyard, cadets spilling onto it from every corner under arched trellises of flowers and fluttering pennants—preparations for the annual Ostera ball in full swing. My palms and pride both sting as if set upon by a swarm of bees, but at least Daniel decided to cut his losses and didn't call on me again after punishment. In my world these days, that's apparently a victory.

Beside me, Arisha lets out a mix of a squeak and a sneeze.

River offers her a white handkerchief, which Arisha grabs just in time to catch her next sneeze.

"Thank—*a-CHOO*." Arisha adjusts her glasses, her freckles

standing out even more prominently against her pale skin in River's forbidding presence. "Flowers. I hate flowers."

"Indeed," says River. "You should see Master Shade. He might have something to help."

The tops of Arisha's ears flush—as do every female's at the suggestion of visiting the stunning healer's infirmary—and she throws me a guilty look before hurrying off, River's handkerchief firmly in hand.

I don't begrudge her the retreat—we both know a dismissal when we hear it—but it still leaves me uncomfortably alone with River for the first time in a month. His peripheral scrutiny notwithstanding.

The male is so large that I feel like a miniature toy beside him, his penetrating gray eyes always seeing entirely too much while revealing nothing of their thoughts. Power and responsibility cling to River's woodsy scent, his broad shoulders and dark hair blocking the wind and sky. Making my thighs tingle in spite of myself.

Silence hangs between us, my smarting hands a reminder of the display he just witnessed—and of the more damning truth about my education that I've managed to keep concealed.

Reaching forward slowly, River taps a single finger against the back of my hand. "When I was a boy, my tutor preferred to rap the knuckles," he says with a hint of smile. "I swear it hurt more than the palms, though a few of my friends disagreed."

Yes, River had tutors. *Royal* tutors. I had a pitchfork and piles of manure. *When you were a colt, River, you knew more by age ten than I do at twenty.*

"Why did you bait Master Daniel back there?" he continues, his voice quiet. Serious. As if he really wants to know the truth. "Is there a quarrel between you?"

My gaze sweeps up River's arm. Neatly trimmed nails, palms calloused from weapons training, muscle-corded forearms that give form to his silk shirt of deep red. Golden cufflinks with the Academy crest. Close as we are, I can feel the heat of his body warming the air between us, see the delicate flaring of his nostrils as his heightened sense of smell takes me in.

"No." I bite my lip, wondering if I should have claimed otherwise, tried to throw River off scent. Too late now. "I…I felt cornered."

River's brow rises. "By being asked to repeat the very arguments you'd put down in your own paper?"

By being asked to display how little I understand of anything in the texts, including the ones I copy from Arisha. "I…I don't know."

All of a sudden, River's presence in my space is too much to contend with. With the male's beautiful face now but a few hand widths away and his fresh scent surrounding me, my mouth longs for his taste so fiercely that I can't think. But if the magic-bonded River would have taken me in a heartbeat, the real one—a born and raised king—might not. Especially once he sees me for the ignorant peasant I am.

I step back, moving so quickly that—exhausted as I am—my balance teeters. Tips. The muddy ground rises toward me in tauntingly slow motion.

Strong hands close on my elbows, River's steady arms absorbing my weight as if it were nothing. Steadying me on my feet, he studies my face with an intensity that sends an unwelcome ripple of want all through my core. It is bloody unjust for the warrior to be smart and beautiful and so damn sure of himself that I feel like a drowned rat in comparison.

River's dark brows draw together. "What happened here?" he asks, touching a finger to my temple.

Trickles of heat spider over my skin, accompanied by a light sting and a hard, fast hammering of my heart. I don't actually know what happened—the cut is one of many I've been collecting on my nightly outings. The very nightly outings River would likely whip me for if discovered. Because I'm just a cadet. Nothing more. Not to him.

"I missed one of Lieutenant Coal's high attacks. It won't happen again." I draw air into my lungs, letting the chilly wind cool the turmoil inside me. "May I go, sir?"

"Of course." River steps back quickly, the loss of his presence beside me somehow both a relief and disappointment. Hugging my books securely to my chest, I rush away, my back tingling with the sense of River's eyes watching my every step.

3

RIVER

River splashed cold water on his face, then curled his hands on the edge of the windowsill. From his study in the keep tower, he could see the expanse of the Academy, now strung up with ribbons and flowers for the Ostera ball that had the whole school quivering with anticipation.

The Great Hall itself had been shut down for the past week as Academy staff transformed it into a lantern-lit, silk-strung extravaganza to welcome spring and fertility. River winced, making a mental note to speak to Shade about tonics—in a walled-off fortress filled with young nobles from ten kingdoms, the *fertility* part could lead to disaster.

Drawing a deep breath, River tried to ward off the personal melancholy the date brought. Ostera was about light and life and dancing. Every seamstress from Great Falls to Grayson was busy sewing elaborate Ostera gowns in the colors of a daylit sky, bright yellows, deep golds, and pale blues.

Surveying the courtyard again, River marked the excited chatter, the way everyone seemed to be smiling at the colored silks.

And, as much as he tried to avoid it, River also marked the now-empty spot at the courtyard's edge where he'd nearly pawed a student a quarter hour ago. Leralynn's phantom lilac scent was still making his head spin, and the hint of arousal River had scented when he brushed her cheeks—*stars*. For a moment, the thought of parting Lera's creamy thighs to expose the wetness between them tightened River's cock.

Taking the rest of the water pitcher, he emptied it over his head.

Leralynn was mouthy and impertinent and heady in a way a cadet could not be allowed to be. But she was also brave and selfless and hurting on a level River was struggling to understand, though it roused every protective instinct inside him. The palm swats Daniel had delivered were more humiliating than truly painful, and yet River had nearly taken a swing at the history master for it. River's control of himself had been so tenuous, he'd not even remained to have his intended conversation with the instructor.

Or maybe River was lying even to himself. Maybe be hadn't been getting away from Daniel as much as going after Leralynn. River had *needed* to look into her eyes, to make sure there wasn't terror lurking behind that chocolate gaze like that day in his study.

River glared at his now empty pitcher, the trickles of water soaking his tunic failing to pull down the stirring between his legs. He was being ridiculous. It was the time of year—the coming anniversary of Diana's death on Ostera eve—that was rousing his senses. Making him stupid. River tossed the pitcher aside. There was a better way to deal with stupid than ogling a cadet.

RIVER'S MUSCLES strained against the force of Coal's blade, the sweat streaking down his back soaking his shirt. The light from the setting sun behind their high grassy knoll reflected off the sharp live steel as River circled his sword away from the clash and sprang off his back leg into a new offensive.

High attack left. Slice up off the parry. Twist in a full circle to gain momentum and strike hard enough to take off a man's head. River's assault lacked finesse but brimmed with enough power that he'd not have dared try it against anyone but Coal.

Coal's blazing blue eyes and familiar face, set in deadly concentration, were as grounding as the movement itself.

Clank. Clank. Clank. The ringing metal called a deadly cadence, the sharpness of the blades multiplying the stakes. Demanding every ounce of attention. Every bit of focus. *Clank. Clank. Clank.*

The blades locked beside River's head, Coal's pressing down, River's up. River's thighs burned, his arms trembling with the effort.

With a derisive snort, Coal kicked River in the chest.

River grunted, the force of the warrior's blow making him stumble back.

"You'll have to try harder than that," Coal growled softly, barely sounding winded.

River's breaths came short and fast, his lungs stinging even as he swung his sword tip back to ready guard, watching Coal's lithe body circle like a predator, black pants and bare torso gleaming in the low sunlight. Did the bastard ever get tired? River adjusted his grip, his sweaty palm starting to slide on the sword's hilt.

That one moment of fidgeting, of losing focus, hurled River right back into the very thoughts he'd come to escape.

Leralynn's image came to him unbidden, River's body aching to know what she would look like in the setting sun. He longed to bask in the glowing skin of her bare shoulders, the deep chocolate eyes that had held so much intelligence and compassion when he'd looked into them earlier today. And mistrust. Smart girl. With a body as lush as hers, Leralynn should be wary of men. River doubted there was a single one in the Academy who hadn't dreamt of her at least once since she'd arrived, and that very thought made him want to brush his scent over her. To mark her as his.

Which she wasn't. Leralynn looked like Diana, but she wasn't River's beloved wife. He knew as much with his mind, though his body refused to agree.

"Should I take a nap while you pull your head out of your ass?" Coal asked.

River blinked, then lowered the blade with a rough shake of his head. Anyone but Coal would have injured him in the past seconds, and River knew it. "Is Leralynn having difficulty in morning training?" he asked.

Coal's jaw tightened. "I'm not rutting with her, if that's what you are asking. I've not even sparred with her myself since we spoke."

"I was asking exactly what I intended to ask," River snapped, even as he knew the sudden jab of fury inside him was meant for himself more than for Coal. Then the rest of Coal's statement registered. "Wait. You've not trained with her at all?"

"No." Tension rippled through Coal's bare torso, and River thought he knew exactly how the man felt to be denied Leralynn's company. Though, unlike River, Coal had at least felt Lera's body beneath him once. River didn't know whether that would make it easier or harder—either way, it made it no more appropriate for either of them.

"What about the split brow?" River asked, calling up Lera's words. "Did she earn it from someone else?"

Coal huffed, hefting his sword in his hand like a predator too long denied his chase. "It didn't happen on my watch. Are we fighting or gossiping?"

River's jaw tightened. With anyone but Coal, he'd have dismissed the words as an understandable oversight, but the warrior before him missed nothing. Especially when it came to Lera. "She lied to me," River said, realizing he'd spoken aloud only when Coal answered.

"Yes, she does that."

River's grip on his sword tightened, the unexpected hurt stinging his chest. He shouldn't be bothered. He was in charge of student discipline, for star's sake. Of course a cadet would lie before admitting something that might get her into trouble. And River was too experienced to take such things personally. Or he should be.

"Fight," Coal growled, the sound primal. Feral. As if River's talk of Leralynn had roused something desperate in the man. Before River could so much as salute, Coal was on him, his sword swinging for River's throat.

Clank. Clank. Clank.

The metal sang again, drowning out the world. Waiting until Coal was midstep, River rushed in, his sword swinging in a high-low-side combination so fast and powerful that Coal retreated a step in his parries. The blades clashed with a deafening, deadly ring that promised injury to any unfortunate limb that might get in the way. When the tip of River's blade opened a gash in Coal's biceps, the warrior didn't even blink. Didn't hesitate either.

Allowing the blade to bite him deeper, Coal used the opening to close the distance with River, even though it meant sliding his own flesh along the sharp blade. River's eyes had only a moment to widen before he felt the sharp point of a dagger that Coal had pulled from stars knew where against the soft triangle of his throat.

"Yield." Coal's voice was ice, his blood still dripping onto River's blade.

4

LERA

The sight of Shade leaning against the fence of our training corral, hands stuck casually in his trouser pockets as he speaks with Coal, sends a ripple of energy through me. In some ways, the two males couldn't be more different, Shade's long black hair, kind eyes, and relaxed shoulders an utter contrast to Coal's crossed-arm glare. Yet, the pair's size and power —not to mention their chiseled, beautiful faces—set them apart from the rest of the group. As does my body's instinctual hum upon seeing them together.

I am not the only one humming, it appears. By the time Arisha and I duck under the training yard fence—Arisha sneezing and nearly hitting her head in the process—the female half of the class has migrated closer to the chatting pair. The boys strut about the edges of the court, practice swords in hand and chests out. One hair away from pissing in the corners just to mark their territory.

Coal's gaze catches me as I straighten, his blue eyes dark and feral. The sudden intensity of even such a causal connection sends a ripple of energy along my spine. Unwelcome energy. The male hasn't come near me since we mated in the cave, always calling a change in rotation anytime we come close to facing each other on the sands. It's taken weeks to build up the emotional calluses to feel nothing for the oversight, and I little want to surrender the hard-won shields over a single glance.

"Are we learning field medicine today, Master Shade?" Katita steps close to Shade and Coal, breaching the two paces of empty space everyone else leaves around them. With her long legs and shining blond hair whispering in the wind, she has the grace and looks to match her confidence. When Shade gazes down at her and smiles, golden eyes flashing in the sun, my jaw clenches so hard, I can hear my teeth scraping together.

"Not today, but I do like the notion," Shade says, clapping Katita on the shoulder. "I will speak with Coal about working it in if there is general interest?" He says the latter part as a question, his voice rising to encompass the ring.

Most everyone nods, the girls all but bouncing on their toes.

I cross my arms. The day has barely started and I already want it to be over—want to go out into the night with my sword and do something I know will make a difference. At least the sclices and Yocklol trees see the true me and find me worthy enough to warrant killing.

"Why are you joining us today, Master Shade?" one of Katita's friends asks, a delicate olive-skinned beauty who's somehow even shorter than I am.

"Because you will be rendering each other unconscious this morning." Coal barely raises his voice, but the entire training pitch falls silent. Feet shift, faces losing color.

Dressed in his usual black pants, today Coal wears a sleeveless leather jerkin over a black shirt that covers his arms to the biceps. Some distant part of my brain registers that this is unusual for him—but stops short when it gets to the ropes of muscle twining around his forearms, shifting beneath his skin as he strides to the center of the ring.

"There are two primary types of chokes," Coal says, making a motion with his finger that has the class circling around him. "Wind and blood. You all will feel both today. Osprey, come here."

I jerk. Me? Why? Coal never chooses Lera the cadet. Not for anything. As he brusquely beckons me toward him, eyes still on the class, I feel that same unnerving tingle rush along my spine as I had when our gazes met earlier.

I stop before him, but the male circles behind me, Shade's sudden alertness making me tense. As he disappears from my sight, I feel dozens of eyes watching my face, waiting for the inevitable—some nervously, other with the eagerness of spectators at an execution.

Shifting my weight, I strain to hear the sound of his silent footsteps, to track microshifts in his metallic scent, but catch nothing.

"Wind chokes—" Coal's gravelly voice is so unexpectedly close to my ear that I jump, and the class chuckles softly. He clears his throat, and silence settles once more. "Wind chokes," he says again, "compress the throat, cutting off the opponent's air. Blood chokes compress the vessels on the sides of your opponent's neck. Right here." Coal's calloused finger traces along the vulnerable spot on my neck, finding my rapid pulse with centuries of experience in taking lives. A shiver races through me. For a second, all I want to do is run. Then his hand disappears, his phantom touch still lingering on my skin.

I draw a shaking breath. *Coal,* I remind myself as I force air again and again into my lungs. *You know Coal. You trust Coal.*

The words that would have put me at ease a month ago now only dry my mouth. Yes, I know and trust the warrior Coal was in Lunos. Not because Coal didn't hurt people—he did—but because I was special. Now, I'm no more than a face in the crowd. One whom he cares little for.

I suddenly want to be anywhere but here in the ring.

"This is a wind choke." He steps behind me again, his body now flush with mine. Hard muscles flex against my back, Coal's heat soaking through the thin fabric of my gray training uniform to spread along skin. After a month of no contract, the intensity of Coal's touch is almost too much to bear. My heart quickens, a zing of unwelcome need rushing through my core and sex. A heartbeat later, the blade of Coal's forearm rests knifelike against my throat, and the sensations change altogether.

Despite the light pressure, I feel each fragile ring of cartilage in my throat, hear their coming crunch beneath a tighter hold. The rush of panic hits me so hard that my ears roar. My hands shoot up to grab his forearm, my body twisting like a fish out of water.

He releases me, his fingertips resting lightly on my shoulder while I rub my throat. My chest heaves with shallow breaths.

"A wind choke is painful from the start," he tells the class, as if nothing out of the ordinary had happened. As if he expected my reaction. And demonstrated on me anyway. "Thus—as you just observed—your opponent will struggle long before her air truly runs out. In contrast, the effects of a blood choke will sneak up on the adversary. Additionally, while an opponent might fight without breath for a time, he cannot function with the blood flow halted. This is also why it is vital to know what a blood choke feels like. You must be aware of what you will and will not be capable of if attacked this way. To demonstrate…"

Before I can stop myself, my body takes an involuntary step away from him.

The class laughs, the grating bellows of Katita's cousins Rik and Puckler rising above the rest. They'd laughed that way in the stable too, as they tried to force a horse's bit into my mouth.

Shade's golden eyes flash in warning as Coal's scent spikes behind me. He grips my shoulders, dragging me back with a primal possessiveness that makes me long to rake my nails down his back in answer.

As if he'd heard my thoughts, Coal lowers his voice so only I can hear his warning tone. "Fight me, Osprey, and I will fight back. I'd stay very still if I were you."

His words are a buzz in my ear, their sound mixing with…with a copper scent of blood. I swallow. Take another breath. The smell is still there, coming from Coal's shirt. As if blood from an opened cut is seeping into the fabric. My magic bucks, feeling its hidden mate. Tangling with it despite my protests.

My head swims, desperate darkness and clanking chains closing around me. *My shoulders scream, the scent of blood and pain filling my lungs. I yank against my shackles as if they might give, but they don't. They never do. Behind me, footsteps get closer, metal instruments clanking against a blood-caked tray.*

I gasp, blinking away the nightmare—the memory. Coal's memory.

I'm on the training pitch, the chill air biting my skin. The class watching. Overhead, a drafting falcon lets out a hunting cry. With my back flush against Coal's hard body, I can feel each of the male's unyielding muscles, the light rumble of his chest as he explains the move. If he felt our magics tangling as I did, he shows no sign of it. I certainly felt them, though. *Stars,* the echoes of Coal's horrors have not been so soul-strikingly raw since they overwhelmed our bond in Lunos, so early on. With flashes like this, I've no notion how the male functions.

A heartbeat later, as his thick arm slides around me, I don't have the time to care either.

My chin drops instinctively, protecting my vulnerable neck. A futile move against Coal, but my mind can't think over my still-hammering heart. I want out of this restraint. Out of this demonstration.

"Cooperate, Osprey." He drives a knuckle beneath my chin, the bruising pressure forcing my head up. In the next second, his arm comes around my neck neatly, the bend of his elbow pressing the vessels on both sides.

For an instant, nothing happens and I think the choke failed. Then dizziness hits, panic riding its wings.

"Stop fighting, Lera," Shade's voice calls through my haze. "Trust him."

No.

No. No. No. Shade, all these cadets, they all think Coal's a human soldier. But I know it's an immortal primal predator who attacks me now. So much more wounded and dangerous than anyone in the Academy can begin to imagine. Trust him? Once, I would have. Now, after a month of the veil amulet squeezing his mind, he is nothing but a beautiful, deadly stranger who rouses my body in a primal way I can't help.

I slam my elbow back into Coal's ribs, the impact waking a strength inside me. Again. Again. My heart pounds against my ribs, Coal's arm a tightening inescapable noose. When I try to take another hit, he arches me backward, reducing my resistance to no more than child's play.

Whistles, then chuckles sound from the class.

"This isn't the time for a sparring match, Lera," Shade orders, a dark blur in my side vision. "Tap out, or stop it."

I can't think. With blackness descending, I slash my nails over Coal's forearm so hard that I can smell the blood leaking through broken skin, its scent mixing with his older wound.

"Enough," Shade bellows.

Coal throws me down to the sand. When our eyes meet, specs of purple dance amidst the blue of his gaze, the roused magic potent enough to show itself in the mortal world. A heartbeat passes, and the magic dies, Coal's chest heaving in a mirror to my own. In that moment, I know that he had felt it after all, the bridge linking our fears and nightmares to each other. Our desires.

"Find a partner you trust enough to let him render you unconscious," Coal calls to the class, struggling to corral his breath, never taking his gaze off me while the sobering crowd looks on in silence. "Or at least to release you if you tap."

As I had not trusted him. That knowledge too is plain in Coal's shuddering gaze as he twists away so quickly that sand flies into the air.

~

THE TOLLING ACADEMY bell nips at my heels, quickening my steps through the dark grounds. A soft spring breeze makes the decorative Ostera lanterns sway almost eerily, carrying the heady scent of flowering jasmine. Despite the morning's training disaster with Coal, the day has improved exponentially with Arisha's news that Gavriel's tests against my last Yocklol sample proved promising. The two caveats to the potion I'm supposed to shoot at the creatures are its long preparation time and short life span. That, and the need to hit the things in the eye.

"We can do a test tonight at nine," Arisha had told me at dinner, her voice dropping to slide beneath the polite din of other finely dressed students, most discussing the upcoming celebration. "Taking the escape route passage into account, that will leave you a twenty-minute window to find a Yocklol and deploy the eradicant. Do you think you can do it?"

Twenty minutes. Provided the Yocklols haven't moved far, it should be possible, though difficult. If tonight's test works, Gavriel will have a full batch for me to use tomorrow night, at the start of Ostera—when the moon's alignment spikes magic's potency. Unfortunately, the flaring of Ostera-spurred magic is also likely to widen the existing rip in the fabric protecting the mortal world.

On the bright side, it means I will have a good reason for leaving the bloody ball early.

Dong. Dong. Dong.

I glare at the bell. *I know, I know.* Eight thirty. Just enough time to change out of my dress into leathers and use the nightly cover to get to my exit point. My blood courses quicker at the thought, the fresh air of freedom and adventure calling on the light wind. Now that I'm not fighting it, I like Lera the fae a great deal more than the cadet.

"Lera!" Despite the formal evening dress code, Tye is in his training grays, his red hair mussed with sweat. When the male falls into step beside me, the scent of his male musk mixes with the pine and citrus that is always Tye, rousing my body to his fake familiarity. The heat of recent exercise radiates from his large, lithe body, his corded arms trembling slightly in proof of heavy exertion.

Training for next month's Prowess Trials. As if they matter. *They do matter. To this Tye, they do.*

"Good evening." I give Tye a curt nod, stiffening against the blaze of desire the sight of him sends through me, my thighs clenching of their own accord. Then I remember the questions the intensity of our coupling gave rise to, and force my mind back where it belongs. "I'm surprised you aren't still twirling around a wooden bar."

He grins, his beautifully sharp face and emerald eyes lighting with a mischief that kindles a fire inside my chest. "It broke." His grin widens, the male not realizing I know him well enough to read through those sparkling green eyes to the uncertainty beneath. "Speaking of breaking things, would you be doing that to my neck if I, say, asked you to accompany me to the Ostera ball tomorrow?"

I trip over my own feet. For a moment, the growing warmth inside my chest spreads south, the image of Tye's feline grace spinning around the dance floor making more than just my mouth water. In Lunos, the five of us came together beneath the magic's pull without true courtship—and the tingling excitement of being invited to a simple dance is both new and intoxicating.

A corner of his mouth twitches, his eyes playing over me. "Is that a yes, I'll come with you?" he drawls. My immortal senses pick up the sweet tingle of Tye's arousal as he leans down to whisper into my ear. "Or yes, you'll attack me like you did Coal? I might enjoy that, though."

My face heats, but not even the morning's embarrassment is enough to douse the excitement. Reality, however, is. I've other plans for the evening, and even if I didn't, I can't answer the questions I know Tye wants to ask. Plus, the other plain truth is that I dance worse than I read. Calling more attention to the deficiencies of my noble upbringing will draw scrutiny. Questions. Especially when I'd have to run out on him at midnight.

No. I'll go to the ball as expected, prop up the wall for a few hours, and retire to more pressing duties. After a month of working male-free, I finally have myself in a fighting set of mind. One that I know better than to compromise.

His eyes dim as if he's read the change in my thoughts. Or smelled it. "You're turning me down, lass?"

"We both agreed that our tussle in the bathhouse was for the pleasure of the moment." I hug my books to my chest, the hurt flashing in Tye's face squeezing my heart. "That's all I was looking for. Weren't you?"

His jaw tightens. "Of course."

Turning on his heel, he strides away before I can say anything more. Not that I have anything to utter. Despite knowing I did the right thing, my stomach pulls tighter—whether in regret over hurting Tye or self-pity over stepping away from the male I love, I don't know.

Dong. Dong. Dong.

Damn. I hurry my pace across the central courtyard, my mind already calculating the location of each piece of gear to make up lost time. To make myself ignore the nagging ache in my chest.

"Leralynn." River's voice hits me in the back just as I'm about to step into the safety of the trees.

I swallow a curse. It is well past eight in the evening, a time when getting through the Academy unharassed never poses a problem—bar the one day when I've a fickle eradicant to deploy. For a moment, I contemplate feigning deafness, but even I know better than to play such games with River.

Turning around, I bow to the male, begging the stars to make whatever he wants quick. "Sir?"

The few cadets still out veer off to give the deputy headmaster a wide berth. I wonder if it's the same distance they'd keep from any senior officer or if, without being aware, they feel the aura of centuries of power that River carries on his shoulders.

He gestures his head toward the reflection garden ahead of us, his hands clasped behind his back as if he is taking a leisurely stroll.

My stomach tightens, my gaze darting to the sky to check the moon's position. Gavriel and Arisha will be making their way to the meeting point by now, wondering where the bloody hell I am.

"Are you expected somewhere this evening?" River inquires with a raised brow, his too-rich voice scattering across my skin.

"The library." Holding up one of my books, I try to conjure up an air of studious intent. "I've a bit of work to catch up on still."

"I'd always thought the library was located in the opposite direction," says River.

"My life would be simpler if you occasionally stopped thinking," I mutter, clearing my throat quickly. "I wanted to change first. Might I go about it, sir? Arisha is waiting for me to study."

"Why the hurry?" His voice lowers enough to send a chill down my spine. "Copying another's work can't possibly be all that time-consuming."

5

LERA

My heart stops.

River waits, the perfect planes of his face unreadable in the moonlight.

My mind races through the past days. I've been careful. So very careful. What does he know? What *can* he know? It can't be all that much. If the male had proof of foul play, he'd be hauling me up to his study, not waylaying my stroll. I force breath into my tightened lungs. He must be fishing for information, looking for me to dig a hole for myself—probably in a renewed attempt to encourage me to leave. I wonder if my common upbringing is as plain to the royal-born River as his high status is to me. If that is why he wants so badly to see me gone.

"I've no notion of what you mean, sir."

He jerks his head toward the entrance of the reflection garden, the order to follow no less strict for being silent.

Schooling my face to what I hope passes for indignation, I follow River's broad back into the vines, trees, and flowers that turn a space barely a hundred paces long into a maze one can wander for three quarters of an hour, especially in the evening's darkness. At once, the normal rhythm of the Academy falls away to hide behind dense hedges as tall as River's head, the thick smell of blooming roses filling the air. Somewhere close by, a small man-made waterfall burbles over smooth stones, further drowning the noise beyond. The ticking time.

Walking with his hands clasped behind his back, River has the straight spine and long, unhurried stride of a king. "Why are you here, Leralynn of Osprey?" he demands, his voice low.

"Why am I where?" I echo the question, my pulse racing. "In the gardens?"

He lengthens his stride, then cuts in front of me so sharply, I stumble back just to avoid running into his large chest. A storm moves in his gray eyes, tightening the world around us with its intensity. River's woodsy scent fills my nose, pushing away the perfume of roses and ferns. "You understood my question well enough, Leralynn. Why are you here at the Academy? It isn't to forge alliances, or you'd have known better than to force Princess Katita to her knees. It isn't for academics, or you'd be doing your own damn work. It isn't to please the Lord of Osprey, or you'd be making an effort to avoid notice, fearing the hell you'd pay should a bad report be sent. So I repeat. Why are you at Great Falls?"

A shiver runs through me, the amulet around my neck burning hot in warning. The last time I went against the veil's magic, Coal paid in screams of agony. My mind races, and there is nothing feigned about the fear rising through my core. Rushing through River's choices, I know I can't deny the first and last options, which leaves only one available route. One that an innocent cadet would certainly take.

"This is the second time you've implied that someone else is writing my papers, sir, which is as insulting as it is untrue. I'm here to study and would very much like to do so tonight." Raising my chin, I step forward to get past the male, my mind promising me that he has no proof. Not yet.

River's palm slams into a tree trunk behind by head.

I jump, the slapping sound echoing through my bones, my lungs breathing in a phantom stench of turned wine and rancid sweat that clings to Zake's clothes. *My heart stutters, my mouth suddenly dry as the man towers over me, his thick arm blocking my path. My shoulders curl, bracing for the coming blow, my breath caught in my throat as my heart pounds—*

"Leralynn?" River's voice splashes over me like ice water, washing away Zake's memory. River, not Zake. Stunning, large, and infuriating *River.* The reality that had momentarily fogged over recrystallizes into focus just as quickly. I scowl at the male whose muscled arm blocks my path and shove the arm away.

River's arm gives only a hand width, a condescending shift along the tree's trunk that sends a jolt of fury through my already primed core. My racing blood heats, now rushing so fast that it rumbles in my ears, feeding the tension vibrating the air between us. "I'm here to study," I say again. "Now let me pass."

As if my deception struck a tender spot, a storm passes over his face, turning his gray eyes to thunder.

"You are lying." His nostrils flare, the restrained, dignified male beside me shifting into the fae predator beneath.

At once, I am aware of how isolated the reflection garden is. *Don't move a muscle,* my mind screams at me even as heat pools low in my rebellious body, my instincts waking despite my mind's orders. I'm a predator now too, and the leashed violence surrounding us is impossible to ignore. A tangle of need races from my sex, down the backs of my thighs, making my toes curl.

River growls.

For a moment, all I can think of is his bedchamber, River's naked body silhouetted against an evening sun. It's been so long since I was allowed to press myself against that body, feel its ridges and contours against every curve of my own. Magic rouses inside me, filling my muscles and lungs with a power that can do nothing in this shackled world, but will try anyway. My face tilts up to meet the fury of his eyes. "With due respect, why do *you* think I'm here, Deputy Headmaster?"

He leans down toward my face, the air between us sizzling.

Wetness slithers along the inside of my thigh, my sex throbbing painfully. I don't know whether I want to put my fist through the male's nose or rut with him right here amidst the manicured ferns. I bare my teeth, flashing the fangs he can't see but no doubt feels with whatever part of him remains fae.

River's pulse hammers hard enough that I can hear its pounding. Once. Twice. Then the male finally speaks. "I don't know." His voice is a low, primal bass. "But I will find out." Shoving away from the tree, he turns and stalks free of the garden, while I press my back against the rough bark.

Dong. Dong. Dong. The distant bell calls, announcing the time window I so gloriously missed and dooming the eradicant batch to spoiling before we ever try it out.

~

"Everything you are, you have, you'll ever become is because of my good graces." Zake's voice snaps along with the deafening crack of his belt. The strap ends wrap around my ribs, making me scream loud enough that the horses whicker in discontent. "When I order a horse saddled, you saddle a horse. You don't lie. You don't pretend he's lame to save yourself a bit of work."

If you took him out again, he *would* be lame. *I swallow the retort because it doesn't matter. Zake works his horses until they break, then puts them down in search of* better stock.

A pain slices through my back, so sharp and deep that my knees buckle. I slide down the wall, pressing myself into a corner.

Zake looms over me, his chest heaving, the scar on his furious red face filling my vision. My breath comes in short bursts, my heart racing so quickly that my hands shake. It isn't over. I know it isn't. My stomach cinches, the gripping fear making me dizzy.

"Get back up and face the wall," Zake says too calmly for the pounding inside my head, his belt slapping softly against his own thigh. "We are not done, and it will be worse for you if I have to force you."

I lurch awake to rushed strokes of a lupine tongue lapping my face, Shade whining softly as he steps all over my chest. Outside the window, a hint of light outside speaks of wee morning hours.

"Bad dreams?" Arisha asks, sitting up in her own bed.

The terrible feeling in the pit of my stomach calms slowly as I try to shove two hundred pounds of wolf off me. "Nothing of consequence." I rub my face, debating the merits of going back to sleep. Maybe I'll take it easy today for once, find some time to nap between classes. My gaze shifts back to the window, the faint gray light dispelling that fantasy in favor of the grim truth tightening my chest. There will be no rest today. It's Ostera eve.

6

LERA

Come ride with me
The horses paw ground.
Come fly with me
There're secrets to be found.

The stunning singer closes her eyes, swaying to her own melody while a string ensemble behind her fills the Great Hall with soul-gripping music, all the way to its high arched rafters. Beneath the silk ribbons and flower garlands of Ostera, cadets and instructors dressed in brilliant shades of blue and gold finery swing across the dance floor, their intricate steps perfectly matching. The hundreds of candles and lanterns make them look like a swirling mass of daylight. Even when royals from different kingdoms connect hands, the basic steps of the dance come easily to the experienced partners. Yes, they've all had dancing lessons. Probably at about the same time they learned to read and ride horses and calculate the amount of grain needed for ten winters in an imaginary kingdom with seven seasons.

"Where are you going?" I grab Arisha's wrist as the girl takes a determined step toward the exit. Dressed in a pale yellow gown with embroidered sunflowers trailing up its bodice, Arisha looks like a proper lady for the ball—or did before the sneezing and face rubbing smeared lip paint and kohl in dark patches over her skin. "You can't leave me alone here."

Arisha dabs her nose. "I need to help Uncle Gavriel get your… things…ready for tonight."

I wince. With me getting ambushed by River last night, the eradicant batch I was supposed to test had gone bad before I could deploy it. My fault, even if Arisha tries to pretend it isn't. Which all means tonight will be it. With the added potency Ostera equinox infuses into magic, we can't let the singular opportunity pass, so Gavriel is preparing the whole batch. Nerve-racking as the thought is, however, I'd still rather be out there in the wilderness than stay here.

"You can handle one more hour." Arisha pats my hand, her voice dropping. "Midnight, Lera. You leave here at midnight, as soon as the requisite Ostera waltz is over."

"Why can't I leave now?"

Arisha looks at me over her glasses. "Because *I'm* leaving now, and that will draw enough attention without you disappearing as well. No one leaves the ball before the Ostera waltz—that's the whole point of the celebration. River is already watching you like a bloody hawk—do you truly want to draw extra scrutiny to yourself just to avoid a few hours of socializing?"

I nod, my throat tight as I watch my friend leave. At the front of the soaring hall, the singer leafs through her music folio while the dancers recover with goblets of punch and small pastries. Laughter and conversation swell, making my urge to flee even stronger. Without Arisha's presence, I feel as exposed as if I were naked, my eyes on constant vigilance to note anyone who might be looking at me too long or, worse, making a move toward me. Each time a boy shows signs of considering taking me to the dance floor, I stride with purpose to some place on the other side of the room.

Not that Arisha made tonight any easier by commissioning this dress for me along with hers, a cascade of vivid blue satin that hugs my waist and breasts, leaving my back bare—and too little to the imagination. It might as well be a beacon alerting the whole room to my presence. I left my hair loose in an effort to cover up more of my skin, but now I think it was a mistake. In the candlelight, its red tones shine almost as brightly as the dress.

I feel someone's eyes again, just as the violins pick up a new song. Turning my head, I discover my chest tightening at Tye's emerald stare. The male looks breathtaking in his sapphire tunic and flowing black pants, his every movement filled with power and grace even when he's doing something as simple as standing still.

I head for the punch. When I look back up, Tye is twirling Katita across the floor, the princess following his lead with a trained perfection that makes my stomach squeeze. The pair are such a whirlwind of color that the others clear the floor just to watch them spin. I don't see why the veil went so far as to insert complicated dancing instructions into Tye's head when it couldn't even deign to teach me how to spell "instructions." *It didn't,* a voice inside me says. *Tye's entertained females for centuries—he knew how to dance all along. You are the one who grew up in a stable.*

Gripping the stem of my goblet with a low growl, I turn away in search of something else to look at. Midnight. So close and yet so far. My eyes snag on Coal leaning against the far wall. Unlike Tye, Coal's only deference to the festivities is a clean black shirt, matching the dark look on his face. Perfect. Whatever else, no one is going to want to come within Coal's killing radius—a fact that I am not above using.

"I'm holding up the wall just fine on my own," he says when I lean against the gilded wallpaper beside him.

"You never know." I take a sip of my punch. Even in his simple black shirt and pants, Coal looks devastatingly handsome, eyes blue ice in the candlelight, strong face sharpened by shadows, pale hair hanging loose to his shoulders. His masculine scent swirls around me, and I have to remind myself not to inhale audibly. After a month of almost zero contact, our coupling is still as fresh in my mind as if it happened yesterday—if anything, it's only grown in potency with no new experience with him to replace it.

Or maybe that's an effect of Ostera too. Everything is more vivid. The magic, the trees, the dreams.

His jaw tightens, the silence stretching between us twisting uncomfortably.

"I'm sorry about spooking yesterday," I say finally.

He keeps looking at the dance floor. "You were right to. I wouldn't let me anywhere near my neck." He runs his hand over his forearm, and I see the outlines of a vambrace with throwing knives beneath the loose sleeve. "If you are taking over wall support, I'll find some other occupation. Excuse me."

I stand alone for some time before setting my punch down on one of the trays. Midnight is still twenty minutes off, and I need a reprieve. Spotting one of the circular staircases leading to the mezzanine, I hold up the front of my full skirt as I climb the steps. A few paces away from the stairs, an ornate set of double doors promises an escape to fresh air. And privacy.

Sending a short thanks to the stars when I find the handle unlocked, I step out onto a balcony so large, it looks like a floating terrace. Unlike the torchlit hall below, the terrace is dark but for the moon above, which adds more atmosphere than light. The sounds of music drift from the Great Hall below, the merriment of overexcited violins a gentle backdrop to the night.

Even out here in the open air, the Academy staff have set out trellises of delicate jasmine and great vases filled with hyacinths, their blue, white, and pink flowers all giving off a slightly different perfume that my immortal senses separate out into soft strands. Crossing the ten paces to the railing, I place my hands on its cool stone surface and look out at the mountains. The forest that beckons with equal parts danger and excitement.

Perhaps it's fortunate that I don't know how to dance, since I can't stay past midnight. It might be difficult to leave if I had something to stay for. Taking in a deep breath of fresh air, I work out the time in my head. I should show myself to the masses again before leaving, slipping back to the dance floor just late enough after the Ostera waltz starts that everyone is already occupied with partners. After the waltz, retiring should raise no eyebrows. Then I change.

Then I go out into night.

A soft whisper from the shadows to my left makes me jump, my hand going to where my sword would usually be. Heart spurring into a gallop, I note a previously stone-still form separating from the railing, the change in wind carrying me an woodsy scent.

River.

7

LERA

"Forgive me for startling you—I hadn't expected anyone would come here." River steps forward, his soft voice an odd contrast to my bounding pulse. Stopping a few feet away from me, he rests his hands in the small of his back, his eyes surveying the star-filled sky. He looks breathtaking, his tailored black pants and crisp blue and gold jacket highlighting every bit of his powerful physique. Despite his perfect posture and soft smile, there is a quiet, melancholy note in his voice that I'm not used to hearing. "It appeared you didn't mark me, and I thought it poor form to keep from alerting you to my presence."

My heart slows. River isn't tracking me—I accidentally intruded into *his* sanctuary. Taking a breath, I look over at him, this time with care. As with his voice, the male's face has a hint of sadness seeping through the controlled facade. My chest squeezes no matter how much I want to be irritated with him over yesterday's interrogation.

"Why are you out here?" I say as the night wraps tightly around us, my words drifting into the darkness. "Do you dislike dancing?"

"I like it quite a bit, actually." His jaw clenches before relaxing with visible effort. When I turn toward him and rest a hip on the railing, the male stays as he is. After several heartbeats of absolute stillness, I lose hope of the conversation continuing, but then his throat bobs as he swallows. "It is one of the many joys I had dreamt of showing my wife."

Wife? A small shock of cold air rushes along my skin. The damn veil amulet gave River a wife? Despite every self-preservation instinct screaming at me to keep quiet, I can't help the question from escaping my lips. "Is she coming to Great Falls any time soon?"

River's shake of the head is so miniscule that a mortal would have had no chance of seeing it in the darkness. Just as his suddenly too-reflective eyes would have stayed safely hidden from view.

"Diana died in a riding accident exactly one year ago, on Ostera eve. She'd galloped her mare ahead of me on the trail, and the horse spooked and threw her. By the time I caught up to her, there was nothing to be done."

My throat closes, the effort to pull air into my lungs suddenly too much. River's pain is so palpable, I can feel it pressing on my soul. "I'm sorry," I say, meaning it. Just as I mean to destroy the damn veil that did this.

He turns to me, the space between us suddenly too large and too small at the same time. The night sculpts his body, the deep shadows somehow making his muscled silhouette as defined as a sculptor's masterpiece. Large as he is, I have to tip my head up to see his face, my eyes skipping over the pointed fae ears to land on his piercing gray eyes, his short dark hair ruffling in the breeze.

"She looked a great deal like you," he says softly. "And had a stubborn streak to match."

I try to smile, but the ache in River's voice makes it nearly impossible. I wish I could say something. To tell him that—that his Diana has not died, that she'd never existed. Better yet, I wish I could say that I'm her. Except that isn't true either. The Diana in River's soul is a peer to him, while the real me standing before him is just a cadet, and a pretender noble at that.

The unfairness of it all makes tears burn in my throat.

In the Great Hall below, the violins play a fast prancing tune. It must look gorgeous with the couples swirling around the floor, the girls' gowns opening like flower petals with each swing. But I don't belong there.

"And what of you?" he asks. "What brings you up here this night?"

I turn back toward the mountain range splaying open before us, my immortal sight and the starlit sky giving me a good view. "I don't enjoy dancing."

"For someone who lies as much you do, I would think you'd be better at it." He says it as a curious fact, his soft tone carrying no hint of malice, as if the night has declared some sort of temporary truce between us.

I shrug one shoulder and leave it at that. Down below, the instruments finish the ditty and change tune. This time, the music is a slow, three-beat piece that makes me think of flying. One, two, three, one, two, three, one, two, three. The notes hit their marks, my core rousing to their beautiful rhythm.

From the corner of my vision, I see River cocking his head, his eyes losing focus as he takes in the same melody that has my thoughts spinning. "The Ostera waltz," he says. "It is bad fortune to sit it out."

"In this place, I'm shocked there is no rule mandating the dance."

He smiles lightly. "There might be." Turning his hand palm up, he extends it toward me.

My breath catches, my stomach tightening with a mix of fear and desire. Despite the fresh spring air, my revealing blue gown is suddenly too hot. Taking a step away, I clutch the railing as if asking for its protection.

His voice softens. "Do I frighten you that much, Leralynn?"

I shake my head, though maybe I should have taken the lie River offers.

Instead of leaving well enough alone, he steps toward me. His nostrils flare gently as he takes in my scent with the same intensity with which he surveys my face, stripping me bare. Reaching forward, he touches my elbow, the contact sending a wave of warmth all through my chest and belly.

"If it's not me you are frightened of, then who?" he asks. "And don't tell me you don't *want* to dance."

"I…" I feel like a rabbit caught in a python's hypnotic stare, my heart beating so quickly that I can't think. Can't see beyond the fleeting moment made of moonlight and violin music, where the rules are distant and time itself has come to a standstill. *One, two, three. One, two, three.* The music calls, my body longing to respond to the rhythm. To River. "I don't know how. The Ostera waltz, I guess."

River frowns. "It's no different from any other waltz."

"No. I mean…" The words fall in a rapid whisper that I can't stop. "I don't know how to dance. Any waltz. Anything at all."

The utter bewilderment in his gaze is so strong that even the self-controlled male can't hide it quickly enough to escape notice. I can't blame him. A noble who doesn't know basic dancing is about as common as one who can't read or work out figures—and Great Falls Academy is a school for the elite.

I clear my throat. "You would have a better time dancing with anyone down in the hall."

Instead of retreating, River steps closer still. "I can't possibly allow a Great Falls cadet to not know a basic waltz." His tone is an irresistible mix of caress and challenge, as if he knows the perfect combination with which to strike at my resolve. Reaching forward, he takes my left hand gently and, upon finding little resistance, lays it atop his bicep. "Plus, I've a secret too," he adds, leaning down toward my ear. "I enjoy teaching."

8

LERA

I'm suddenly shy as River draws me into the powerful frame of his arms. A clean soapy scent wafts from his clothes, weaving with his natural woodsy smell. Even as he grabs my waist firmly, he pushes against our clasped hands, engaging a gentle tension between us. His sculpted face is suddenly so close to mine, it's an effort of will not to close the distance. *One, two, three, one, two, three,* the music calls, and River sways to it, shifting his weight from foot to foot.

One, two, three. One, two, three. One, two, three.

I start to move my feet, but River's hold tightens gently. "Just listen to the beat. Let it fill your body until the tension is too much to bear."

I've not seen this side of River before, not even in Lunos. For a heartbeat, I expect the moment to dissolve, but I find him opening to the music instead, his pulse matching the melody's rhythm. I draw an uncertain breath, but the security of his hand on my waist holds me steady. Despite being so close that my lower right ribs press tight against River's taut body, the position manages to feel powerful instead of lewd.

One, two, three. One, two, three. One, two, three.

River sways, each movement winding an invisible spring.

"Ready?" he asks.

"No."

"Let me lead," he says into my ear, his final pause seeming to compress the energy of the world into a single movement. "Stop thinking and let your body listen." He squeezes my hand once, and, with the first step, the male moves *through* me. Powerful thighs step between mine, propelling the pair of us across the wide empty terrace.

"Left. Right. Together," he murmurs, his body molding mine into the motions, making us rise and fall and twirl.

Wind hits my face, the stars starting to spin. For a moment—just a moment—I feel like I might actually be dancing, River's perfect movements embracing uncertainty, guiding my body with gentle cues of pressure and step.

We spin. Again. Again. A—

I step on him.

His hand only tightens around me, a steady assurance that he isn't letting me go. He sways again, finding the rhythm before thrusting us into motion.

Left foot. Right. Together. I recite the instructions in my head. *Right—no*

This time, I somehow manage to crash into the male, only River's firm hold preventing me from tripping over the hem of my own dress. Heat fills my face, a bouquet of embarrassment and regret. He invited me into the magic of a dance—and not just *a* dance, but *the* dance, the night's crown jewel to mark the clock turning to Ostera.

And in return, I'm body-slamming him.

"This isn't happening," I say, pulling my hand from his grip. "I can't learn how to dance in the course of a single song."

"You are right," River says, but instead of releasing me, he only tightens the grip. His gaze pierces me, powerful and steady and deep enough to brush along my soul. "Can you trust me, Leralynn?" he whispers. "Not forever, but just for this song."

I nod, and suddenly, I am in the air, my body flush against his as he spins us to the rising music. Faster and faster, the breeze filling and lifting the layers of my blue dress. My breath quickens, my lungs opening to the hyacinth-filled air. In the night sky, the stars circle us in perfect harmony to the song. To us.

More strings join the chorus, the Ostera waltz rising to its inevitable climax. River takes us into a spin so fast and powerful that the world disappears in a swirl of speed and color and streaking stars. When the final note vibrates through the air, he brings us back to the same railing where we started, his eyes locked on mine as he settles me back to the ground.

I feel as though I've been running, my breath quick with energy that wakens all my senses. Around me, the world rocks into gentle focus, but I can't take my eyes off River's, the mix of joy and pain in his eyes gripping my soul.

He gently loosens his hold.

I tighten mine.

"Leralynn," he warns, a tremor racing through his muscled frame. The male's pulse beats so hard that I see it in the hollow triangle of his neck. "Thank you for the dance."

I try to let him go, but my fingers won't obey my command. The heat from River's body envelops me, everything but his piercing gray eyes falling away into irrelevance. I draw a shaking breath, feeling him do the same. The bicep beneath my left hand coils, the calloused fingers holding my right palm softly scraping my skin.

"Lera. We need to stop." His words hitch, and when he tries to step away again, I feel the hardness pulsating between his thighs. An oh-so-familiar hardness that I haven't felt in far too long. "This is wro—"

"No." A desire as powerful and primal as the male himself grips my chest. My fingers dig into River's flesh. My mouth tingles with the need for him, my whole body as desperately tight as the mystical strings of the Great Hall violin. Rising to my toes, I grip the back of his neck and suck on his lower lip.

"Stars take me," River rasps, his hardness giving a tight jerk against me. With the next heartbeat, he lowers his head, covering my mouth with his. His lips are soft at first, as if seeking permission—despite the thundering need making my thighs so wet that I'm sure he can scent it. It's almost surreal, the press of his warm mouth, after more than a month of missing my commander, longing for him from afar.

When I open for him with a soft, helpless moan, River cracks. His tongue plunges into my mouth, an inaudible growl rumbling in his chest. Claiming me with a primal need that turns more possessive with each stroke of his tongue. His hands come around to grip my head and back, trapping me between his powerful arms and body, the restraining hold magnifying each sensation.

His woodsy taste makes my head spin just as the stars did. Within his strong hold, I feel safer than I have since stepping foot into Great Falls. When he scrapes his canines along my lips, the sting of edged pleasure shoots down to my core, echoing from my bunched nipples, my thighs, the arches of my feet. My sex clenches, my damp underthings sliding along sensitive skin.

His hand tangles in my hair, and I moan into his mouth. My hips press forward, my mound seeking the pressure of River's large thigh, the rock-hard muscles shifting beneath the warrior's skin driving up my need.

Dong. Dong. Dong.

I jerk, the bell's rich toll driving ice down my spine. No. No, it can't be midnight. Not now. Not yet. My fingers dig deeper into his flesh, trying to stop time.

Dong. Dong. Dong.

Inside my soul, duty pounds against desire, each extra heartbeat of stolen time with River worth the safety of all realms.

Except it can't be. Not with others' lives at stake.

I pull my mouth back, River's panting breath filling my ears. His gray eyes narrow, his beautiful face straining with a mix of confusion and restraint. With questions I can't answer.

"I… I have to go." I tell him, pulling back more roughly than I should. I've no choice. Another moment in his arms and I know I will damn the whole world to hell before leaving. "I—"

River steps away so quickly, cold air rushes to fill the void between us. His eyes are wide now, his hands grabbing his head, making his dark hair stand up in tufts. "Leralynn." River's chest heaves, cracking open my heart.

"I'm sorry," I whisper, backing away beneath the final *dong, dong, dong* of the tower bell.

My last sight of the terrace before I rush out the double doors is that of River standing with his back to me, his shoulders hunched as he braces himself against the rail.

9

LERA

"You are cutting it close," Gavriel steps out from behind the cluster of whispering trees guarding the escape tunnel entrance. He's draped in his usual dark robes, his thinning brown hair poking up in wild tufts that speak to long hours bent over a desk. Holding out a bow and quiver, he checks me over with a scrutinizing gaze—though I'm not sure what he can possibly see in this light. I pull the final part of my outfit on before taking the bow—an armored leather vest that laces up the side, the hardest place for a sword to reach. In my fitted black pants, boots, and long-sleeved tunic, my hair in a tight braid down my back, I feel far more myself than I did only moments ago in that gown—now crumpled in a beautiful blue heap behind the usual bush.

I sling the quiver over my chest, Gavriel's eyes widening at my brusque movements. "Have a care. Those arrowheads are saturated with eradicant. Unwrap them carefully before firing—and remember that you need to hit the Yocklol's eye. This is all the eradicant we have, and it will sour in forty-five—no, forty—minutes. No diversions before you deploy it."

"I know." I make my voice strong. Or think I do, until Gavriel frowns at me with perceptive brown eyes. Of all days for Gavriel to pay attention, of course he'd choose today.

"Are you feeling ill?" Stepping forward, the librarian touches my forehead, and it's all I can do not to jump back, the memory of River's touch still searing through me. Gavriel's frown deepens. "Your life is more vital than killing those Yocklol trees, Leralynn. If you aren't feeling well—"

"I'm fine." My heart pounds, my words coming with a snap I don't intend. "I'm mad at myself for being late. Let's get this done and go to bed." Without waiting for Gavriel's reply, I open the trap grating and slip into the darkness. I'm already on the floor of the tunnel when Gavriel's final words—ones not intended for my hearing judging by the mutter—reach my ears. "Be careful, Lera. Please."

I AM ONLY HALF surprised when, a mile into the hike, Shade's wolf trots up beside me, his gray fur and yellow eyes gleaming in the moonlight, black muzzle opened in a soft pant. How the animal—or Shade himself—gets in and out of the Academy is still a mystery to me, but one I am happy to leave alone for now. Reaching around the back of my neck, I take off the amulet, feeling a weight lift from my skin, the slight haze in my mind clearing.

Beside me, Shade sneezes. Some small creature chitters in the branches above us, scared from its rest.

Tucking the veil amulet securely into a pouch around my neck, I follow the now-familiar trail to the Yocklol trees, the memory of River's lips fighting for my concentration so much, I nearly trip over a root. "Things aren't supposed to be this complicated," I tell the wolf, who blinks at me with bright yellow eyes that seem to say *Want to chase a rabbit together?*

I scratch Shade's ear, which doesn't require me leaning down any, and pick up my pace. By my calculation, I've only ten minutes of the eradicant's effective window left when I reach the first of the yellow Yocklols. Thanking the stars that all five—no, now *six*—of the things are near each other today, I ease the bow off my shoulders and carefully unwrap the arrowheads. The one beauty of this arrangement is that I should be able to hit the trunks from far enough away to stay clear of the writhing tentacles.

The memory of River floods me again, the dismayed look on his face as I stepped away making my stomach clench.

Stop it.

Bracing my shoulder against an oak, I take a few calming breaths, trying to think of something happier. River's lips on mine. Exploring, claiming.

The taste of him, after having tasted none of the males in a month, felt as intoxicating as Tye's strongest brandy. Is intoxicating me still, apparently, despite the effort I've put to focus on my mission.

Except I best sober up quickly. Ostera is here, and the moon continues shifting along the sky with each passing minute. I have to keep my mind in the now, not in memories of a bed long ago. My hand brushes against the rough bark, grounding myself. When I look at the Yocklol trees again, I can finally think clearly.

Which is when I notice the six eyes are open. Blinking. Watching.

I swallow, turning about. Someone or something had to have been here recently enough to have woken the things. I'd chalk it up to an unfortunate animal if one or two had wakened, but all six? I take a deep breath, but the wind is blowing against my back, the scents it carries limited to ground already covered. A glance at the moon has my heart speeding again. Whatever else is out here tonight, I'll have to deal with it later.

Nocking the first of my ten arrows into my bow, I pull the string back to my ear, aim at the first open Yocklol eye, and release.

The arrow hits with a soft thud, its head crumpling before falling to the ground. If that is supposed to have happened, Gavriel forgot to mention it. Either that, or I missed the eye. I am still pulling the second arrow onto my bow when a darkened spot appears on the Yocklol's yellow trunk, making the thing look like a bruised banana.

Relief rushes through me, and I shift position for a clear shot at the next Yocklol, nocking my next arrow as I move. Focusing on my next target, I let my mind go blank as I pull back on the bow. Take aim along my forearm. Breathe in. Out. Hold and release.

The arrow flies as straight as the first one did, managing to catch the Yocklol's eye despite the tree's sudden shift. I wonder if the thing is smart enough to sense that something is amiss or whether the movement was simple coincidence. Making a mental note of it to ask Gavriel, I draw my third arrow and pull back.

Shade whines.

So much for coincidence. Over the extended arrow tip, I mark all the Yocklols moving away now, the two I hit earlier limping behind the deadly herd. Yellow tentacles slither up and down, concealing the target eye.

"Smart bastards, aren't you," I mutter, wincing as a slimed yellow vine flicks an errant squirrel. The small animal runs off, unaware that it's already dead. My teeth clench. Yocklols are a toxic blight that not even the horrors of Mors want around, and they need to wither. Tonight. I will make sure of it.

Another whine sounds from Shade's wolf, but I trust him to stay away from the thrashing vines. With the trees moving, I will have time for one or two shots at the most before I have to find a new firing point, and the minutes are already racing by me.

The bowstring pulled back to my ear cuts into my fingers, my eyes narrowing on my shifting target as my breath stills. The third Yocklol's eye comes into view and disappears behind a waving tentacle. Again. Again. *Now.* I release the arrow.

For a second, I think the sharp pain along my forearm is from my own snapped bowstring, the arrow's wild flight an accident of a poor shot. Then Shade's snarl twists me around to discover a pair of dark-cloaked figures sliding silently from the trees. The one on the left pulls off his hood, his pointed ears and elongated canines sending first hope, then fear thudding through me.

Glancing down at my arm, I discover blood seeping through a slice in my leathers, the dagger that left it now on the ground. The insignia on the hilt scratches at my memory. I know it. I've seen it before——in Lunos.

"Move, and you are dead," the male says, his hard eyes nearly as black as his hair. "How many of you are there here?"

"Of us?" I lick my lips. "You mean fae? It seems you'd know more than I."

The male snorts. "Don't toy with the Guard, girl. You crossed Mystwood with a key. Where is it? How many others came with you?"

Guard. The word triggers the missing link to the insignia, though it brings me no closer to explaining the faes' presence. The Night Guard, a renegade group of fae who pledge their loyalty to the dark realm of Mors, has no more business being in the human world than…than I do.

Yet, here we both are.

"What are Mors's wanna-be lapdogs doing in the mortal realms?" I ask, my mind racing to decide whether the arrows or the sword sheathed down my back would be of more use.

The male snarls.

At my side, Shade's wolf bunches his powerful muscles and launches himself at the male. So much for conversation.

Dropping my bow, I pull my sword in time to parry the blade of the second fae, whose curves reveal her gender just as her swing shows off centuries of training.

My muscles strain beneath the force of her blow, the stark difference between fighting a fae warrior over a human cadet a rude reminder of reality. The female's sword presses down on my blade, forcing my own edge closer and closer to my throat. Her pale blue eyes find mine, their chilled indifference more frightening than any roaring fury.

My arms tremble, the muscles screaming from the strain. I know I should be moving away, staying free of the game of strength, but the fear of what that blade will do to me if I miscalculate sends my heart into a gallop. Makes me hesitate.

Her blade moves another inch closer. With a grunt, I shift to my right, redirecting the force of our battle.

The locked blades snap free of the impasse, my balance wavering. I step to regain my footing, taking another slice along my shoulder for it. The pain is distant, the leather armor taking some of the force. Seeing the female's blade rise into the air, I kick her exposed ribs a moment before I realize the opening was a trap. Catching my leg, the female slams me into the ground, her sword slicing my thigh.

Stones dig into my back. Shade's primal growls cut through the haze of my beating heart, spurring me on. My hand tightens on the hilt of my sword—only to discover the female's boot pinning my wrist to the ground.

"Happy Ostera." The Night Guardsman bares her canines, her cold pale eyes carrying all the emotion of a stone as she raises her bloodied sword—this time aiming it at my heart.

A lupine snarl rips the night, a great mass of gray wolf slamming into the fae atop me. The female falls to the side, rolling over her shoulder to regain her footing with a whip of her silver braid.

The wolf circles, his muzzle bloody, his hackles raised.

Gasping, I try to sit up. Blood leaks from my thigh, filling the air with a thick copper scent and making the world sway.

The wolf twists toward me, a flash of bright light leaving Shade's fae form standing where the animal had been, chest heaving, yellow eyes wide with fear.

In one stupid heartbeat, I register the male's Ostera finery, a golden tunic over billowing black pants. In the next, with a bolt of panic, I remember that I'm not wearing my veil amulet.

Then all thoughts disappear as the female, recovered from Shade's blinding shift, closes in with a growl.

"Behind you!" I yell, pointing through the haze to the female warrior, her bloodied sword held high. Gripping the hilt of my blade, I toss it to Shade.

The female's eyes narrow, her gaze quickly sweeping from her downed companion, his throat ripped open, to me, to Shade. With a face that holds too little fear, she steps back, the air around her rippling before swallowing her whole.

"That's not possible," I mutter stupidly, staring at the spot. "You can't step into the Gloom from the mortal world." Or *was* impossible. With Ostera's surge of magic, the rip in the mortal world's protective fabric may have widened for good.

Then my eyes shift to Shade, and all thoughts of the Gloom disappear.

The male's breaths are ragged, his yellow eyes taking in the forest as he prowls toward me. The scent of battle hangs on him, mixing with blood. Stopping a pace away from me, Shade lowers my sword, holding out his free palm toward me.

"I won't harm you, little cub." His low, gentle voice carries no note of recognition.

10

SHADE

Shade's mind roared with confusion that he had no time to unravel. The last coherent image he recalled was the sight of Leralynn of Osprey's brilliant blue gown as she left—fled—the Great Hall. The dress's fabric had flowed behind her in the moonlight, accentuating both the girl's curves and the tug she always seemed to have on Shade's soul. Shade couldn't help following her outside, both to steal one more glance and to escape the uncomfortable stares of the female cadets in the Great Hall. Vestiges of laughter and violin music drifted into the night behind him.

Then he was here. Fighting, his mouth filled with the taste of foreign blood. Even now, Shade's heart still pounded with energy, his breaths quick and deep as he tried to orient himself. Having been losing time for over a month now, discovering himself in places he didn't remember walking to wasn't new, exactly. He'd even woken in the forest before. But it was still disorienting as hell—and this was the first time Shade found himself jerked into the middle of battle. *Why? How?*

Even as Shade asked himself the question, he could feel the answer hovering at the edge of his consciousness. Knew, somehow, that it hadn't been the arousal of combat that yanked him into the now. It was something else.

Some*one* else.

Despite the night, Shade saw the girl clearly—from her pointed ears and elongated canines to her tattered black combat leathers and those deep chocolate eyes that pulled Shade so strongly that he knew he'd run through flame if that was what it took to get to her. Which made as little sense as Shade being here in the first place, yet was just as true. He frowned at her. *Stars,* she was small. And hurt.

And very possibly dangerous.

Shade knew this *creature* should terrify him, that shackling the fae and marching her at sword point to the Academy's dungeon was the right thing to do. Yet he felt only awe toward her—awe and worry. Having smelled the girl's blood and pain, Shade wanted——needed——to fix it.

If she let him.

"I won't harm you, little cub," Shade said, kneeling beside her. The effort it took to keep from pouncing on her and running his hands over every inch of her trembling body in search of wounds drove him mad.

"Shade?" The girl's weak voice tightened his throat as much as the word she'd uttered. This girl, this *fae female*, knew him.

"How do you know my name?"

She opened her mouth as if to speak, then shut it, shaking her head. Her fingers dug into the ground in apparent frustration. She couldn't tell him—because something prevented her from speaking of it, or because she was too injured to do so?

The healer inside Shade surveyed the girl's body, his mind struggling for dispassion. With her leathers on, there was no way to gage the extent of her injuries, and Shade needed to locate those before giving in to the pull to cradle the girl against his chest.

The girl grabbed his wrist, her soft fingers and moonlit eyes making his skin—and all other parts—waken.

"We need to leave," she said. "The barrier is weak here. The Night Guard might return." The girl pushed herself up as she spoke, though her walking just now was out of the question.

Still, she had a point. While Shade little liked the thought of moving her before he could assess her injuries, none of it would matter if the Night Guard—whoever that was—came back for another round. Shade considered his options. Where to take her? He couldn't bring a fae into the Academy without her being arrested, and even if he could, it was farther away than he liked. One of the large caves in the mountain range was an option but would lack even the starlight's illumination. A stream a quarter mile off would have to do, its clean water, mossy bank, and relatively good defensive position the best they could hope for at the moment.

Slipping his hands under her, Shade pulled the girl against his chest, her small body feeling perfect against his. For a heartbeat, that contact seemed to be enough to make the world regain the meaning it had lost—a feeling that usually surfaced only in Leralynn's presence.

Brilliant. Shade went from secretly obsessing over a student to imagining himself connected to an immortal fae. Magic. This female and the abrupt, overwhelming bond Shade felt with her had to be the work of magic, didn't it?

Shoving away the implications of those conclusions, Shade focused on the girl in his arms. "What's your name, cub?"

She shook her head. As if she couldn't tell him. Or wouldn't.

All right, they'd work that out later, once Shade discovered how badly wounded she truly was. Perhaps the girl had something to do with the time he'd been losing. *Later.* A healer. He was a healer—and he had to be that now first and foremost.

Setting the girl down on the moss beside the rushing stream, Shade pulled a knife from his boot. "I'm cutting off your armor and clothes," he explained, lest the cub thought he intended the steel for her. "I need to see where your wounds are."

"You could ask me. The answer, by the way, is *on my thigh.*"

Shade snorted softly. "Noted. However, what hurts or bleeds the most isn't necessarily what's most grievous, so you'll bear with me as I make up my own mind." He pushed her down gently. "The armor and clothes are coming off, cub."

Having enough experience in the infirmary to know better than allow time for debate, Shade made short work of the straps and cloth, the sight of the girl's naked flesh filling him with a flash of heat. Lush breasts with nipples peaked in the cool air, flat abdomen, a mound with auburn curls to match the locks framing her face.

Blood, Shade snapped at himself, running his callused hands over the girl's soft skin. *You are looking for blood. Punctures. Hidden wounds. And your cock doesn't get an opinion.*

"So who is the Night Guard, and why do they wish to kill you?" Shade asked, as much from curiosity as to distract the girl from his exam. In addition to the thigh puncture, the girl had a long bloody gash along her arm and several lacerations around her ribs and shoulder. Considering the battle she'd been in, it was better than expected.

"Fae who don't want to follow Lunos's rules and ally with Mors instead," she said through clenched teeth. "I hurt less before you started prodding me."

"I believe it." *And it will hurt more still before I'm done.* "Deep breaths, cub." With one look at her tattered black shirt, Shade took off his tunic and laid the soft fabric over the girl's upper body before pulling off his undershirt. Several rips had the fabric in strips, one of which he placed next to a sturdy stick about the length of his hand.

"I don't like the look on your face." The girl's voice shook slightly, her attention following his motions suspiciously. Like many warriors Shade knew, the girl would clearly rather face a swordsman trying to kill her than a healer trying to help. "What are you planning exactly?"

Crouching beside her head for a moment, Shade cleared a lock of auburn hair from her face. On the side of her neck, the girl's pulse pounded a quick rhythm.

"I'm planning on wrapping some cloth around your thigh," said Shade.

"You're planning more than that."

He sighed. "I'm going to put a bit of pressure to help stop the bleeding. And the arm will need stiches, though I've no supplies on me. Maybe the ribs and shoulder as well." Shade touched her cheek, the skin soft and sensuous. In the forest about them, the rustle and snaps of twigs spoke of animals scurrying about their night. In their world, all was well. Shade caught the girl's gaze. "Can you trust me not to hurt you more than I must?"

Despite the fear and pain leaking into her scent, the girl nodded.

Shade swallowed, savoring her trust. Then, unable to stop himself—or question why it seemed right—he leaned down to brush a light kiss across her forehead.

Trapping the girl's leg between his thighs, Shade made short work of packing the wound before wrapping the wad of cloth tightly into place. Threading the prepared stick through the knot, he wrenched down on the dressing, the girl's whimpers lashing his heart. "It's all right, cub. I'm done with this."

"I...want...to kill you."

"I know." He brushed a hand along the girl's shoulder, every detail of her body calling for his attention. The large eyes glistening with unshed tears, the lip she'd bitten, the slight tremor to her muscles. Sliding his hands under her shoulders, he scooped the girl into his lap, her cool, silky skin flush against his bare chest.

Despite the pain he'd just caused her, she leaned into his touch, pressing her cheek against his shoulder.

Desire and possessiveness shot through Shade at once. Magic. It had to be magic, this maddening craving for a girl he'd never seen before yet somehow knew with every fiber of his being. Despite the fine tremor from the chill, the girl's muscles were taut beneath her skin, her full breasts and curves calling to his hands with a siren's song. Shade longed to hear her voice again—longed for a great deal more than that, judging by the painful twitching of his cock—but for now, her words would have to be enough. "How do you feel?"

"Like I lost a fight." Nestled against his shoulder and without enduring more prodding, the girl was clearly at greater ease.

"You did lose a fight." His arms tightened around the girl, though he was uncertain who was comforting whom. The solid warm weight of her in his arms filled his soul, her round bottom against him turning his ache into a throb.

A slow smile tugging the corner of the girl's mouth said she felt that very throbbing hardness beneath her just fine.

Face heating, Shade went to place her back on the ground, but the girl tightened her grip on him instead. "I need you, Shade. Now. Please."

His heart stopped. He licked his suddenly dry lips. "You—" *You don't know me,* he wanted to say, but knew that was somehow not true. "You are hurt."

"I know. But you'll make it better," the girl whispered as her hand reached for his head, tugging his mouth down to her parting lips. "The *why* of that you'll need to work out for yourself."

The scent of lilacs hit Shade first, followed by a hint of sweet arousal from her shifting hips. Then…then came the press of a warm mouth, a tongue inviting his into a slow, maddening dance.

Shade froze, his heart pounding with a sudden predatory desire that overtook need and want. He tried to focus on what the girl had said, he truly did, but it was impossible. With her delicious taste overwhelming his senses, her lilac scent rousing his soul, he couldn't think. Couldn't control the urge to take her, no matter the warnings the healer in him shouted or the common sense the man in him had.

No, he could no more stop himself from angling his mouth deeper over the girl's than he could have resisted breathing.

He intended to be soft, to follow her slow dance. To savor the sweet taste of her that tingled his tongue. He lost that battle the moment the girl's sharp canines brushed against his lower lip.

Heat surged through Shade's spine, making his cock pulse so hard that each beat of his heart was agony. Gripping the back of the girl's head, he took her mouth with a savage possessiveness. Claiming. Demanding. And when, instead of yielding to his pressure, the female roused to it—her hand tangling in his hair and yanking him close—there was no more thought of any kind to be had.

A growl that was anything but human rose inside his chest as he pinned the girl to the soft moss. His mouth still on her, he plunged his hand between her thighs to find her sex wet and hot and calling to him. But he wanted more than to bed her. He wanted to claim every inch of her blazing body.

Shade slid two fingers into her without mercy, the spiked scent of her arousal raking down his chest and thighs and cock. Yes, he would be inside her soon, making her tight, hot channel his own. But first, first, Shade wanted to savor all of her. Properly.

Pulling free from the girl's mouth and sex, Shade held himself up over the girl. Her pupils were wide and glassy with a desire that matched his own. Her lips parted, her breath as quick as her racing pulse as she arched up toward him. If she felt the pain of her injuries now, the sensation must be as distant as Shade's common sense. And in a few moments, she would feel not even that.

11

LERA

Shade's body looms over mine, his yellow eyes fevered, black hair swinging around his sculpted face. His bare chest and shoulders are a field of rippling tan muscle. My heart speeds with anticipation, the magic inside me recognizing its mate, the vital connection with him it needs for survival. I need Shade inside me as I need air, the craving so primal that I shake with it, a moan escaping my lips.

Shade's canines flash in pleasure at the sound. Since I knew him before he'd donned the veil, with my own amulet removed, I see the male for what he is, my body already bucking for more, my damp sex clenching around the emptiness I long for him to fill.

Flexing his arms to lower himself toward me, Shade brushes his sharp teeth along the exposed skin of my throat, stopping on either side. The predator inside my mate growls, its claim as ancient as the magic itself. Not human. Neither of us.

The pressure on my throat increases, Shade's sharp canines tightening to the edge of pain. A blade of heat rushes down my skin, making my breasts tingle, the backs of my thighs suddenly prickling. My toes curl, each moment under Shade's power somehow more exciting, more unbearable than the one before. When Shade's hand slides between my wet thighs, I clench my legs together in an effort to capture it.

Dropping a knee between my legs, Shade shoves my wet thighs apart. Cold night air brushes along my hot sex, my gasping breaths loud enough to send the wildlife dashing for cover. Lifting his teeth from my throat, Shade covers my mouth with his, swallowing the sound. Down below, the male's strong finger opens my folds, the callused pads running up and down my sex. Toying with me.

I growl.

Shade's eyes flash. His pupils are wide, the gold around them as bright as glowing embers. Pulling free of me, Shade licks his fingers, the fevered need in his gaze rising with each suckle.

The desire the male radiates is enough to make my breasts tighten to aching. Hidden beneath Shade's breeches, his bulging cock tempts me with the taste denied for so long. My magic bucks, finding the strands of his. Tangling. Yanking against restraints with all the enhanced power of the equinox.

Shade gasps. Pulling away, he raises his face to the starlit sky and draws a shaking breath. Another. His arms tremble, his thighs clenching around a great pulsing bulge. "You are hurt," he rasps. "You can't fight me off. And when—if—I start, I won't be gentle. I can't." A shudder rakes his strong body, his breaths quick and shallow. Despite the chill, his temples are damp with sweat. The scent of him, like earth fresh from rain, fills the air between us. "If you want to stop—"

"I don't." *I can't.*

Shade growls. His eyes flash, the magic in them taking over. "If you move too quickly, I will hunt you." A warning.

"You can try." Baring my teeth, I rip his flies open, his cock springing free. The long velvety shaft rocks beneath its own weight, the moist tip of it glistening in the starlight. Making my mouth water for it. I rake my nails along Shade's shoulder, and he sheathes his cock inside me in a single hard thrust.

I gasp, his size filling me completely.

Without waiting, Shade pulls back and thrusts again with a groan, the great length of him taking me by surprise no matter how many times I've felt it. *Thrust. Thrust. Thrust.* The thick head of his cock hits the sensitive ridges inside my channel, sending zings of spasming pleasure rippling through my back and thighs.

My channel clenches around Shade's shaft, but it is still not enough. Gripping his waist with my legs, I push my hips up into him and—I scream as a blaze of pain shoots through my wounded thigh, tears springing to my eyes. Inside me, I can feel the closeness of Shade's healing magic, its desire to knit my flesh together—just as I feel the shackles of the mortal world holding everything down.

Shade pulls free of me.

"No!" I grab his shoulders.

Brushing me off him with a single, powerful motion, Shade flips me over the heap of clothes piled high on the moss. My backside is suddenly high in the air, my legs bent, my face pressing into a shirt that smells of Shade.

But I can't see him. Can't grab him.

Gritting my teeth against the stabbing in my thigh, I try to flip back over—making it all of two inches before a biting slap on my bottom sends a different kind of blaze all through my skin.

I yelp, clenching my backside, only to discover Shade has spread my thighs, his fingers stroking inside my folds. The male's deft fingertips brush ruthlessly along either side of my apex, the sting from my bottom echoing all along the swollen bud. Magnifying each sensation. Molten flame consumes my throbbing sex, pushing me to the edge of an abyss.

Then the head of Shade's pulsing cock is at my entrance again, sliding easily through the wetness. In and out, in and out, the sound of his hips smacking my backside reverberating through the forest.

I barely catch my breath when I feel Shade's hands on me again, one reaching around to stroke my apex while the other cups my right breast, rolling my nipple. Shade's large body engulfs mine, holding me from all sides.

Too much, my wounded body screams at me, my breaths coming as fast as the rushing stream beside us. The pulsing inside my channel, the spark of pain on my thigh, the escalating zings streaking from my breasts to my sensitive bud. The pressure building inside me is exquisite, my whole shuddering core knowing that something must give.

His gasps tickle my ear, his throbbing shaft sending ripples of vibration through me. His hand shifts from my breast, desperately digging into my hips to get more purchase, pulling me back harder against him in a frenzy. The abyss looming before me is surely large enough to swallow us both. Yet it does not.

The pressure grows, squeezing my need, my lungs, my magic. His finger quickens along my apex, flickering left and right and middle.

"Leralynn!" He bellows suddenly, the tension between us finally giving way. Shade's magic floods our connection, searing my wounds just as the ecstasy of release shoves me over its own cliff.

Agony and elation weave together, the warmth Shade spills inside me spreading like the strongest of spirits. I shudder. Once. Twice. With the third great spasm, I arch toward the stars, screaming Shade's name as the world flickers around the edges.

12

LERA

After a few minutes wrapped in a haze of exhausted release, the world returns into focus with my naked body reclined against Shade, the male using a stream-dampened cloth to clean my thighs. Despite the smooth strokes of Shade's hands, his heart pounds against his ribs. Blinking, I realize the dressing he applied to my leg earlier is gone, my once-deep wound now shallow and no longer bleeding. Not my usual fae-enhanced healing, but much more. As if some of Shade's healing magic actually staked its claim, even the mortal world's shackles unable to fully contain the power surge my coupling with the quint male brings.

Or else the wards protecting the human world have cracked further still in Ostera's honor.

I try to sit up.

Shade's arms tighten around me, his earthy scent caressing my skin. Shifting me to the crook of his shoulder, he focuses his beautiful face on mine, his high cheekbones and strong jaw shadowed in the scant moonlight. The air thickens between us, questions and sensations saturating the small space. The memory of Shade inside me still stirs my body, the loss of him tingling like a phantom limb.

Reaching out slowly, he runs a knuckle along my cheekbone. "For a moment, when we were connected, I knew who you were," he whispers. "But I don't anymore."

I swallow, the memory of my name on Shade's lips squeezing my chest. I press my cheek into his touch, savoring the feel of his hand along my skin. Pretending, for a moment, that we are in the *before*. "I know."

"And… Do you know me?" he asks, his yellow eyes penetrating.

My throat closes, my pulse picking up the beat. I don't know what might trigger the amulet, whether answering even that question might turn the magic on Shade.

"You do know." Shade's jaw tightens as he answers his own question, his hand falling away from my cheek. "Tell me. Who are you? Who am I? Why have I been losing time, finding myself… How did I come to be here?"

"I can't say it." I rub my face, missing the male's touch.

"Try." His voice hardens. "We've shared quite a bit more than information just now. You owe me a chance to understand."

I wrap my arms around myself, the loss of contact with Shade's skin leaving me chilled to the bone. Maybe Shade is right, maybe speaking the truth will fare differently from forcing physical evidence of it, like I tried by having Coal touch his ear. Maybe this moment now is too precious to let pass. Licking my lips, I find the male's eyes. "You are fae, Shade," I say quickly, despite the warning bells tolling in my soul. "We came from Lunos together, wearing an amulet that was supposed to make humans believe we belong in the mortal realms. But—"

I cut off as Shade's eyes widen—not in surprise but in sheer undiluted agony. *No.* Clamping his hands on either side of his head, the male rocks, gasping for breath.

No, no, no. This can't be happening again. I've only just recovered from Coal's agonized scream.

"Shade!" My gut clenches. Twisting to my knees, I brush my finger along his strong pain-lined face. "Breathe. It's all right. I'll stop."

Holding on to my gaze like a lifeline, Shade continues gasping a minute longer until his breathing finally slows. "I heard you speak, but your words turned to daggers," he says, his voice breaking. "I could hang on to what you said no more than I could hold a blade with my bare hands."

The image is so on point that bile rises up my throat. I'm afraid to speak. Afraid of doing anything lest it challenge the amulet's veil. I only realize that tears roll down my cheeks when the male reaches out to brush them away with his thumb.

"It's all right, cub." Drawing me to him, Shade smooths my hair, his palm large and so, so warm.

"No, it isn't." I force the words past my tight throat. "I have to go."

"No." He grabs my arms, his eyes now clear. Intelligent. "Just because you cannot speak of some things doesn't mean you get to run from me, cub. Not now, not ever."

I shake my head, my fingers running along Shade's cheek, savoring the stubble-roughened skin. "I have to go," I whisper again. "We both do. We can't talk, and we can't stay here forever. You know that. Plus, the Night Guard is still about."

Predatory yellow eyes narrow on mine. "I will find you again," he says, this time the words coming as a mix of threat and promise. "I will work out the truth of this, and I will find you."

When I open my mouth to reply, his lips descend upon mine with a claiming force that takes my breath.

Gripping the back of my head, Shade plunges his tongue deeper still, each stroke more possessive than the one before it. Heat rushes from my mouth all the way to my swollen apex, which rouses again immediately. My body flinches from the sheer intensity of Shade's kiss, but the security of his grip keeps me in place, turning the spreading flame into a bonfire that has my thighs trembling.

I moan into Shade's mouth, my tongue trying and failing to match his. I struggle against the force of his kiss again, my heart speeding until…until I stop fighting, letting myself feel the full force of Shade's desire, trusting the male as he makes my soul soar to frightening heights.

A whimper escapes me when he starts to pull away, the sound turning to a short yip at the string of pain along my upper lip.

"You bit me," I sputter.

Still holding me in place, Shade laps the tiny drop of blood from my lip, his eyes glowing with lupine intensity. "I claim you, cub," he whispers, finally allowing me to pull back. "Now and forever."

I touch my lip, the sting morphing to a warmth that spreads through my skin. "You marked me."

He shrugs one shoulder, a bit of color touching his face. "If you are going to go, you better do it now," he murmurs. "I don't know how much longer I can keep myself in check."

Right. Over my panting breaths, the night still feels like a dream. When I climb to my feet however, the sensations flooding my body reassure me that everything that happened was, in fact, real. Gathering what's left of my clothes and armor, I cover myself the best I can. "Don't look," I tell Shade as I start toward the gathering of thick oaks a few paces away. I don't know how his looking actually matters since the moment my own veil amulet snaps into place, it will spin a story of its own, but I want to tempt the magic as little as possible.

Once behind the cover of the trees, I take the magical relic out of its pouch and swallow. Shade claimed me. But will he find me amidst the humans? Before the terror of his possible failure paralyzes me, I fasten the amulet around my neck and disappear into the woods.

A cadet keeping clear of an instructor lest he catch her out of bounds.

By the time I meet Arisha on the other side of the escape tunnel—waiting with a patient smile and my rumpled dress and cloak in hand—my throat is so tight that I can barely pull myself together enough to explain my disheveled state. Shade held me. Claimed me. Called out my name. And would not recognize me now if I walked right into him. I can hardly explain why this is so agonizing to *myself* right now, let alone my inquisitive, too-watchful friend.

"I only managed to hit two Yocklols before the *Night Guard* appeared of all things. It seems they've obtained a key to Mystwood *and* managed to step between the Light and Gloom in the mortal realm," I force myself to say over the sorrow and longing pounding my soul.

"Stars." Arisha sucks in a breath. "Plugging a leak of errant magic seeping through faulty wards is one thing, but going against the Night Guard… "

"Could they be responsible for the crumbling wards?" I ask. "Why are they here of all places?"

"Likely the same reason your quint came——this is where the rift in the protective fabric starts."

"Fair point. Well, unless the rift expands, the Night Guard fae have no more access to magic in the mortal realm than I do, so at least we are even." I try to shrug one shoulder in feigned nonchalance but end up wincing instead, my traitorous body reminding me of just how sore and drained I am. Whatever dance Shade's magic did with mine while we mated might have healed the worst of my injuries, but I am still a certifiable mess. "On the brighter side," I say, starting our trek back to the dorms, "Coal is likely to break me in two in the next morning training, and then I will have to deal with none of this mess. That *is* right, right? Your uncle doesn't have some prophecy that says a fae comes back from the dead to do work?"

"Actually…" Arisha shoots me a sideways glance that makes my stomach sink on instinct.

"What?"

"The good news," says Arisha, "is that you need not worry about Coal in the morning."

"And the bad news?"

"I didn't want to distract you earlier, but you are to report to River tomorrow morning. The suspicious sort that he is, he'd like to watch as you complete your assignments." Arisha tries for a smile that doesn't quite reach her blue eyes. "Look at the bright side, do this once, and we'll have breathing room for a while."

13

LERA

Stopping halfway up the long, winding keep stairs to River's study, I press my back against the cool stone wall on an off chance that brilliance might strike down upon me at the last moment.

It doesn't.

My mind spins with the taste of a forbidden kiss, of River's stunned gray eyes. Of his hunched broad shoulders silhouetted against the railing as I ran from the balcony.

Of what transpired between *Shade* and me since then.

I scrubbed the healer's scent—along with other smells of the night's fighting—off myself early this morning. But there is nothing I can do for my memories.

Focus. I shake my head. *One problem at a time.*

The satchel with books I can barely read and math I can't begin to understand hangs over my shoulder, its weight heavier than any weapon. Despite tossing in my sheets for what was left of the night, I've no solution for the looming disaster. The moment River pushes, there will be no hiding the extent of my ignorance. And then… *Then you'll deal with the practical consequences,* I tell myself firmly. He can punish me for cheating, force me to repeat the classes for the next decade, lock me in my chamber until I improve. But he can't expel me from the Academy.

And he can't ever unknow what he will discover about me. King, meet stable girl.

Swallowing the bile rising up my throat, I force my body back into motion, the spiraling staircase somehow managing to be too long and too short all at once. The bustling Academy grounds glimmer through tall narrow windows, escape growing farther and farther away. Stopping at the second level from the top, I survey the antechamber to River's study, the pair of benches where visitors are to wait currently empty. The double doors leading to the study itself are thrown open, revealing a room burned into my memory despite a single visit here. Wood-panel-lined walls, a bookshelf, a fireplace—the flames currently banked.

River stands in front of his desk, his back toward me. With his arms braced on the table's edge and his attention down on something he must be reading, his back forms a muscular triangle beneath a black silk shirt. His shoulder blades are especially pronounced against the soft fabric, which tapers to a narrow waist and fitted pants that outline the male's muscular backside and thighs. His woodsy scent fills the room, marking it as his.

The sight of River's perfect, powerful frame dries my mouth—and the male hasn't even moved a muscle. Hasn't acknowledged my presence either, though surely his immortal senses have alerted him to my coming. In the silence, I can almost hear the phantom chords of the Ostera ball, River's sure steps spinning us with a waltz that makes the very stars dance. Biting my lip, I press my thighs tighter together, my body reacting to his sheer physical presence even while my mind screams its warning to me. That was a noble lady he had been spinning. Not me.

The heartbeat of silence between us turns to two. Three. I clear my throat. "Sir? You wished to see me."

"Yes." He still doesn't turn, though his back muscles bunch beneath his shirt. His hand moves, apparently pulling another paper out for his inspection as he motions to a high-back chair a pace away from him. "Take a seat."

I walk slowly, my hands fingering the strap of my satchel. "I'll stand." The words come out softer than I'd intended. I clear my throat and try again. "I'd prefer to stand, sir. If that is all right."

River turns, his broad chest and square jaw enough to make a stone dampen. "All right." He waits, bracing his hands on the desk behind him in a way that makes his shirt stretch over his abdomen.

Stopping at the chair, I'm suddenly not sure why I insisted on standing. Certainly it does little to diminish the sheer difference in our size, with my head barely reaching River's shoulder.

"You should know that when I issued orders for you to report here, the Ostera ball…events had not yet happened." His voice is a soft rumble that vibrates my core. *Events.* His dance. Our kiss. My running off into the darkness. My hands tighten on the back of the chair. River straightens, pulling down on his already perfect shirt, his face an unreadable mask. "What I did was inappropriate, Leralynn. And I both beg your forgiveness and offer assurance that such indiscretion on my part will not be repeated."

Ice douses my core. Indiscretion. I'm a bloody indiscretion.

"Understood, sir." My voice is so distant, I can't believe it belongs to me, my heart hammering against my chest.

He draws a deep breath, his shoulders straight but seeming to bear even more weight than I am used to seeing upon them. "All right. With that said, judging from the books I see you've brought, I imagine you are aware of my original reason for summoning you." He runs a hand through his hair, one of his only tells of discomfort. "However, given my subsequent poor choices on an unrelated matter, I don't believe myself to be in a position to oversee you. So I will instead simply lay out the facts and let you walk out that door to make your own choices. You are not required to say anything regarding my suspicions or allegations, but I request that you not lie to me either. Can you agree to that?"

I swallow, my mind tripping over River's words as I repeat them in my head. Say nothing and walk out. Too good. The offer sounds too perfect to be true, and yet I can find no hidden hook in it.

"Leralynn?" River prompts, then clears his throat. "If you do not wish to be alone in a room with me, I understand."

"No." I raise my hand, simultaneously realizing both River's misinterpretation of my silence and the small glowing coals of indignation that his previous words roused inside me. Spinning on my heel, I stride to the still-open double doors and pull them shut. "I've no problem being alone in a room with you," I say, striking back at him. "You didn't force something on me that I didn't want, and I will not let you rewrite history to imagine it that way. I'm perfectly capable of making my own choices about who I kiss."

He raises one dark brow, his gaze brushing from the now-closed door back to my face. "Relieved as I am to note that my actions have not doused that spitfire spirit of yours, my position at this Academy makes any overture coercive." He holds out his hand, forestalling anything I was going to say. "In either case, let us return to the topic of my original summons."

Putting his hands into the small of his back, he inclines his head toward me. "Several of your instructors have expressed concern about whether the work you submit is done…independently. My intention was to have you work here for the morning, to reassure both myself and your teachers that the material you submit is, in fact, your own. Or to address the issue by harsher means if it is not."

A shiver runs down my spine, and it's all I can do to keep myself from taking a step back.

He shakes his head, not even pretending that he missed my sudden tension. "None of that is going to happen, Leralynn."

I let out a breath in spite of myself.

River sighs. "I am not at all certain I am doing the right thing, but as I refuse to insist you remain in my isolated company, I will simply remind you that, eventually, you will face exams and leave the matter at that."

Exams. I'd not thought I'd be here long enough for those. "What happens to students who fail?" I can't help asking.

"Great Falls Academy is prohibited from expelling students directly, but we make the consequences unpleasant enough that most withdraw their enrollment or choose to alter their study habits drastically." River's gaze locks on me, something about the way he says the words making them sound like a desperate warning instead of a threat. Tapping a finger against his desk, he walks back to his seat. "You may go."

Tension that I didn't know was holding my body immobile suddenly releases its grip, relief flooding my blood. A reprieve. A stay of execution. All I need to do is walk out the doors, and I can return to the niche I've carved out for myself over the last month. I work alone, powerful in the safety of being who I am—no matter how short it falls of the males' standards. And now, without River looking over my shoulder, I will have months of easier breaths. Months to fight unmolested by night and survive the Academy the best I can by day. He need never learn the truth of my ignorance or of my cheating. As for exams, I'll deal with those when they come. If they come at all.

Everything is exactly as I could possibly wish it. So why am I not happy? Clenching my jaw, I wait for a delayed uplifting of spirit to flutter through me. It doesn't. It can't.

"River," I say quietly.

"*Sir.*" His voice has an edge.

"Sir." I shut my mouth, the words catching in the back of my throat. I need to keep silent. Turn around. Walk out the door and thank the stars for making the male leave me alone. And yet my legs will not let me move.

Maybe I don't want the reprieve. Don't want for River to turn a blind eye to my cheating, for Coal to release his wrestling holds, for Tye to take no for an answer to a dance. Maybe I don't want Shade to look away when I ask him to. All the things that I've struggled for. Maybe I want none of them. Not really.

Whatever punishment he will inflict for my cheating, I think it will hurt less than him turning his back on me.

With a suddenly trembling hand, I reach into my satchel and pull out my history text. Opening the book to a random page, I lick my lips as I stare at the long words. "'Ckriee-del's inch-insulation…insinuation that it would consider…consider…'" My voice breaks on the long words as it always does, my heart pounding harder with every misread syllable. River unlikely even remembers a time when he tripped over such things. My face heats, my chopped words echoing in the small wood-paneled room. I tighten my grip on the pages, the words swimming before me. "'It would consider any buildup of ships a provo…provo…'"

"Provocation," he says very quietly.

"Provocation," I echo, gripping the book so hard that my knuckles blanche. "'Ckridel's insinuation that it would consider any buildup of ship a provocation, led to the core-create…'" The words blur, my traitorous eyes stinging. I should have chosen a different sentence, one that I had some chance of reading. *Stars,* I should have walked out the door when I had a chance.

I realize he is beside me only when his large hands take the book from my grip. Putting a knuckle under my chin, he tips my face up to meet his. For the first time since I met the male, I can't bring myself to look into his eyes. Can't bear the disgust and disappointment that I know will lurk behind his gaze no matter how schooled his features.

"Might I deduce that your mathematics skills are little better?" he asks. "And that neither the work nor the application you turned in to the Academy were your own?"

I nod. Ironically, no lie there.

He blows out a long breath. "Why are you telling me this now?' he asks. When I keep silent, the grip he has on my chin tightens, a note of command entering his tone. "Look at me, Leralynn."

The journey up River's large muscular body to meet his eyes is one of the longest I've taken.

"Good," he says as our gazes meet. Mine vulnerable, his commanding. I hate how much weight that one syllable of River's praise carries. His eyes stay on mine. "Now. Tell me why you're telling me this. I would have let you walk out the door."

"Because… I didn't know what else to do." The truth rushes from me in a whisper.

He nods, as if that answer is somehow acceptable. "Who else knows? Your roommate, Arisha of Tallie, I presume?"

I shift my weight, but he does not allow me to escape his gray gaze, his control somehow frustrating and calming all at the same time. With no escape route left, surrendering the last of the truth is somehow easier. "Arisha believes I'm just having trouble keeping up with everything because I've been busy. She doesn't realize the extent of…of what I don't know." I force a hint of a smile I don't feel onto my face. "So, in other words, the Academy is about to see its first cadet who fails exams *multiple* times. A first time for everything, right? Now you know it will happen. In case you don't like surprises and all."

He shakes his head once, his sharp eyes cutting right past the fakeness of my smile. "I'll help you."

"What?" It's my turn to stare at him.

"Reading, mathematics, the basics everyone here takes for granted. If you are prepared to work, to really set your mind to it, I will help you with all of it. In confidence." He lowers his hand, leaning back on his heels as if to give me a bit of breathing room. "It will take all you have Leralynn, and I may—will—push you harder than you think I should. But if you trust me to teach you, I will." He pauses, looking uncertain for the first time. "Do you trust me?"

I take a deep breath. "Yes."

14

OWALIN

The chamber fell silent as Owalin, Captain of the Night Guard, strode to the kneeling female. Beatrice's wounds bled still, the copper scent of her blood and fear filling the air. She was right to be frightened. In the decade since Owalin obtained the key to Mystwood and led his regiment to the mortal realm, his warriors had never been compromised. Until now.

"Yori and I were certain the female was alone," Beatrice told the chamber, her chin raised despite the slight tremble in her voice. Blood and sweat plastered long strands of silver hair to her face, her pale blue eyes twitching between the floor and Owalin. "Alone and young. It would have been a swift capture and valuable intelligence had the shifter not appeared."

"You had no leave to engage," Owalin barked at her before checking his tone. This was about planning and information, not punishment. Punishment would come later. After years of work at Great Falls, the threads in the tapestry shielding the mortal realm from magic were finally starting to fray. Already there were points where stepping in and out of the Gloom was sometimes possible. Just a bit more prying and Owalin's warriors would be able to successfully tap into their immortal magic.

Once that happened, taking the Academy would be a swift matter. Any peoples who thought penning the children of ten royal kingdoms together was a bright idea deserved to be taken. Just as Owalin and the Night Guard deserved a realm of their own.

Owalin returned his glare to the kneeling warrior. "The wench saw you step into the Gloom?"

"Yes." Beatrice flinched. "It was my only way of making it back alive. I judged that reporting the presence of other immortals was of greater value than keeping the Gloom a secret."

Owalin drummed his finger on the table's edge. Beatrice had a point. Any immortals outside the Night Guard would be under Council orders to protect the mortal realm—and once Night Guard warriors became able to access magic, so would the other bastards.

Ensuring no other fae prowled the mortal realm was the whole reason Owalin had funded the human inquisitors so actively scouring the continent. Owalin was rather proud of himself on that front. How many others would have recognized the hidden opportunity in a stray lord's anti-fae movement and turned the silliness from a liability into an asset?

"Master Zake, why is there an immortal on my lands?" Turning to the only human sitting at the table, Owalin raised a brow. "I was under the impression that your people were combing the alliance to eradicate any hint of fae sympathizers. How the bloody hell did an actual fae immortal slip their grasp?"

"You are the one who's been dumping experimental refuse into your own yard," Zake said. Around forty, the lord was large and—by human standards—muscular. With a thick head of wiry brown hair, Zake had amassed a series of scars, including a long slash across his face that gave him a perpetually displeased expression. "If you shit where you dine, you can't expect to keep from attracting those Lunos rodents."

Owalin flashed the man a warning look. A year ago, he'd have done a great deal more than that, but the human lord had proved useful. Spurred by some personal slight, Lord Zake had half the bloody continent busy turning on neighbors and eradicating fae craft. Most of the *craft* was imagined, of course, but any occasional artifact or text that got caught up in the process made it right back into Owalin's hands. By the time the Night Guard was ready to attack, the continent would be prime for the taking, the humans having no notion of what was happening until it was too late.

Which meant Owalin had to swallow an occasional insult. Keeping

Zake was akin to keeping a hunting dog—you couldn't expect the pooch not to lick its backside in public once in a while.

"Let me restate my question," Owalin said harshly. "How has your network of fae-hunting inquisitors overlooked an actual fae intruder?"

"My people are seeded in the cities and towns, Grayson being the closest to here." Zake's tone finally shifted to something Owalin could tolerate. "We don't comb the wilderness. So unless the wench and her shifter have taken residence in the forest itself, the only location I've no visibility into is the Academy itself. They will not allow outsiders, even my inquisitors, inside the walls."

Owalin pursed his lips, mentally examining and discarding one possibility after another before settling on an approach that was as simple as it was powerful. "Very well, Master Zake. Then let us not be outsiders. Please discover what employment opportunities might exist at this prestigious institution. In fact, I'm confident we can assist in creating the appropriate vacancies as needed."

PART II: DUNGEONS AND DREAMERS

1

COAL

"I do miss the sight of that pretty, bent-over ass greeting us in the stable, but this will have to do." The guardsman's voice, reaching Coal through the thin walls of Czar's stall, grated on his already dark mood. The clanking of metal bits the guards had been sorting earlier had sounded so much like the phantom scrape of chains that Coal had paused twice to brace his forehead on Czar's shoulder and breathe through the flashes of pain and darkness. Shade had said time should snuff out nightmares, but time, plainly, had opposite plans when it came to Coal.

The one—the only—time the nightmares had quieted for two days was after Coal had coupled with Leralynn in the cave, the storm raging outside a harmony to the one exploding between them. Not a solution to be indulged in again, though Coal still held on to it in the privacy of his memories. But that was a month ago, and each day since, that precious lifeline thinned more and more.

Another man whistled. "You went and drew that yourself, Kreger? Quite handy with a pen when 'tis to your cock's benefit, I see."

Feet shuffled, and Kreger squawked indignantly, startling the horses. "Give it back, you bastard."

"I will. But this beauty is meant to be shared. You aren't the only one with an aching cock, you know." The man laughed, raising his voice. "'Ey, Coal. I know you're here. Come take yourself a look. If this doesn't lift your mood, I swear you are a lost cause."

Coal straightened from where he was cleaning Czar's hooves—the stallion was liable to kick any of the stable hands who came within range, leaving his care to Coal alone—and looked out from the stall. Two stocky dark-haired guards tussled over a scrap of paper, the taller holding it out of the shorter one's reach. The pair picked a poor day for it—not that there were many days now that Coal didn't feel his leash on violence straining to the breaking point. Waiting for half a reason to escape.

"Give it back to him and leave for your patrol," Coal called, though it was a waste of breath. Until the damn dance was resolved, neither bastard was going anywhere. Fine.

Hoof pick still in hand, Coal strode out of Czar's stall and ripped the offending sheet from the taller man's hand. Midday sun slanted in through the high windows of the immaculate stable, catching a corner of the parchment. Coal was halfway to handing the loot back to its owner when the familiar lines of a girl's face, sketched in easy pen strokes, leapt out of the shadows, gripping his stomach. Unfolding the parchment all the way, he stared at the unmistakable mock-up of Leralynn, her legs parted open to reveal a wet entrance, swollen with need. An entrance he knew all too well. The drawing didn't come close to doing it justice. Just as it failed to capture Leralynn's heaving, pink-tipped breasts, the memory of which was well burned into his mind.

Coal's hand tightened on the page, darkness hovering at the edge of his vision. "Do you have more?" he asked, his words a cool distant noise at utter odds with the hot rush of blood filling his ears.

Kreger's bloodshot eyes narrowed for a moment. "Maybe." He licked his lips, a hint of a smile creeping onto his face. "In my barracks. But it will cost ya."

The darkness was tinged red now. "Take me there," Coal heard himself say, his voice a cracking whip, his body already in motion.

2

LERA

Sunlight streaking through the window of River's study illuminates my graphite slate, tiny specks of dust hanging starlike in the light's beam. I try to concentrate on mathematics. I really do. But with River looking over my shoulder, one wide, callused palm braced on the back of my chair, and the other flat on the writing desk, I can't think over the heat of his body, his intoxicating male scent. Woodsy, mixed with soap and a hint of the chalk we're using. This close to him, I hear the phantom song of the violin all over again, the stars rushing across the sky as River twirls me through the Ostera waltz. *One two three. One two three. One two three.*

In the wake of the Ostera celebration and during the ensuing liberty week that the Academy grants cadets, River has made good on his offer to tutor me through my lagging academics. Ostensibly, I report to his study to fulfill a clerk's function—it's far from protocol for the deputy headmaster to work one-on-one with a cadet, especially a cadet who's one assignment away from flunking out of the Academy—and this arrangement has raised no eyebrows in the two days since we started it. In truth, my literacy and computation skills have left River wincing multiple times a day. Including now.

"How exactly do two *and a half* soldiers dig a latrine?" Taking the chalk from my hand, River leans lower to add his marks to the slate, his neat dark hair and clean-shaven jaw only inches from my face. From my lips. *Focus, Lera.* We may have avoided raising eyebrows, but I've discovered the real risk of tutoring: being so close to *this* version of River, one who's not yelling at me or issuing a command, is wreaking havoc between my thighs. In just the span of a couple of days, these moments, whether I care to admit it or not, have become precious to me—too precious. I feel a warm finger on my chin, directing my gaze back down to the slate. "Pay attention." River writes with the same crisp efficiency as he does everything, the muscles beneath his white silk shirt equally at ease working out mathematics as wielding a sword. "You need to remember what you are actually counting."

I cut River a sideways glance, meeting his beautiful gray eyes with a quirked brow. "It might help if we counted something more pressing than latrine ditches," I say carefully. The presence of the Night Guard that I fought on Ostera night changes the landscape of the magic threat we are facing—as does the Night Guard's discovery of *my* presence. There has to be a way of conveying as much to River without either triggering the veil amulet's defenses or getting me thrown out of the study. "Such as the number of fighters at the Academy who can stand against magic-tinged foes."

"Alas, you are counting ditches." Straightening, River crosses his arms and gives the slate a meaningful look. One of the largest males I've seen in Lunos, he is downright overpowering in the mortal world, carrying the cloak of responsibility on his shoulders without ever tripping. Or yielding. His biceps and shoulders press tantalizingly against his shirt. In the warmth of the study, he's hung his jacket over a chair and undone his top buttons, revealing the flare of his tanned pectorals. He's become less careful around me as we've studied, caught up in his work, the strong planes of his face unselfconscious in concentration. With every cuff he loosens and shirtsleeve he rolls up, he becomes more distractingly beautiful. "If you spent half as much effort studying as you do trying to meddle in issues I've ordered the cadets to keep clear of, you might have a chance of passing your exams. Let us get back to it, if you please."

Beneath the writing desk, my fingers curl around the smooth satin of the dress I chose for the day. The amaranth fabric is light enough to be comfortable while staying formal, while the long skirt and covered sleeves conceal the fading bruises and cuts of my encounter with the Night Guard's blade. "Just tell me one thing—have you ever heard of fae pledging allegiance to Mors? They—"

"That's enough." River's face hardens, his low, sensuous voice taking on familiar gravelly steel. "When I give a cadet an order, I expect it followed. If you intend to take up arms, you better get used to obeying your superiors whether or not you like their decisions. Do I—"

River cuts off, both our attentions sliding toward the door and the two sets of approaching footsteps beyond. The third set of visitors in under two hours. With the constant traffic coming into his study, I'm not sure how the male manages to get anything done. But he does. River has his competent fingers on the pulse of everything. Except the very mission we came from Lunos to accomplish.

By the time a knock sounds on the double doors, River is already there, waiting for me to cover up my work. I didn't know it was even possible for someone to be so attentively considerate and bullheadedly frustrating at the same time. As I shove the last of my books into a drawer, River lets his visitors inside.

"Good morning, sir," he says.

Hearing the honorific, I quickly rise to my feet as Headmaster Sage strides into the study, his signature wet cough, hawkish features, and gleaming bald pate arriving with him. Walking in beside him is a man I've not seen before. Tall and trim, he appears to be in his early thirties, with short black hair combed back from a pronounced peak and a sharply attractive face. His eyes, a stormy mix of blue and gray, survey River in a single glance before sliding across the room, brushing over me dismissively.

"River, allow me to introduce Master Han," Sage says, waiting as the men bow formally to each other. "Han is a well-positioned Prowess trainer and will be joining the Academy's instructor cadre to prepare Tyelor and the others for the upcoming Trials. He has been in the circuit for a decade now, and fielded more gold medalists than any other practitioner in that time. Han, Commander River is in charge of the Academy's day-to-day matters. You and I will work directly, of course, but River can see to any special requirements you might have."

"Your servant, sir," River tells the newcomer politely, a flash of concern in his features that only I know him well enough to catch. He turns to look back at Sage. "I wasn't aware that anyone but Tyelor intended to compete."

"A fact that I intend to change shortly," Han cuts in before Sage can answer. His cool, velvet-smooth voice sends an uncomfortable ripple across my skin. "As Master Sage and I have discussed, athletics is one of the world's greatest unifiers. With the royal offspring of all ten of the alliance kingdoms together, fielding less than a full team is a mistake. And with the Academy's strong physical preparation, I feel confident I can adapt interested cadets to be competitive in the less exotic events—unarmed combat, swordplay, perhaps archery."

Sage nods along eagerly to Han's speech. "I recruited Tyelor with the notion of returning the Academy to the Trials, and Han will move on that vision. Not only will this weave the royal-born cadets together, but it will bring their *parents* together as well." The hungry glint in Sage's eyes betrays the honors he already imagines being showered upon him in the wake of victory.

I make a small noise, the pen in my tight hand suddenly breaking with a loud *snap*. Sage didn't recruit Tye—the veil did. And now the little man is turning that kernel of warped memory into a continent-sprawling affair. So much for Lunos not interfering with the humans. I don't know what this new direction means, but it can't be good.

For the first time since walking in, Han's eyes swing to meet mine straight on. Though there is nothing but guarded greeting in the man's gaze, its contact makes nausea tickle my throat, my magic churning in its mortal shackles.

"Was there something you wished to say, Cadet?" Han inquires.

River shoots me a look that makes any retort dry up immediately, unease swirling in my stomach. *Tread carefully,* his gaze says. If River is nervous, I'd be a fool not to listen.

"No, sir." I answer quickly, pulling the reins of my self-control tighter still and staying silent for the rest of the brief visit.

"What do you make of Han and the Prowess plan?" I ask River a few minutes later, once the study is free of visitors but for their lingering scent. A sickly musk for Sage and something sharper, like cayenne pepper, that crept from Han's muscled body.

"My opinion on the matter was not sought." River motions for me to bring out my books, ready to return to the fascinating calculations of ditch digging. Any sign of worry in his sculpted face is gone, back behind that thick, impenetrable curtain. "Neither was yours."

"Doesn't stop us from having one."

"It stops me from discussing it with you," River says, that stern voice returning, storm-gray eyes unreadable. No matter what I do, each hour since the forbidden kiss on Ostera night is turning the male more and more formal the moment we stray from academics, his inner sense of student-teacher etiquette on high alert. I almost wish it didn't happen, for the wall it's erected between us—but then I remember his warm, velvet lips on mine, the press of his hard body, the soft gravel of his voice in my ear as he led me through the dance steps, and I wish I could spend another eternity in that moment.

Shade, on the other hand, has gone missing altogether since our moment in the woods, having sent a note of intention to spend several liberty days off Academy grounds. My chest clenches with the certainty that my male now prowls the woods, desperately searching out a mate who isn't there. I know how he feels, which only makes my worry for him greater. Without Arisha and Gavriel finding me when I first arrived here, giving me a sense of purpose with our nightly missions, I might have gone mad with loneliness weeks ago.

My heart squeezes painfully. One male is looking in the wrong place and the other is two mere steps away but refusing to look at all.

"Leralynn." River's sharp snap jerks me from my thoughts. Adjusting the rolled-up sleeves to perfectly creased perfection, he throws a pointed look at my empty slate. Right. Latrine ditches and soldier halves.

This time we manage a full half hour without interruption, River leaving me to struggle through a set of calculations while he catches up on his own work. When the next set of approaching footsteps sounds, however, River barely has time to jump out of the way of the swinging door, much less properly greet the liveried visitor.

"Sir!" Rabbit, having streaked in like a small dust vortex, smashes into River's thigh and bounces off. Panting, the boy jabs toward the window, his narrow chest heaving. "A brawl. A real big brawl," he says between gasping breaths. "With blood and shouting and everything. By the guards' barracks."

"I don't imagine a brawl by the guards' barracks is going to last very long, Rabbit." River's voice is battle calm as he shrugs into his red wool coat, fastening the buttons with precise, economical motions. "Do you know which cadet chose such a brilliant location for a fight?"

"None, sir." Rabbit shakes his head vigorously. "It's Master Coal against a dozen of the guards themselves."

3

LERA

A faint humming has started in my head as I try to make sense of Rabbit's words, River's study growing distant.

"Stay here, Leralynn," River orders. He takes one more heartbeat to hold my eyes, a heartbeat he can't spare, just to press into me the importance of what he's saying. "That isn't a request."

Knowing better than to argue, I keep my eyes trained on my studies until the sound of River's and Rabbit's steps fades from earshot. That settled, I rush down the stone steps and streak through the hedgerow separating the academic quarters from the training pitch. Worry for my male casts all thought of rules or repercussions aside, his name ricocheting through my mind with each whoosh of blood through my temples. *Coal. Coal. Coal.*

The sounds of fighting coming from the guards' barracks at the base of the towering Academy wall pierce my immortal hearing, spurring my steps and thoughts. Coal makes no habit of fighting lesser warriors, not without provocation. And even then, his battles are swift and meaningful, not brawls.

Or at least that's how it used to be.

"Stop!" a man shouts at me as I dart out of the hedgerow onto the edge of the wide grassy training yard. A half-dozen Academy guards are already spreading out to keep curious cadets away from the fray at the far end. Distantly, I can see a heaving mass of bodies in various states of dress—some shirtless and barefooted, some in full red uniform. Some wielding fists, others charging in with whatever they'd found at hand—from pitchforks to chair legs. It's too thick to see Coal. "Get back to the dormitory right now."

Right. Ducking back into the fragrant green corridor, I rush along the thin walkway, sunlight dappling down through lush overhanging branches. This time, I emerge on the other side of the patrol, near the riding ring at the top of the training yard. A nearby guard catches sight of me and lunges with a surprised shout, but I roll over my shoulder to clear his grasp. Cursing sounds behind me, but the guards have no time to chase a lone runner, not with a smattering of the Academy's cadets coming out of the woodwork to see what all the fuss is about.

"Whoa there, lass." Tye emerges suddenly from the corner of my vision and snatches me with the skill the guards lacked, his large lithe body swinging me in an easy circle. I curse and try to squirm free, but he holds fast to my upper arms. The male smells of pine and citrus and sweat, the wet patches on his sleeveless gray tunic speaking of active training. His hair is damp at the roots, a mess of fiery strands, and his green eyes are brilliant in the sunlight—and firm. Jerking his chin toward the barracks across from us, he shakes his head. "You don't want to go anywhere near there. Trust me."

"Yes, I do." I squirm out of his hold successfully this time. "But feel free to return to twirling around the wooden bar if you don't want to help."

Cursing, Tye falls in step with me, jogging to the perimeter of the fight, which is partially obscured by a wall of observers now—guards, mostly, with a few instructors and stray cadets sprinkled into the mix. Over their heads, on the other side of the fray, I spot River walking away. "Where the bloody stars is he going?" Tye asks.

With a shrug, I push my way through the watching crowd and take bearings, all my fae senses on high alert. It *is* a brawl. Shouting and a thick scent of fury fill the air, more and more men rushing in with whatever weapons they find underfoot. A rock. A piece of chair. Bare fists. In the center, Coal spins a wooden staff—which I think started its day as a broom handle. In spite of everything, Coal in battle is a breathtaking sight—his low blond bun gleaming in the sun, sleeveless black tunic revealing every flick and bulge of muscle in his arms and shoulders, beautiful, sharply carved face set in deadly concentration. His blue eyes glitter, cold as ice chips.

The wood in his hands twists quickly enough to appear a solid circle, one that has already done untold damage. I wince at the sight of a half-dozen men writhing on the ground, one with bone sticking clear out of a broken forearm and what seems to be paper stuffed into his mouth. The several sergeants shouting orders to stand down are drowned out by infuriated grunts and screams, the downed guardsmen's friends rushing with vengeance-filled cries.

In contrast to the guards' hot rage, Coal's face is so cold and haunted that I am not sure the male knows where he is. As if having heard my question, the magic inside me stirs, flashing with images of shackles and despair and agony so vivid that my throat closes.

"Coal won't stand down," I tell Tye quickly. "Not unless there is no one left around to fight. I don't know where the hell River went, but stopping the guards is the only option."

Tye pauses for one more heartbeat, then curses under his breath as he nods, his lanky body shifting smoothly into a battle stance that makes me think of the tiger hidden inside him. Every muscle coiled, ready to spring into action, fierce green eyes speckled with silver in the sunlight. When he speaks next, the casualness in his voice belies the deadly warrior I know he is about to unleash. "You want right or left flank, lass?"

"Right."

"It's yours." Tye's unquestioning confidence in me sends a ripple of warmth through my readying muscles. With the discipline born of centuries of combat, the male waits patiently for me to get into position, marks our first target, and signals.

We rush forward as one, scooping up the swinging guard and throwing him into the crowd, which at least has the sense to hang on to the thrashing man. One down, a dozen to go. My heart pounds, my breaths full and deep. Despite the silly amaranth dress, I feel right. Alive. Strong.

The second guardsman we go after is swinging a pitchfork around, the erratic movement managing to clip Tye before he grabs the guard's arm. "Behind you," Tye tells me calmly, bending Pitchfork's wrist hard enough to relieve the man of his weapon.

I turn around in time to see a fist swinging toward my head. Large and muscled and too slow to compete with my immortal body. I parry the blow and shove the idiot against his friend, the pair tripping each other in a tangle of limbs. When I turn back, however, there is a new slew of attacks separating me from Tye. Some—the more intelligent half—seem to have pegged the pair of us as being on Coal's side and thus viable targets; the others swing blindly at anything in their path.

The scent of fury and sweat thickens the air, the men surrounding me blocking my sight. A few paces away, howls of pain and thuds of wood mark both Coal's position and the growing casualty toll falling to his staff.

A thick, mustached man with a bleeding brow snarls at me, launching himself forward.

I step off his path and the man falls to the ground. Behind me, someone steps on the hem of my dress, the tug unbalancing me long enough that yet another idiot blunders into the mess, shoving me atop the original mustached man.

The man roars with a fury that says his common sense is long gone. When he grabs for my breast, my own wits disappear as well. Baring my teeth, I lunge at the man's throat—reining myself back at the last moment to sink my elbow into his nose instead. A spray of blood shoots into the air, splattering my dress and the sand beneath. I roll to my feet in time to find myself a new choice target, men separating from the sidelines to—

A horse's sharp whinny pierces the air. Dirt flies high from beneath a rearing stallion's heavy hooves. A shout of warning races through the mob with the speed of wildfire as a familiar horse and rider wade through the fray. Making only marginal attempts to keep his stallion from stepping on anyone in his way, River rides right into the center of the crowd. He's magnificent—and terrifying. His eyes are hardened steel, every angle of his face tightened in anger, his shoulders square under his crisp red jacket. The same men who refused to step aside for their sergeants' orders and Coal's deadly blows scurry like cockroaches from the horse's hooves. Even Tye rolls over his shoulder to make way.

Stars. Within seconds of River riding his horse into the rioting circle, the fighting is finished, Coal swinging his staff against empty air.

The deputy headmaster's gray eyes flash with thunder as he surveys the scene from his stallion's high saddle. No fewer than two dozen guards, plus Tye and me, are in some state of disreputable dishevelment, a good portion of the would-be mob having some injury to show for the experience. I tense when River's eyes brush mine, flashing with an icy fury that says I've disregarded the wrong male's orders.

Raising his voice, he bellows for three of the guardsmen's sergeants, the noise making me flinch. The men stretch out before him so quickly, I'm not sure they've dared take a breath since their summons.

"Everyone, take a knee, *now,*" River demands in the tone of a general who knows he'll be obeyed—and is. Even Coal, his staff still in hand, stops swinging to kneel on the dirt. My body moves to obey before my mind catches up to my motions, the power of River's demand reverberating through every fiber.

In a moment, the training yard rings with silence.

Turning his horse back to the sergeants, River keeps his voice loud enough to be heard by all. "Take the injured to the infirmary. Everyone else can cool off in lockup until I say otherwise. No exceptions."

4

LERA

I flinch as a metal grating slams into place behind me.

Tye is already striding forward into the large damp cell where the two of us have been relegated, broad shoulders relaxed under his gray tunic, which now has a long tear down the front. He looks down at it, snorts softly, and pulls the thing off, muscles flaring in the dim light. Having once been an active fortress, the Academy's central keep has a dungeon serious enough to hold prisoners of a major battle. A pair of slits near the ceiling provide entrance points for sunbeams, the light drawing two sharp lines on the uneven stone floor. Our cell is about ten paces on each side, with numerous manacles bolted to the wall and hanging down from the ceiling.

At first, I think the accommodations are intended to hold many people at once and then…then I notice a hinged wooden table in the center of the room, a rack holding leather lashes standing not far away. Bile crawls up my throat. The guards didn't throw Tye and me into just any cell—they chose the interrogation chamber. *River* chose the interrogation chamber.

Clapping my palms over my mouth to keep from losing my breakfast into the dark spattered drain, I press myself into the corner. My breath quickens, drawing lungfuls of stale, moldy air that feels like it hasn't been inhaled in decades—and it probably hasn't. River's ice-cold gaze pierces me over and over, mingling with the bruises I saw him leave on Tye's flesh a month ago. With the violence I know he doesn't hesitate to dole out.

A new shiver grips my throat as I wonder if the room itself is River's warning of what's to come. The echo of a leather belt's tiny whistle a moment before it lashes across my back fills my memories, Zake's furious face towering over me. Morphing to River's. Bile burns my throat anew.

"Stop that, lass," Tye says lightly, though he doesn't look in my direction, as if giving me space to calm down. Whistling a lilting tune, he tests the grating, then perches on the torture table as if it were a bench set there for his convenience. "These are just accommodations. And not the worst ones either, so far as these things go."

Tye would know. At least the real Tye would, having spent a good deal of his life in and out of lockup before the quint magic's call connected him to River and the others. Has this Tye's veil-magic-spun life sent him into trouble as well?

I swallow, trying to focus on that thought. On anything except where we are. What someone might do to us here.

Soft footsteps tap the stone, then Tye is before me with a whisper of warm air, brushing a lock of my hair off my face. His beautiful sharp face and emerald eyes fill my vision—eyes that see more than I'd like. His silver earring winks in the low light. "Think logically for a moment, lass," he says gently. "If someone intended to hurt us, they'd hardly give us access to weapons."

"Weapons?" I ask.

Tye waves at the rack of whips before stepping away from me a little too quickly. Aside from teaming up in the fight, we've not exchanged more than a few words in the month since our coupling in the bathhouse. Tye has his reasons and I have mine, which doesn't make missing my friend—my male—any less painful.

Grabbing onto a set of chains hanging from the ceiling, Tye pulls himself up, his body perfectly taut. "These aren't bad," he says, spreading out his arms until they are parallel to the ground, every muscle in his bare chest and stomach coiling impossibly. The cross-like position makes me want to rub my shoulders, but Tye holds it with ease. Catching my gaze, he grins and flips himself over, landing on the stone floor with a flourish.

I shake my head. "You are insane."

"So I've been told."

I try to smile, to show some gratitude for his effort, but I can't unsee horrid stone walls surrounding us. Can't forget River's furious gray gaze as he stared down at me from his horse. As if…as if I betrayed him. Took advantage of the tentative trust we've built, forged in secret study and shared moments, and used it as permission to disregard his orders. The male plainly regretted letting me glimpse his true self, hidden behind the mask of a commander's coldness. And now, now he was ensuring I regretted it too.

The worst part is that River is right. The Leralynn who stays meekly behind while Coal faces trouble, she never existed. Never would. The Leralynn I'd let River believe me to be is as imaginary as Lady of Osprey.

Of course River wants vengeance.

I glimpse the chains hanging from the ceiling again, so like those clanking in Coal's nightmares, and swallow a lump. Coal. River locked him up too. Somewhere close by. The very last place Coal should ever be.

Pressing my back against the wall, I slide to the floor.

"You don't want to do that," Tye calls, sitting atop the table again. When I glance questioningly toward him, he jerks his chin at the stone beneath me. "Sit on damp stone. However long River decides to have us cool off here, it will be that much less pleasant in cold soggy clothes." He pats a spot on the table beside him.

"You want me to sit on…there? Where they question people?"

"If it's the sitting you object to, I can think of something more interesting," Tye drawls before stretching like a cat, every hard square of his abdomen on magnificent display. "You know, most females would consider themselves fortunate to be locked up in a dark room with me and no other entertainment to be had."

Heat floods my face. Having already risen before the bastard finished his sentence, I plot a course in the opposite direction from him, into the farthest, dankest corner of the cell, where the scent of mold is most cloying. The thoughts and sensations flooding my mind make actual thinking difficult, but I do anyway, taking stock of where I am—of how abruptly my mission has ground to a halt. Just this morning, I was plotting my next Night Guard reconnaissance outing with Arisha and Gavriel's help and looking forward to another tutoring session in River's heady presence. Now the latter is furious with me, Shade is prowling the woods, Coal is locked up with only his demons for company, and Tye… Tye is playing games.

Damn the male. He flirts on reflex, unable to help himself, but I know he has no plans to follow through. Even after a month of little contact, the intensity of our coupling in the bathhouse still turns my insides to molten heat each time I trespass on the memory. I was naive to think I could bed the male, enjoy the sheer physical pleasure of it, and walk away without scorching my soul. The connection is too strong, the wound too painful to keep ripping open. Not when I know that this Tye's priorities lie solidly with his precious Prowess Trials, while mine are solidly elsewhere.

My hands curl into fists. It isn't fair how easily a few words can undo a month of hard-won calluses. How the dungeon walls can leave Tye unscathed but insist on closing in around me.

"That wasn't amusing, Tye." I quicken my step as if there is anywhere to go, only to trip over a manacle. The metal ring clatters across the stone floor, the sound raking my nerves, sending echoes of pain and darkness reverberating through me. Making me flinch as if branded.

As if I'd heard it before. Been held captive before. Been questioned and punished and made to scream—I cut myself off with a jerk. Coal. *He* has been held before, not me. It is *his* flash of memory that gripped me just now. *His* nightmares that will only get worse the longer River maroons him in the dungeons.

Yet, it's Coal's fear as much my own that's stealing my breath just now. And yet, the knowledge doesn't make the darkness any less crushing.

I don't realize Tye is moving until he's beside me, his strong arms pulling me from the corner I've somehow burrowed myself into. Before I can blink, I'm gathered against his warm, hard chest, wrapped in his citrusy scent. His warmth surrounds me, making my muscles relax on instinct.

"It was a *little* amusing," Tye says impertinently, even as he strokes my back and head like a kitten. The smooth touches along my hair fill me with safety. With a sense of *now* to stand against the phantom memories I shouldn't have. Tye's knuckles brush my cheek. "I know, I'm a horse's arse."

"Yes, you are," I tell him. *But stars, I want you anyway.*

5

TYE

Tye *was* a horse's arse. And he well knew it.

Despite Lera being oblivious to it, any male with a cock would thank his lucky stars to be locked in with her, Tye being no exception. Her deep brown eyes confused the senses, her hair a fiery auburn silk that positively begged a man's fingers to get tangled up in it. Worse still, he knew what it felt like to be buried deep inside all that lilac-scented warmth. A fact of which his lower body was painfully aware. But that was no excuse for even hinting at the many things he wished to do to the lass.

First, Lera had made her preference for Tye's staying away quite clear. And second, she deserved better than him under any circumstances. Tiga's death was proof enough of that. And yet being near Lera made Tye feel alive, like fog lifting from the world to reveal all the colors and smells.

He breathed out slowly, willing his body to settle despite Leralynn's intoxicating lilac scent. Worse still, standing this close to her, he could smell the slight hint of the lass's misguided arousal. That sweet musk alone had his cock pulsing hard enough to make the room spin.

Tye forced his hand away from Lera's soft skin, bracing on the small of her back instead. Her amaranth dress, in tantalizing tatters from the fight, felt smooth and cool beneath Tye's touch. The fabric fell perfectly over her curved hips and full breasts, though the bright cloth would look even better pooled on the floor, the lass's creamy flesh bent over that wooden table, her legs… Tye shifted his weight, trying to evict his cock's thoughts from his mind. "Go sit down, lass."

Lera started forward obediently, her body tense. With her gaze free to wander the dungeon, the lass's arousal waned, a shot of fear turning her scent. Her eyes had taken on that hunted look again, darting from wall to hanging chains to shelved whips as if something might be hiding there. As if the damn implements would leap from the holds and let themselves loose on her flesh.

Tye's gaze narrowed, a strange twinge of worry growing in his chest. Lera's fear seemed to go deeper than the large cell, beyond a cadet's normal anxiety over being punished. And they were being punished—punished, not tortured.

Yes. Something was wrong. Walking into this cell had woken demons in Lera that were now clawing their way out.

Well, not on Tye's watch. He might be in the dark as to what exactly was making terror lurch in those beautiful brown eyes, but that didn't mean he couldn't be the one to make it go away.

Unable to stop himself, Tye gripped Lera's waist and, ignoring the indignant squeak, hoisted her up onto the table in the dungeon's center. Another step, and he positioned himself between her thighs, their eyes for once level with each other. As he trapped Lera's gaze with his own, preventing it from scanning the dungeon, Tye could see the pulse in her neck start to slow, the hunted fear in her eyes wane. Good. A few moments later, the lass's fear-tight muscles softened enough to let her breathe easier.

"There we go," Tye said softly. The notion that—despite the manhandling— the lass still trusted him, was so gratifying that it nearly made Tye purr. He ran his thumb over Lera's high cheekbone, watching her eyes flutter, his whole body longing to wipe the vestiges of her fear away. "It's just a room, Lera. It's people who hurt you, not anything in here. If someone wished you harm, they'd hardly need all these toys for it." A corner of his mouth tugged up and, because he *was* an arse, Tye added, "I could prove it to you if you want."

Lera snorted softly, a touch of humor in her eyes—which was a miracle as far as Tye was concerned. "You sound very certain of yourself."

"I am." Oddly enough, Tye wasn't lying. He *was* certain. Knew exactly how he'd go about turning their cell from a chamber of horrors into one of pleasure, guiding the nervous tension in Lera's body to mindless release. As if he'd done such things before, many times with many women.

Which, of course, was utter nonsense. After all, Tye had been with Tiga for most of his romantic life. Hadn't he? His mind itched, as if memories were trying to hatch through a hard shell. A familiar feeling. Small and feisty as Lera was, she made Tye feel as though he wore blinders, only able to see the world fully when she was close.

A spot on Tye's chest burned suddenly, and he rubbed at it, shaking his head. No, of course, he was just speculating as to what one *could* do in such a chamber—envisioning the pleasures a man might offer a woman given the tools at hand. It was nothing more than imagination mixed with a healthy dose of desire and cockiness.

"What are you thinking?" Lera asked, making Tye realize he'd gone quiet.

"Some very explicit thoughts that involve your screaming in ecstasy," he muttered before catching himself.

The heady scent of Lera's arousal once more spiked the air, reminding Tye of exactly how she tasted. Everywhere. Tye's whole body heated, and he simultaneously longed to splay the lass out on the table before him and to gather her against his soul.

Lera swallowed, a delicious pink blush rising into her pale cheeks. "That… Us. It would be a very poor idea."

"Agreed," said Tye firmly, clearing his throat. The memory of their last coupling had driven him mad for weeks. They couldn't do it again. Shouldn't.

But anything was better than having Lera spiral down into terror again.

He looked around the dungeon cell, his mind racing against the tension starting to rise into the lass's shoulders. That odd sense of expertise teased him again, an uncanny set of ideas of the many, many things he could do here. Maybe there was a way to offer her pleasure without losing himself. Not coupling exactly, but… "Do you want me to distract you, lass?"

Leralynn frowned at him suspiciously. "What do you mean, precisely?"

Tye grinned and cupped the back of her head with his wide palm. Leaning close to her ear, Tye nipped the bottom lobe. "Precisely, that I am a very good distraction." He grinned, breathing her in. "Also, the one nice thing you should know about the chamber here is that no one can hear us—so feel free to scream my name as loud as you wish."

This time when Lera opened her mouth—probably to call him a colorful type of bastard—Tye captured her soft lips with his own. She stiffened for a moment, then yielded with a nearly inaudible sigh that sent currents of need shooting into Tye's cock so fiercely that he groaned.

Resisting the urge to take Lera right on the table's edge, Tye slid his hands under the dark pink shoulder straps of her dress. Pulling the satin down over her breast, he considered the chest wrap for a moment before lifting her with one arm to slip the dress all the way off with an efficiency that made the lass's brows rise. Apparently, Tye was also exceedingly good at undressing women.

6

LERA

I *shouldn't do this. Shouldn't let Tye do this.* The thoughts repeating in my mind lose potency with every stroke of Tye's hands along my skin. His emerald eyes study me with a predatory intensity that makes my sex clench, my thighs slick. Somehow, the male has gotten my dress, undershorts, and chest wrap all off within the space of a few heartbeats.

With a low growl, I slip off the table and plant my hands on Tye's hard chest, fully intending to push him away and put a long, cold cell between us. Then he cups my rib cage in his large palms and flicks his thumbs over my nipples, taking my mouth so suddenly and deeply that I can't help but moan against him. His large body blocks out the damp cell, his pine-and-citrus scent pushing away Coal's phantom memories, River's furious gaze, Zake's descending whip.

I reach for his flies, suddenly desperate for more distraction, intending to make him as naked as I am. Whatever this is, however ill-advised, it's working. The anticipation of feeling Tye's muscles beneath my hands makes my fingers tingle, but it's the bulge in his trousers I plan to enjoy first. To savor the hardness pulsing there.

Before I can so much as undo a button, Tye catches my wrists in a viselike hold, the wicked sparkle in his gaze sending a shiver along my spine.

"What—" I start to ask, but he is already moving on.

Transferring both my wrists into his one wide hand, Tye binds them together in front of me with my own chest wrap. He drinks in my whole body with his gaze, brushing his palms lightly over my arms. Across my abdomen. Through the coarse auburn curls between my legs.

I release a long breath, my eyes shuddering closed, each touch of Tye's callused fingers waking my body more to his presence. Heat plays along my skin, warding away the dampness of the dungeon's stale air. Emerald gaze capturing mine, Tye drops his hand lower still and—

I gasp, rising onto my toes as he plunges two fingers into me. A tiny pang of indignant shock followed by warm pleasure ripple through me at the intrusion, my breath quickening. But before I can get accustomed to the sensation, Tye pulls the hand free and grins at the sparkling wetness coating his skin. The smile splitting his perfect face, deepening the lines around his mouth, makes it disorientingly beautiful. I feel dazed, unable to move.

"I think we are on the right track," he says, sucking his fingers clean.

I'm still blinking at Tye's antics when he cups my bottom, pushing me a few steps forward. With swift, sure motions, he lifts my arms and loops the loose ends of the wrap binding my wrists to the chained manacles hanging from the ceiling.

"Tye?" I yank, trying to bring my arms down. The restraint sways but yields nothing to my effort. I yank again, harder. My heart stutters, my blood swishing anxiety through my veins. Anxiety and excitement. "What—"

"Look at me, lass." Tye's low, self-assured tone demands my gaze as firmly as the knots he sets. The moment I lift my eyes to his all-consuming green ones, heat fills my skin. Despite my mind's protests, a trickle of moisture slides from my sex and snakes down the inside of my thigh. *Stars.*

Feet wide apart, Tye steps in front of me, his bare chest and torso a shadowy field of muscle, lightly damp with sweat. His mouth curves appreciatively as his callused hands roam my skin once more, massaging my aching breasts and stroking my hips. "Almost perfect," he whispers into my ear before settling his foot between my legs and pushing them wide apart.

Cold air brushes my hot sex, my fluttering attempts to close myself meeting Tye's braced knees. Running two fingers skillfully between my slippery folds, Tye traces the hood hiding my quickly swelling apex.

"You can't escape my touch, lilac lass," Tye whispers into my ear, the words—which should rightfully make me cringe—sending a zing of excitement all the way to my sex. The mix of unyielding restraint and Tye's utter focus on me is intoxicating, my emotions spinning between anxiety and safety. Desire and frustration. "You can do nothing but feel. And enjoy." Tye teases the hood again, running the tip of one finger oh so casually across my bud.

I moan, my toes curling in my boots. More. I need more.

Tye pulls away.

My teeth grind together so hard, they squeak.

A small tug at the corner of the bastard's mouth says he marked my reaction. Was planning it all along. With fingers slicked in my own wetness, Tye circles my nipples. One, then the other, until the sensitive skin tightens into peaks and my breasts feel so full, they ache.

"You have gorgeous breasts, Lera." Eyes on mine, he puts his mouth on one thick nipple and sucks.

I gasp, the pull on my breasts joining the low throbbing in my sex. I try to cover myself, to close my legs to do something—anything—to ease the growing pressure. But I can't. *This is wrong,* a voice inside me tries hollering again. *You're naked in a dungeon chamber, restrained and...and stars,* if all that doesn't somehow drive each sensation higher.

Tye's hand drops to my sex again, stroking my folds in a maddening harmony to the insistent suckles above. Forward and back, forward and back, until my hips thrust toward him greedily, my toes so tightly curled inside my laced boots that my legs shake.

Without warning, Tye slides a finger into my channel just as his teeth close slightly over my tender nipple. The tiny sting of pain morphs into a scalding pleasure that washes through me like a storm.

"Stars." I whimper. More. I need more. I need *him.* My arm jerks toward the pulsing bulge in Tye's pants, the restraints catching me ruthlessly. My channel clenches around Tye's finger with greedy desperation.

Releasing my nipple, Tye soothes it with little laps of his tongue that starts to drop lower and lower along my flesh until he is on one knee, hands gripping the insides of my wet thighs.

I half expect guards to burst in at any moment with how loud I'm being. Then I remember that this chamber is soundproof, which only heightens my feral arousal. Tye blows on my hot tissue, his strong hands keeping me utterly open to him. Leaning closer, he swirls his tongue around my nub, which pulses so fiercely, I can barely stand. I grab the chains for support, small whimpers escaping as the world narrows.

Lap. Lap. Lap. Tye's tongue teases my engorged apex, my whole sex feeling too tight to bear. *Lap. Lap. Lap.*

I pant, reaching for the approaching abyss. My heart pounds, sweat trickling down my temples. Tye caresses the whole length of my hood, then takes my bud into his hot mouth and sucks.

I barely bite back a scream, every muscle in my body tight. Pleasure so intense, it hurts, rushes through me. Hitting me again and again. I gasp, my legs buckling as release thunders through me.

Wrapping his arms around me, Tye holds me tight through the exquisite spasms. When he seems confident I will not collapse, he lets me take up my weight, a satisfied smile on his face. "Did you enjoy your distraction, lass?"

"No." I pant. Growl.

He cocks a brow, looking genuinely bemused. "Your body says otherwise."

I swallow, unable to think. "You. I want you."

Tye stiffens, something unreadable flashing through his eyes, and starts to step away. "That wasn't the—"

I don't care. Leaning back into my binds, I hook one leg around Tye's hard waist, yanking him closer.

Tye's eyes widen as our hips collide. Wrapping my other leg around the male's waist, I hook my ankles together, my hips grinding against his hardness. Leaning my neck back, I savor the heady energy pulsing through me and indulge my one utterly unfair advantage—I nip the so, so sensitive ear tip that Tye doesn't know he has.

Tye hisses, gripping my hips for balance, his fingers digging in so hard that I yelp.

"Leralynn—" His voice is guttural, a mix of purr and growl that echoes the tiger he shifts into in Lunos.

"You started this, kitty cat." I grind into him again.

The male's emerald eyes darken, the swirling lust blowing away uncertainty with a storm's force. His hips move against mine as if of their own accord, a groan escaping his throat as his fingers dig into my backside. Drag me closer.

My heart quickens, my dilating eyes losing focus of everything but the pulsing body between my thighs.

Strong hands lifting me easily, Tye moves me against his length, his body taking over.

I nod, baring my teeth, nodding for him to hurry up.

In another heartbeat, Tye pushes my legs down with a predatory growl and yanks at his flies. His cock springs out of its binds so forcefully that the shaft smacks my flesh, our mingled breaths echoing harshly against the stone walls.

He pulls away, out of reach of my legs, and drinks me in like a master musician contemplating his next note. Letting the pulsing pause stretch the tension. The hot glaze in Tye's green eyes would almost make me nervous if I weren't trembling with need.

He runs one finger from the hollow of my throat down between my breasts to the top of my mound, eliciting a tiny noise in the back of my throat. Then, with no warning, he takes my mouth, teasing my lips open with his tongue before thrusting in with a surge of desperation that echoes my own. Makes the magic inside me flare against its restraints as fiercely as my body does.

Hooking his hands under my thighs as if I weigh nothing, Tye presses his hardness against my dripping sex and shifts his hips, running his bare velvety length up through my folds and down. Up and down, the wet sounds joining our heavy breathing. I moan against his mouth. Bite his lower lip. His cock slides against my bud with increasing pressure, making me tremble.

"Stop teasing me," I gasp. And know instantly that it was a mistake.

With a jolt, Tye disappears behind me, leaving me cold and gasping, struggling to find my footing again on the rough stone. In the next moment, his hot hands trace my ribs, my waist, my hips. With one hand pressing into the small of my back, bending me forward slightly so my bottom juts out, he swirls his other down my thighs. Across my swollen, pulsating bud.

I moan, bucking my hips and pulling against my binds, demanding—begging—that he fill the emptiness inside me. Even with that, when the head of his cock presses against my wetness again, the sheer width of it makes my heart stutter with anticipation. I inhale, readying my muscles for the invasion…but instead of moving inside me, Tye stays at my opening, pulsing, then spirals the tip of his finger around my still-sensitive bud. The tightening circles send waves of throbbing need through me.

I shudder. Then shudder again as Tye's slickened finger circles my *other* opening.

Oh stars. Everything inside me clenches. Even after so many couplings, with Tye and River both liking to claim my backside as readily as my channel, the thought of it still makes my face flame. Every time. No amount of knowing I'll enjoy it soon enough stops the doomed attempt to escape the inevitable.

It's no exception now, and I squirm like a wildcat despite the thick wetness coating my sex and thighs. Wetness that Tye doesn't fail to mark as he tightens the pressure on my backside, his low growl vibrating through me. "You're in a dangerous position to bait a hunt, lass." His voice is rough, on the knife's edge of desperate. With no warning, he surges forward, burying himself to the hilt inside my channel. I scream. And instantly, I push back against him, urging him to start moving. Tye returns with a resounding slap that shocks my nerves awake. Another slap stings my other cheek, hovering at the very edge of pain. Making everything more potent. Aching. Needy.

Hands gripping my hips, Tye pumps once, twice, again, our wet skin meeting loudly in the stone chamber. I wrap my hands around the binds to take his force.

The cock disappears from my sex, and Tye's finger slides into my tight back hole again, twisting in and out. In and out. Bringing me to a cliff's edge and backing off.

"Bastard," I growl between clenched teeth.

This time when Tye's hand comes down on my backside, it lights up a blaze.

I yelp, but even as I do, my voice morphs to a moan of pleasure as Tye buries his cock in me again, bringing me to my toes. His cock and fingers plunge into me together now, filling everything. My sex. My backside. My whole utter world. And when he increases the pace, alternating the rhythm of the two, there is no holding back the tsunami of sensation.

I scream again, every fiber in my body tightening at once. The agonizing waves of pleasure ripple from my sex, raking across my back and legs until even my teeth feel the unyielding pulsing. *Oh stars.*

I collapse against my binds for the second time, my bones liquid.

Tye pulls me upright against his hard chest, squeezing my breasts with his wide callused palms, and I pant, resting my head against his shoulder. He bites my exposed neck lightly. Tweaks my nipples. Runs one hand down to my mound.

It takes me a few moments to realize that his cock is still in me. Hard. Throbbing. And starting to move all over again, slowly now, languidly. "You didn't…what…" I can't make my tongue move.

Tye brings his velvety lips to my ear, his voice warm against my neck. "I wanted to see your face."

Pulling away, the male steps in front of me, and I almost come again just at the sight of him. Every ridge of muscle in his body is tight, his incredibly broad shoulders narrowing to taut hip flexors and a cock so hard, I can see it pulsing. His damp skin is burnished gold in the dimness of the cell, his red hair highlighting emerald eyes that rake over me with so much raw hunger that I almost want to shrink back.

Those eyes grip mine as he slides his hands under my bottom and lifts me, urging my legs around his waist. The pressure eases from my shoulders and I sigh—which turns into a low groan when, in the same motion, Tye guides his cock deep into my channel. He gives me no quarter, pulling back and burying his cock even deeper. With his size and strength, Tye moves me easily along his shaft, our faces close enough to share breath the entire time. My ankles cross in the small of his muscled back while my arms grip the binds, my breasts pushed up and bouncing with each thrust. With each powerful stroke, all control fades from Tye's gaze, replaced by a fierce need that pierces straight to my soul.

As shackled magic inside me wakens, I mark the shudder running along Tye's powerful body and fear that our plan of light distraction from this cell's horrors has just failed spectacularly. He pounds into me now, our heavy breaths and the *slap slap* of our pelvises echoing off the walls, every tendon standing out in his neck. His biceps bulge as he holds me in place. His pulse hammers so hard that I hear the *lub-dub* of his thumping heart. Feel the throbbing of his cock. Everything inside me coils tighter and tighter, the gaping hole of the abyss spreading once more beneath me.

Thrust. Thrust. Thrust.

"Lera!" Tye shouts my name as his hips press into me the final time, the warmth of his release sending me over the cliff.

Searing waves of pleasure explode from my apex, shooting outward along every nerve and fiber inside me. Again. Again. Shock after shock, until I feel the binds at my wrists loosen and fall away, until I'm draped like a rag doll in Tye's arms. Shaking. Satisfied. And in oh, so much trouble.

7

LERA

This... This is exactly what was not supposed to happen. I rub my hands over my eyes as Tye helps me back into my dress and pulls on his pants, his own gaze sliding everywhere but my face.

"Lera..." Tye says finally, forcing his eyes to meet mine. "This, you... It was genuine. Everything I felt. We felt. But the reality of my life is that—"

"You want to twist around a wooden bar that I couldn't care less about," I say flatly. Because there is no point in coating it with honey. I've things to do, magic to fight. None of it supports simpering around a male who is following a fiction. Despite the intensity of our coupling, the way it wakes my magic, there can be no *us* unless Tye wants to join my team.

And he doesn't. Tye has other priorities. The best thing to do—the one thing I just failed at miserably—is to keep the intensity between us from interfering with our lives.

Tye hops up to swing himself on the dangling chains again, as if looking for familiar territory. The sculpted muscles of his chest, arms, and shoulders tighten with perfect control as he holds himself in the impossible cross position again. Then, he brings his legs up at a right angle to his body, his toes together and pointing. Belatedly, I realize he has no shoes on. He trained without them and didn't stop to dress before the fight.

I sigh. Even with three lung-shattering releases behind me, watching Tye move threatens to arouse me again, and I quickly find somewhere else to be looking.

Instead of sanctuary, my gaze trips over the rack of whips, my stomach clenching reflexively. At least Tye didn't try to include those in his *distraction.*

"I didn't think you'd enjoy those no matter what I did," Tye said, following my gaze without permission. Damn him.

My jaw tightens. "Would you?"

Tye turns himself upside down, his red hair flying in the low light, but continues talking as if both his position and the topic of discourse were normal. "Not for pain, no." He frowns at himself, then shakes his head like a dog trying to dislodge water. "It's the second time today I've felt certain about something I don't recall ever trying," he mutters. "Odd as it sounds, you make me feel as though something grand prowls just at the edge of my world."

My breath catches, and I feel my gaze sharpening on Tye. In Lunos, even when I was mortal, coupling with my males tightened my control over magic. I wonder if as much might be happening in reverse, with the males' essence strengthening when we join. Heart quickening, I lean forward, bracing my forearm on my knees. "Tell me more. How—"

I cut off as the door of our isolated corridor croaks open, inopportune footsteps tapping the stone at a swift, confident pace. Tye's head snaps toward the sound, and he settles himself back to the floor with casual grace. By the time the visitor makes his appearance a few heartbeats later, Tye is lounging beside me, his body surreptitiously angled to cut off the path between me and the door.

For the second time today, a pair of cold gray-blue eyes sweeps over me with dismissal, a strange discomfort following in their wake, like ants crawling just under my skin. Han's attention is riveted on Tye. Though of a similar height and build, the instructor's short, combed-back hair and harsh gaze is at utter contrast to Tye's mischievous red mane and feline grace.

"Have you met your new Prowess trainer yet?" I ask Tye under my breath.

"He has not," Han answers, surveying the male with a disgust typically reserved for lame roaches. "If he had, I guarantee you he would not be here now." Han unlocks the door, swinging it open. "Come with me, Tyelor. Now."

Tye's hand touches the small of my back. "You mean both of us, sir."

Instead of replying, Han strides into the cell and grabs my wrist in a viselike grip. With a rough yank, he pulls me over to the stone wall, clamping my wrist in a bolted manacle. "Have I answered your question clearly enough?" Han demands, turning back to the male as if I no longer exist in his world. Han points to the door. "Whore on your own time, boy. Until the Prowess Trials, you are on mine. Move."

Tye doesn't move, his muscles bunching. I can practically see the thoughts sprinting across his face. *Don't do it, Tye.*

Han sighs. "If I need to make the wench less attractive to you, I will," he says, lifting the back of his hand. The intended trajectory of the blow is clear enough to make me press back into the stone. Han snorts. "Personally, Tyelor, I believe my expertise would be best used on the training pitch, directing *your* actions. But we can approach this any way you want."

"Leave her alone." Tye's words come out in a snarl that he checks with visible effort. "I am at your full command, sir. There is no need for further clarification."

"Good." Turning his back to me, Han waits for Tye to exit the chamber before following him out, the grated door left swinging open in their wake.

I wait until the pair's footsteps fade before letting out the breath I didn't know I held. Then I use my free hand to open the manacle.

It stays closed. I frown at the latch, realizing the damn thing was constructed to click locked without a key. Wonderful. With a frustrated growl—and too little thought—I yank at the metal with all my strength.

Click.

The sound comes from inside the mechanism, like a metal tooth snagging a new hold. The band around my wrist tightens, digging into my skin. The manacle may need a key to open, but apparently, it needs nothing to tighten down on itself.

Uncertainty slithers down my spine. "Guards," I shout, despite knowing the chamber is designed to contain sound.

No answer. No steps. Only the slight creaking of the open door, still swaying on its hinges.

Right. Forcing my breath to slow, I lean back against the cold wall. River knows I'm here. However mad he is, however little he may want to lay eyes on me right now, he won't leave me inside forever. In truth, it's only been a couple of hours since the riot and someone has already come to get Tye. If River intends to come for me himself, it might be a couple of hours more until he has time for it.

My chest tightens at the thought, but this time, I'm smart enough not to pull on the metal again. I'll deal with River when he comes, and when that happens, he won't find me whimpering and cowering.

Minutes tick by with agonizing slowness.

An hour.

More.

I memorize the entire stone wall in front of me, every crumbling crack and patch of moss. I close my eyes and tune my hearing, waiting for a single sound of life beyond these walls—another prisoner, a bird. Hell, I'd even take a mouse.

Nothing.

My stomach lets out a disgruntled rumble, my muscles starting to cramp. Ripping the hem of my dress, I stuff the soft fabric into the little space left between my skin and the manacle's cold metal. The satin cushion helps protect my skin, but nothing can be done for the height of the restraint, which keeps me from sitting unless I want to badly strain my shoulder. A shoulder that's already strained from long minutes of being bound overhead—though, then, I didn't feel it through my haze of arousal.

Dong. Dong. Dong. More hours tick by, the sound of the Academy's bell barely seeping through the dense stone.

Dong. Dong. Dong. My shoulder screams. Despite the padding, the metal eats into my flesh, especially where it presses the bone. The slits near the top of the cell darken with the setting sun, the temperature plummeting—and my last reserve of calm with it.

"Hello?" I can't help calling, hating the tremble in my voice—the weakness I can feel creeping in with the dark. "Hello? How long am I to stay here?"

The words echo off the stone but there is no answer. Nothing. Not even a shout to keep down my voice. It isn't fair. *It was a fight, River. It was just a damn stupid fight.*

For Coal's sake, I hope he is far, far away from here by now. That he isn't having to watch the last rays of sun arc across the wall, the dungeon's damp cold crawling under his skin.

Maybe River has simply forgotten about me, relegating the little lying cadet to the back of his mind. That thought sends dread spiraling through me in new waves, the ceiling pressing lower, the walls closing in. Crushing me. The dark chamber suddenly feeling less like a cell than a crypt.

I wait another long hour, counting off the seconds with barely moving lips, then bellow for the guards again, this time with all my might. My lungs fill and empty until I'm too hoarse to keep going. The last one ends in a harsh sob. My chained wrist has gone numb. My head pounds now with hunger and thirst. I hear a steady drip in some corner of the cell, and even that taunts me.

No one comes. No one is going to. Despite the growing night, neither food nor water have appeared, only a darkness so complete that I see nothing but the vague outlines of chains and shackles. Finally, I close my eyes, the need to sleep so profound that it transcends the pain.

That's when the images start.

A clank of metal tools; a crack of a whip slicing through the stench of pain, my grunt echoing off stone walls; a melodic voice of a woman who holds my soul before abandoning me without a word; a swirling darkness waiting to choke me each time I dare try to sleep.

I shove myself free of the nightmare, panting against my arm. Coal. Coal must still be locked up as well. Somewhere close. *Stars.* It's an effort of will to force my lungs to accept a full breath of stale air. I knew the male's nightmares were spiraling—I felt it during those few intense moments when we touched in the past month. But I didn't realize just how bad things had gotten.

After being shut for a day in a dungeon, Coal's horrors are spilling with enough force to breach the gap between us. I jerk against the chains, not caring how the manacle tightens and cuts into my skin. My vision swims once more, though this time, it's different.

My face presses into a stable wall, Zake's rank breath tickling my neck. There is no sound but the horses' soft nickering, the hammering of my racing heart, and the tap-tap-tap of a wide leather strap against Zake's thigh. There is no escaping the coming whipping. Not now. Not ever.

My back will soon be a map of angry bleeding welts, fresh wounds over old bruises. The leather strap traces my bare back almost gently as Zake seeks his first target. No matter how often it's happened, how prepared I am, the agony is always fresh. The paralyzing helplessness of it. I bite my knuckle to suppress a moan. The terror of how much worse it will be if I fight him.

"Everything you are, you have, you'll ever become is because of my good graces," Zake snarls into my ear. And then it starts.

8

COAL

Coal little blamed the guards who threw him into the cell for ensuring he fell face-first against the rough stone floor. He had, after all, cracked the bones of five of their comrades. Or maybe six. He'd stopped counting sometime after the grunts and screaming began to bleed together into nothing but white noise.

"Maybe I'll just forget to take these off." The larger of the guards yanked the ropes binding Coal's hands behind his back, making his shoulders stretch painfully.

Getting his knees under him, Coal rose to his feet. He could already see how a spin kick to the man's temple could lay the guard out. Maybe for an hour. Maybe forever. The man's partner was so young and nervous that he'd more likely piss himself than interfere.

Coal's gaze found the large guard's dark eyes. "Maybe." It was all the self-control he could manage, with all his being still screaming for violence. By the time Coal had finished destroying Kreger's lewd art collection and room and—very likely—wrist, enough of the guards' friends had arrived at the barracks to risk rushing Coal.

They'd had no idea how much he welcomed the assault. That they'd been doing Coal a favor.

"You're insane." The man shook his head, slicing through Coal's binds before backing out of the cell. "Like a rabid dog."

The sound of the closing lock ricocheted through Coal's body. Yes, the guard was right. Coal was rabid. But the image of Lera's naked body turned into fodder for a bastard's cock still made murder spill into his blood. He didn't know why, and he didn't care. All he knew was that some deep-down part of him screamed *not yours* and planned to make sure the bastards knew it.

Coal rubbed his wrists, pacing the small cell. Had he had his wits about him this morning, he'd still have ensured Kreger never drew another cadet—much less Leralynn—for as long as the man lived. However on the edge of darkness as Coal had already been, the whole mess had happened without his control. Which would make for an unpleasant conversation with River later.

Leaning back against the cold stone wall, Coal felt the adrenaline begin to drain out of him by necessity. The body could only hold on to battle's sharpness for so long. He knew what would come if he let go of his mind in this dark, foul place. Knew what it would trigger—and was too exhausted to fight it.

Time passed. He had no idea how much. He'd spent enough time in cells to know not to count the seconds.

His lungs tightened as the sun sank below the Academy's walls, as the air cooled. His breath, harsh now, came out in puffs of condensation.

His hands were shackled, his shoulders screaming from the strain. The taste of blood and fear choked him, blood from his last beating crusting along his skin. The islanders who'd held him for the past year never intended to let him leave. Never let him take his life either, no matter how he tried.

A noise scraped against Coal's hearing. He shifted, the sores beneath his shackles sending lightning bolts of agony down his skin.

"You aren't alone." A feminine voice sounded behind him, soft steps circling until a young woman with intelligent brown eyes came to stand before him. She was small, barely reaching Coal's shoulder, yet she filled his world with a lilac scent that drowned out all else. One of the islanders he'd not seen before.

With a gasp, Coal roused himself, scrambling against the damp floor for a link to reality. The woman, whose name Coal never learned, had kept the shards of his sanity together—only to destroy them all in a single blow when she disappeared without a word. Coal knew the wound was his own fault for having entrusted himself to her, but that made it hurt no less.

It was the woman's scent that Coal remembered most. A lilac so clean and crisp, it could drown out the stench of fear. Coal never expected to breathe in such a lilac scent again—until a cadet named Leralynn of Osprey walked into his world, grabbed a blade, and ripped every abscessed memory wide open.

A *cadet*. And yet when Coal took her in the cave that month ago, his soul had woken. For the first time since escaping the islanders, he had felt alive, the scents of the forest's pine and rain-wetted earth so potent, he tasted them with each breath.

Coal strode to the bars, his hands wrapped around the iron. Staying away from so much as touching her for a month had stressed Coal's self-control to the limit. He was too honest with himself to pretend that the growing nightmares had nothing to do with the strain. He had slipped once. Just once, when he chose Lera for a choke-hold demonstration because he could not bear the thought of another's arm at the girl's throat.

Spinning, Coal struck his fist against the metal, the pain singing through his bones and flesh. Physical pain was easier to endure than the one gripping his chest. Even now, days later, he remembered every second of that exercise. How anxious Leralynn had been, how little she trusted him. Standing so close to Lera, her small, tight body pressed against him, Coal had breathed in the lilac with the hunger of a starved man.

Yet the moment he had, the woman from the islands appeared, the vision of her melding with the cadet in Coal's hold. Fury had risen in Coal's chest, the pain of abandonment spurring a flash of chains and questions. And then…then Lera had fought him like a cornered animal. The same girl who, a month ago, had stood up to River—despite the threat of a whipping that terrified her—all to protect Coal, now couldn't bear to trust him in broad daylight before a class of others.

Lera's fear of him, the breach in her trust, had unraveled Coal at last. Yes, the guard who'd brought Coal here was right. Coal was rabid. And the sooner he was put down, the better.

Sitting on the hard stone floor, Coal listened for the tower bell marking the passage of time. He little expected River to come for him today—the man liked to be in control before doing anything and would take time to calm down. Plus, it now fell to the commander to clean up the mess Coal had made, which—had the positions been reversed—Coal would have eviscerated River for.

The walls of Coal's cell closed in on him, the edges of his vision blurring in preview of the too-familiar terrors. Knowing what was to come made Coal's heart race no slower, however, his lungs stretch no less with bit-back screams. Pressing himself against the wall of his cell, he settled in for a long night of seeing chains and whips and heated iron. His mind did not disappoint.

Not until full dark settled and Coal suddenly smelled the scent of sweet hay and the lathered sweat of hard-worked horses. Felt helpless dread fill him as a large man with dark coiled hair loomed over him, blocking out all the light of the stable, twisting him as easily as if he were a child.

"Everything you are, you have, you'll ever become is because of my good graces," the man's voice snapped along with a deafening crack of his belt. The strap ends wrapped around Coal's ribs, making him scream loud enough that the horses whickered in discontent. Terror clawed at his throat—terror and a strange sort of resignation. "When I order a horse saddled, you saddle a horse. You don't lie. You don't pretend he's lame to save yourself a bit of work."

The whip fell again, and Coal screamed again, unable to stop himself. Tears blurred his vision of the rough wooden stable wall.

Each hiss and crack of the whip felt stamped upon his mind as much as his body. The whip fell again, again. Until the pain made darkness close around him.

9

RIVER

Striding down the stairs of the dungeon corridor, River breathed in the damp air, the keys in his hand clanking with each step. His head pounded, the ache pressing on the back of his eyeballs and pulsating against his skull. He'd barely had time to piss since the brawl yesterday morning, much less eat, sleep, or wring Coal's neck, as he was desperate to do.

The six guards still laid out in the infirmary—a dozen others falling into the walking wounded list—made unscrambling duty schedules alone a nightmare. That was before even considering who disobeyed whose orders, and how command needed to be restructured. Adding to that, the Academy's top healer had chosen this time to bloody disappear, and Sage was in a rightful fit. At this point, River little cared for how the problem started—he'd gotten a mix of explanations ranging from cocks to women—a well-trained regiment of soldiers didn't have a right to degenerate into a mob.

Which brought River back to Coal. And the cadets. River paused, running a hand through his hair. He'd forgotten to send word to Leralynn canceling the morning tutoring session, but she'd hopefully work out the reason for his absence from the study. More likely than not Lera would be glad for the reprieve—given that her disobedience of his direct orders to stay in the study was another matter to be dealt with. Another issue he was looking forward to very little.

One problem at a time. River started walking again, reining in his focus. In the shadow of what the islanders had done to Coal in captivity, leaving the man in lockup overnight hadn't been ideal. But Coal had been in the heart of the mob, and anything less would have had the guardsmen revolting. How much further River would need to take discipline was dependent as much on Coal himself as anything else. Which meant River had to be very, very careful, especially when he opened the door, lest Coal did something to get himself into hotter flames.

Drawing a lungful of moldy air, River coughed loudly before turning the final corner, small empty cells lining both sides of the wall, the damp ceiling less than a foot from his head. The Academy had been a fortress once and still had the facilities to hold more prisoners than it could ever see. With Coal having no line of sight to the corridor, River little wanted to surprise the man who might well have spent the night punching stone walls to ward off nightmares.

River braced himself for that too. Braced himself for many things.

None of them included finding Coal kneeling on the floor, his hands braced on his thighs as if it took all his concentration just to keep breathing. Sweat glistened on his arms and tight face, matting his loose blond hair. *Stars.* The whole cell stank with acrid fear.

River paused to collect himself, hiding away the self-loathing he felt for making this happen. Then his cool voice rang through the bars of Coal's cell. "Good morning."

Coal stayed still, his gaze locked on the floor. "Let her go." His voice was rougher than usual, as if he'd used it up talking—or screaming.

"Let who go?" Had Coal actually lost his mind overnight? River swallowed a curse. "Coal." Shoving his own frustration aside, River spoke softly, as if soothing an anxious stallion. "I'm going to open this door now. Then we are going to walk out of here. Do you understand?"

Coal's face snapped up, his blue eyes so dark, they seemed tinged with purple. "Leralynn. Let her free, and then you can deal with me as you wish." Coal's voice was strained but fully lucid despite the absurdity of his words. "She was caught up in the fray, nothing more. Punish me, not her."

"Leralynn and Tye were released yesterday," said River, a shiver running along the length of his spine. "They were left to sit a few hours in the questioning chamber, but no more than that. I assure you."

"She is still here," Coal snarled, uncoiling smoothly to his feet. His hair hung loose to his shoulders, matted with the same splotches of blood that covered his torn black tunic and bare arms. The knuckles on both his fists were raw and bleeding, as was his lip. His chest rose and fell with quick breaths.

Quickly calculating the path of least resistance, River decided that nothing he could say was likely to make an impact. Phantoms. Coal was imagining phantoms, he had to be. And you didn't talk someone out of that. "I will make you a bargain, Coal. We go check the interrogation chamber, and once you see for yourself that no one is there, you and I will have a different conversation. One in which you will cooperate fully. Is that agreed?"

"Yes."

River clicked open the lock, the intensity of Coal's insistence making his heart patter in his throat. As Coal moved to stride out the door, however, River blocked the male's path with his arm. "Have I your word?"

Coal's nostrils flared as he pushed past River's hand and sprinted down the corridor to the stairs, as if following some internal beacon. Down, down, down, the man's soft steps took the crumbling stairs two at a time, River following close behind to the lowest level of the hold. The one where air was even more precious, from which not one sound escaped.

The heavy door to the questioning corridor opened with a screech of rust, releasing the sound of a girl's whimpers into the dank air.

River's face drained of blood. Quickening his pace, River rounded the final turn to find the questioning room not empty at all. Lera knelt on the floor, one of her arms in a too-high shackle, blood covering both the metal and her skin. As if she'd been pulling against the shackle all night, until her strength finally waned.

Her normally vibrant auburn hair hung in lank strands over her blanched face.

"Good stars, who did this?" The words spilled from River's mouth before he could stop himself.

Coal's ice-cold eyes cut River off at the knees. "You."

Shoving past him, Coal rushed into the cell and crouched beside the girl with a slow gentleness that River had never seen in him. Instead of yanking Lera into his arms, as River would have, Coal shifted her just enough to take the pressure off the overstretched joint and examined the bloody manacle.

Leralynn whimpered but didn't cry. Perhaps she had no tears left to shed.

River shifted his weight and felt Lera's eyes lift to watch him over Coal's shoulder. Fury and fear and pain saturated her chocolate gaze, though she was fighting like hell itself to put up a facade of strength.

It took all of River's self-control to play along, keeping his face schooled and seemingly unaware of her state, all while bile rose up his throat, threatening to make him vomit.

He'd done this. Ordered Leralynn held without following up to ensure the instructions were executed as intended.

The pang of envy at watching Leralynn lean trustingly against Coal's chest squeezed River hard enough to take his breath. Shuffling the key ring, he pulled up the small one for the manacle and took a step toward the pair. At least he had something to offer, late as it was.

Coal's head snapped around, a low primal growl filling the room. River raised his hand to show the key, but the fevered glaze in Coal's blue eyes was as clear a warning as a tiger's roar. River wasn't to come any closer. For any bloody reason.

Moving slowly, River slid the keys along the stone floor and backed out of the cell. He wasn't welcome beside Leralynn. Not now, and very possibly not ever.

10

LERA

I am afraid to breathe too quickly; the rhythm of slow steady inhalations has warded off the night terrors for hours now. My body is numb. Separated. So long as I don't move, the world feels distant, as if a curtain of thick cotton has settled around my senses. All I taste are mouthfuls of stale air. In and out. In and out.

Hinges squeak.

With excruciating slowness, my gaze focuses. The cotton keeping my senses at bay disappears as I blink at the figure rushing inside my cell, bringing unwelcome reality with him. A heady metallic musk fills my senses, drowning out my own stench of stale sweat and dried blood.

"Leralynn." Coal crouches beside me, leashed violence simmering behind his devastatingly beautiful face. His usually bound hair hangs down to his broad shoulders, framing a strong jaw and blazing blue eyes. On the stone floor, lines of sunlight speak of morning well on its way. I've been here all night, and I wager Coal has too. No, I know he has—I felt him. Despite Coal's slow movements, his muscles—the very air around him—vibrate with tension.

Our gazes lock, the connection powerful enough to make nothing else matter for a moment.

Then Coal reaches for me, sharply carved muscles moving with liquid grace beneath the thin black cloth of his tunic.

Without meaning to, I push back into the stone. With the exception of the ill-fated choke-hold demonstration, the male has avoided physical contact with me for a month now. The rest, the flashes of memories and pain, those took place in my mind alone. I have no reason to believe he sees me any differently now than he has in the past four weeks. Even with our gazes locked, my wary body doesn't know what to expect from itself at the warrior's touch.

"I'm going to take the pressure off your shoulder." Coal moves slowly, lifting me off the stone floor onto his bent knee, his hands bracing my shackled arm. The shift releases compressed veins and nerves, blood flowing back into my numb limbs with scorching agony.

I bite back a scream, but Coal's silent, intense gaze stays on me. *I know,* his blue eyes say. *I know.*

Once I am able to breathe again, I lean into the male's shoulder while he checks the manacle holding my wrist. Beyond the world of the two of us, I finally mark another figure in the dungeon cell.

Still stopped at the open door, River stares down at my crumpled form. The patient male who helped me read is gone, a cold, powerful commander in his place. A commander whose orders I disobeyed. There is no emotion in River's chiseled face, his back as straight here in a dungeon cell as on the parade grounds, his dark brown hair just as flawlessly neat. *This is what happens to those who fail to abide by my word,* each harsh line of his sculpted body enunciates in silence. *I warned you, didn't I?*

My heart hammers against my ribs, my breaths quick through the streaks of pain raking my cramped muscles. River left me here to break me. Punish me. But stupid as it is to tempt his wrath just now, I still lift my chin high, not giving River the satisfaction of seeing me cower.

River steps toward me.

Coal growls, the sound anything but human.

Stopping, River slides keys across the floor instead and leaves without a word.

I hate the relief that washes over me with River's departure, but savor it anyway. When Coal releases my shackle, the raw skin beneath stinging at the open air, I'm more than a little glad River can't see my flinch or note how my fingers dig into Coal's arm.

Giving the swaying world a few moments to settle, I go to stand. Coal catches my waist in time to keep me from landing back on the floor. It takes two more tries for me to conquer my buckling knees, but at least I never make a sound. Not that words seem necessary with Coal.

Coal doesn't touch me as we wind through the dungeon hallways and step outside—blinking like newborns in the harsh sunlight and inhaling deeply of the fresh spring air—or as we cross the entire courtyard back to the student dormitory, but he stays close enough that I can hear the short puffs of his breathing. The few cadets out and about the courtyard follow the pair of us with their gazes, their eyes burning into my skin. Shutting out the stares, I focus my thoughts on the safety of my room, counting the steps until I can hide away.

"Lera!" Arisha opens the door the moment I start turning the handle, her wide eyes taking me in. Dressed in a yellow spring dress, the girl looks like an awkward sunflower with her frizzy brown hair making up the petals. "What happened?" She reaches for me. "The last I heard, a certain muscular idiot started a brawl and then—"

Coal clears his throat.

Arisha lifts her gaze, her body freezing in place.

Pushing me past Arisha into the room, Coal shuts the door behind us. The entire small space, with its neat white walls and tall sparkling window, suddenly feels filled to the brim with Coal's presence. With his masculine scent and sheer size, he's as out of place here as I'd be in the guards' bathhouse. "Make yourself busy elsewhere, Tallie."

Arisha's face swings toward me in assessment, then back to Coal. Putting her hands on her hips, she glares up at the male who towers head and shoulders above her. "No." Her soft voice mixes with the sharp tang of anxiety she always has in proximity with Coal. "But I think *you* should."

Coal stays put.

Arisha narrows her brows and steps right up to him, like a nearsighted, determined goat, her pale, freckled cheeks tightened in anger. If I could move, I'd throw my arms around my friend and hold her forever.

Coal pivots out of Arisha's way. "Did you just try to evict me. Physically?" he asks slowly. "To intimidate me into backing out the door?"

Arisha swallows but lifts her face high. "Yes."

"Did you misplace your mind?" Despite the ferocity coming off him in waves, Coal sounds genuinely curious.

Arisha scowls at him. "It might have worked."

"Very doubtful." Coal sighs. "Lera is hurt."

"Thank you for clearing that up—I was confused as to what all the blood was about." Arisha pushes her glasses up the bridge of her nose. "And you look little better, in case you were wondering."

Coal's blue eyes flash. "I wasn't."

Time to intervene. Yanking at its ties, I let the tattered dress slump to a pile at my feet, then, wrapping a blanket around myself, sink into the divine softness of my bed in my underclothes. "Coal helped me back to the room, Arisha. The blood isn't from him. I...I was wrapped up in yesterday's fight at the barracks, and River had me held overnight. I'm going to get some rest now. There is little more to it."

"There is—" Arisha and Coal say at the same time, stopping to glare at each other as soon as the words are out.

I glare at both of them. "I'm *fine*."

"Like hell you are," Coal snaps at me, just as Arisha shouts, "You are not fine."

Turning back to Arisha, Coal crosses his arms. "I'm not leaving."

"Neither am I."

The warrior's jaw tightens. "Fine," he says finally, pulling his hair back into its usual tight bun as if preparing for battle all over again. "But if you repeat anything you see, hear, smell, or even bloody *think* in this chamber for the next hour, I will make your life so painful, your hair will have bruises. Do you understand?"

Arisha's throat bobs, but she squares her shoulders toward Coal. "And if you harm Lera, I'll work out a way to castrate you in your sleep."

"This changes nothing when you are on the training pitch," Coal says. "I'll still expect you to do at least one halfway decent push-up. And punish you when you don't."

"Agreed," says Arisha. "And any cooperation now is not a sign that I like you."

"Agreed," says Coal.

"Do I get a say?" I ask.

"No." The pair answer together, this time not even bothering to exchange dirty gazes.

11

COAL

Crouching beside Lera, Coal suddenly realized he didn't know what to do next. Everything about her filled his consciousness, from the racing pulse that made the hollow of her neck tremble with every beat, to the tightness on the side of her jaw where she clenched her teeth to conceal her pain. Her large chocolate eyes had a guarded look that tried and failed to hide the penetrating stubborn intelligence lurking inside her. Intelligence and pain, a hurt that extended a lot deeper than her strained arm. One day, Coal would find that man he'd seen in Lera's nightmares and repay him in kind for every beating.

"Shade is still gone." Arisha set a very well-stocked basket of bandages, salves, and other healer's supplies on the bed beside Lera. "But this might be of use. I'll get some water." The door clicked softly behind her, leaving the dorm room suddenly far too silent.

Coal raised a quick brow at the impressive basket, then returned his attention to Lera. The girl's small body had an ethereal beauty that made her the object of every man's fantasy—obviously, given the brawn—but to Coal, it went deeper than that. Coal remembered Lera's body taking him inside, melding with his in an explosion of power and ecstasy and connection that he'd so expertly destroyed in the month since.

"Let me see the arm," Coal said, the words too collected to be his own. Maybe Arisha was right and him staying here was a mistake. He'd coupled with Lera and then ignored her for a month, only to spy on her nightmares while she sat shackled in a dungeon cell. That he'd not done the spying on purpose—didn't even know how the hell it happened—little changed the facts.

From how Lera pulled her arms away from him, she was of similar doubt about the merit of Coal's presence. "I can take care of it myself, sir."

Sir. Because Coal was an instructor and Lera a student. He'd gone out of his way to remind her of that, and now he was paying for it.

"You could." Arisha had returned, and, ignoring his better sense, Coal dunked a cloth into the washbasin she brought over and dabbed the blood on Lera's arm. "But you didn't get to this state on your own."

"Neither did you," Leralynn said quietly.

Seeming to sense the intensity in the room, Arisha once more slipped out.

Coal paused, then dipped the washcloth back in the basin, turning the water a soft pink. Was Lera referencing the fight or something else? The probing light in her eyes made Coal feel far too seen. His chest tightened suddenly at the eerie notion that he might not have been alone last night. That the tunnel of memories he'd stumbled into might have gone both ways. "I'm not sure what you mean," he said, hoping to the stars the lie sounded genuine.

A muscle in Lera's jaw ticked. When she tried to pull her arm back, Coal held it firm. He wasn't letting her go. Not yet. The next swipe of the washcloth was harder and longer than Coal had intended, and he opened his mouth to apologize for hurting her—until he noticed what was on the skin beneath. The half-healed slash creeping from beneath Lera's raised sleeve came from no shackle or training weapon. Coal was fairly certain no one had pulled an edged weapon in the last morning fight, but even if they had, this mark was a bit too old for that.

A fight. Leralynn had been fighting. Coal frowned at the mark, his memory suddenly scraping up River asking him about another injury of Lera's. One that Lera had told River came from training, though Coal knew it had not.

Lera yanked against Coal's hold, this time hard enough to reclaim the limb.

Lifting his head, he captured her guarded gaze, ignoring the wave of possessive instinct that made him want to pull the girl against him. The same possessive instinct that made him also want to wring her neck for playing them all. "Who are you fighting when no one watches, Leralynn of Osprey?" he asked.

Lera's face closed off from him, the distance between them suddenly a cavernous void. "I'm not sure what you mean."

She flung his own words back at him.

Coal cursed. Even if he'd avoided the topic himself a few moments ago, this outright lie stung. More to the point, whatever Lera was doing clearly wasn't safe. "You want to try that again?" His voice dropped to low command.

"You want to tell me why you've gone out of your way to avoid training with me for the past month?"

"You know exactly why," Coal snapped with more force than he'd intended. "I'm an instructor, and you are a cadet. What happened between us in the forest cannot happen again. Keeping clear of me is the best thing for you."

Lera leaned forward, bracing her good arm on her knee. Small, injured, exhausted—and yet she still managed to harness as much power around her as River could. It made Coal proud and furious at the same time. Especially when she spoke, enunciating her words with scalpel-sharp precision. "Then, keep clear."

Coal closed his eyes. He deserved that. But it still hurt. The feel of Lera's body leaning against him in the cell, trusting him to care for her even for a few moments, was the most precious sensation to have touched him in the whole bloody month. And he was ruining it royally. Opening his eyes, he softened his voice to one of consolatory reason. "Whatever is happening, I might be able to help. Trust me, Lera."

"All right." Lera tipped her head. "You want trust, Coal? You start. How have you been sleeping lately?"

Coal's heart skipped a beat, a tremor running along his skin. Had the girl overheard River's and Shade's concerns, or had that tunnel of last night's nightmares truly run in both directions? The notion sounded too insane to entertain seriously, but Lera seeing his memories was no more absurd than him seeing hers. And that had happened, hadn't it? Well, even if it did—especially if it did—this line of conversation was going no further. "That isn't your concern," he said, his voice hitching with his racing heart. "Not now, not *ever*, Cadet."

The moment he said it, he knew he'd gone too far.

Lera snarled softly. "You dreamt of clanking chains and heated irons. The stench as they came up behind you so—"

"Shut. Your. Mouth." His gut twisted, bile burning as it rose up his throat. Pushing away from her, he rose to his feet.

Lera stood in answer, the blanket falling away from her ethereally beautiful body, now vibrating with shattering fury. "What's wrong, Coal? Don't like what you're hearing?"

"I don't like who is speaking."

The chill that settled over Lera's eyes twisted Coal's stomach, the bang of the iron door falling into place between them echoing through his soul.

With a nonchalance that eviscerated him, Lera jerked her chin toward the door. "You should go, sir. We might give River and the others the wrong impression if you stay in my bedchamber too long."

12

COAL

Coal crossed the Academy grounds blindly, unaware of cadets' wide eyes as he passed, of anything but where he was going. She knew. However it happened, Lera saw the jagged, shattered pieces of Coal's soul—and found them as vile and pathetic as he did. The nightmares that were getting worse, the darkness ratcheting tighter around Coal's neck each day. He could barely look at his own reflection nowadays, knowing his memories had somehow been laid open for Lera to sort through... Coal had barely made it out of the cadets' barracks before losing what little food his stomach held.

Even if Coal stayed away from Leralynn completely, transferred the girl to another class, and never ever crossed paths, the truth would still saturate the air. He couldn't do it. Couldn't face Lera again. Worse still, if that strange bridge between them reopened again, the darkness haunting Coal might assault Lera as well.

A rabid dog, one of the guards had called Coal. How very accurate.

Opening the keep door, he took the keep stairs toward River's study, two at a time—only to find the man descending the steps.

"Coal?" Stopping on a wide landing with a window overlooking the courtyard below, River arched a dark brow. With his arms behind his back, he made the weight resting on his shoulders seem easy to carry—

though the fatigue lining his eyes spoke the truth. Well, at least Coal would shortly be getting rid of one of River's problems.

"I wished to give you a chance to rip into me properly over yesterday." Coal slid his hands into his pockets. "I will be leaving after that."

River pinched the bridge of his nose. "I've been unable to find Shade for the past bloody day, and you've managed to both corner him and somehow wring a clearance to return to active duty from his jaws?"

"No. But I am resigning my commission. You are within your rights to have me arrested over a number of charges by now, but whether I leave in shackles or free, I will be off the grounds by nightfall."

River surveyed Coal with opaque gray eyes that gave no hint of his thoughts.

A tight band closed around Coal's chest, the passing heartbeats sounding louder and louder in the heavy silence. Coal had served under River and Shade for as long as he could remember, and the thought of breaking all ties with the men cut as sharp as a blade.

"I will consider your resignation and let you know my decision by nightfall," River said finally, as if discussing a proposed change of vendor for cleaning oils. Perhaps he had been waiting for this awhile now. Hoping Coal would realize the toxic effect he had. Straightening his already neat coat, River started down the steps. "Meanwhile, I am on my way to discuss Leralynn's unintended overnight captivity with Master Han, whom I'd expected to release her. You may join me if you wish."

"Who the bloody hell is Han?" Coal asked, falling in step.

DESPITE MOST OF the cadets enjoying the week of holiday liberty, using the time to ride out to the small town near the school, the training pitch at the far end was in active use. From what Coal could see over the expanse of freshly cut grass, Han was working ten cadets—all royal born, save Tyelor of Blair.

The royals, all dressed in training grays, were holding a plank position along the fence. Sweat dripped from their hair, leaving dark clumps in the sand. Judging by Princess Katita's trembling arms, they'd been at this for some time already. Unlike the others, Tye was climbing a thick rope rigged to hang from a sturdy tree branch some twenty feet up. Moving closer, Coal noted an iron anvil tied to Tye's ankles, the metal both increasing the weight to be hauled up the rope and preventing Tye from using his legs to help the climb.

"We are all waiting on you, Tyelor," Han was yelling as River and Coal made their final approach. Tall and muscular, with neat black hair, the new man had a warrior's body and a sharp smell that made Coal think of cayenne pepper. Dressed in a tight-fitting gray shirt and black pants, Han moved with a speed and balance that spoke of violence despite being plainly unarmed at the moment. Tipping his head back to watch Tye's ascent, Han raised his voice again. "Every single damn person in this corral is waiting on your pleasure, Master Tyelor. Your feet will be on the ground in the next five heartbeats, or this training starts over. For everyone."

Coal gave River a sideways look. Tye's body was already shaking, and, as Han's threat registered, the athlete pushed his pace at the expense of control. Not a good combination twenty feet up in the air, in Coal's opinion—though he trained soldiers, not athletic competitors. Twisting upside down around a bar was not a good idea in Coal's mind under any circumstance.

"Four," Han called. "Three."

Tye touched the top branch and started scrambling down, gripping hand over hand, his chest heaving.

"Two," Han bellowed.

Tye flinched, making a too-hasty grab for the rope. Coal foresaw the inevitable a moment before it happened. Tyelor's hand slipped, and he slid down the remaining fifteen feet of the rope, the hemp burning off his skin to leave streaks of crimson behind. By the time Tye fell to the ground, his knee striking the anvil's edge, blood dripped freely from his palms.

Han kicked the sand, sending the grains into Tye's eyes. "Pitiful and sloppy."

Tye showed no emotion, his chest heaving as sweat ran down his face.

"I've no notion what child's play you called *training* up to this point, but I assure you, it won't be the case any longer." Han pointed at the rope. "Again."

River strode up to the corral fence, waiting in that silent way the commander had of getting attention. As usual, the method worked. Han approached the spot a moment later, a small smile tilting his lips.

"I see you've already begun assembling the new team," River said mildly.

Han leaned his back against the fence and nodded. "I have. One moment, sir." He snapped his fingers at the royals, whose heads swiveled to him at once. "Two laps around the Academy. The last one done will be running extra every day for the next week. Go."

The cadets scurried off, Katita and two of her cousins leading the way. With all students but Tye gone, Han split his attention equally between his climber and River. "I presume you came to check on your troublemaker, sir." Han nodded toward the rope. "I feel confident that after today, Tyelor's desire to get into brawls or break any other Academy regulations will be curbed effectively."

"I'm heartened to learn that. However, I came to discover why you failed to remove Leralynn of Osprey from the holding cell yesterday." The chill in River's voice was enough to set any man's spine crackling with ice, but Han seemed too busy watching Tye's progress to mark it.

"Who? Oh, the wench. She isn't any concern of mine." With a dismissive shrug, Han pitched his voice up. "Move, Tyelor. Bathe in self-pity on your own damn time."

Coal felt a growl rise up his chest, but River beat him to it. Clamping a hand on Han's shoulder, the large commander jerked Han around to face him.

"First, that is the last time you refer to any female at this Academy as *wench.*" River's voice was low and dangerous as he stared down at Han. "Second, you were told to set both students free and instead shackled the girl and left without a word. Explain yourself."

Han glanced at River's grip as if examining an unsightly slug. "First, Commander River, Leralynn of Osprey—as well as any other student not on my training team—is utterly irrelevant to my position here. I left her cell door ajar and kept her shackle loose enough for anyone with half a brain to work their wrist loose with a few minutes of effort. Beyond that, I expect the *young woman's* training instructor to take responsibility for her." Han's eyes cut to Coal, the blue-gray in them lined with distaste.

Coal bared his teeth.

Han snorted, returning his attention to River. "Either way, certainly the guards at the prestigious Great Falls Academy can subtract one from two and know there is something left over. If Leralynn's disposition wasn't reported back to you, then either your people's arithmetic or communications skills are lacking. Both of which, like Leralynn herself, are not my concern. Now, let go of my shoulder, *sir.*"

River released Han, and Coal swore the commander nearly wiped his hand on his trousers before putting it behind his back.

Han turned to Coal. "While we are on the topic of cadet oversight, Lieutenant Coal, please allow me to make myself clear in light of some recent history I've learned. I little care who you rut with, so long as it isn't any one of my athletes. You let your cock, tongue, or even your stars' damned eyes touch any of my students, and I will cut off your sac and stuff it down your throat. I do hope that is clear enough. Excuse me, gentlemen."

Coal realized he was moving only when he felt River's hand dig painfully into his shoulder.

"Leave it," the commander ordered, half dragging Coal off the pitch.

Coal's nostrils flared, the pounding in his ears making the whole bloody world pulse in front of his eyes. The moment he and River cleared Han's sight, he twisted toward the commander so quickly that the other man had to jump back just to keep from being slugged. "Did you hear—"

"Yes, I did." River matched Coal snarl for snarl. "I heard a man who knows his authority comes from Sage tell me exactly where the lines in the sand are drawn. And, point of fact, the bastard was right. I ordered everyone into custody, so the responsibility to keep track of them was mine. Had the guards not been in utter disarray, they would have reported the situation as Han expected. They didn't, and I was too preoccupied to notice. That is not a mistake someone with the power to lock people up is allowed to make."

"That's it?" Coal's voice was too calm and quiet for the blood rushing in his ears. There was little point in pushing when River got like this. No, action would come later. "And Tyelor? Or was that near neck-breaking fall also somehow your fault?"

"If Tyelor—and the rest of the cadets in that corral—find Han's methods unpalatable, there is nothing stopping them from walking away." River clasped his hands behind his back, his broad chest pressing against his red jacket. Reminding Coal of just who was in control. "Unless Han starts physically forcing the athletes or expands his power outside the team, I've matters of greater import to address than how a Prowess coach handles his *entirely voluntary group*. As for what he said to you—"

"Don't." Coal turned on his heels before the fury raging inside him flashed too brightly in his eyes. He was done here. Done but for one last thing that River would do better to know nothing about. Not until it was done. After that—after that, nothing really mattered.

Coal waited atop the Academy's high wall, crouched against the deep shadow of the night. The curfew bells had sounded hours ago, though with Ostera liberty, several errant cadets were still trying to talk their way past the harried guards. But Coal wasn't watching for them. He hunted someone else.

Despite being assigned quarters in the instructors' wing of the keep, Han was yet to move in, his rooms empty. Which meant that sometime tonight, Han would leave the Academy. Most likely, he'd head to one of the two small inns in the Great Fall's village, though it little mattered. By the time Coal finished his chat with the man, Han wasn't going to be arriving at either destination—not unless he crawled there.

Han had shackled Leralynn to a cell wall and left her there. Alone and frightened and in pain. Just the memory of the coppery scent of her wrists, her numb fear, made Coal's blood simmer. For that, Han would pay. The man might have a silver tongue and leverage enough to talk circles around River, but none of that would save him from Coal.

The three hours Coal spent waiting passed swiftly, his heartbeat staying level even when Han finally walked out the Academy gate, the night breeze carrying hints of cayenne pepper toward Coal. Han wore casual clothing now rather than the instructor's red, a soft white tunic tucked into fitted black pants, and tall boots. That white shirt would be easy to spot in the woods—and a pleasure to ruin. From his perch, Coal watched as the man chose one of the wooded trails instead of the main road and started down the path at a leisurely gait. With Han's speed and the direction in mind, Coal jumped softly from the wall and cut through the woods, beating Han to the small clearing Coal had spotted. Crossing his arms over his chest, Coal leaned back against a thick oak and waited.

The smell of cayenne pepper announced Han's approach even before the sound of his soft footsteps brushed Coal's ears. Entering the clearing, the man spotted Coal and snorted softly, his blue-gray eyes filling with the same derisive loathing Coal had marked at the training courts.

"To what do I owe the pleasure?" Han asked.

"You left a girl chained to a dungeon wall." Pushing away from the oak, Coal stepped toward Han. "River might have to swallow the horseshit you spew, but I've no intention to."

"Are you here to *fight* me, Coal?" This time, Han actually laughed, his face crossing the line from handsome to cruel in an instant. "And here I thought you were just spanked for as much last night."

Coal's hand curled into a fist, Han's gaze narrowing at the motion.

"You know…" Han's tone changed, amusement disappearing. "On second thought, I think I'd welcome the exercise." The shift of Han's hips was the only warning Coal had before Han's boot slammed into his ribs, the force of the blow lifting Coal into the air.

Coal's back bounced off the very oak he'd leaned on moments earlier, the impact a distant thud. Rolling over his shoulder, he dodged the next attack, his senses coming into focus.

Han crouched in a fighting stance, his chest moving as evenly and slowly as Coal's own. When Han's lips pulled back to expose a set of bright white teeth, a guttural primal growl escaping from his chest into the forest, Coal knew that only one of them was walking out of the clearing alive.

And Coal little cared who it would be.

13

LERA

"I don't like him," I tell Arisha, hugging a pillow to my chest. Without Shade's wolf in my bed, the mattress feels too large. The male has been gone two full days now—who knows how far he's gone in search of the mysterious fae girl. *Stars take me.* "I don't like the whole notion."

"There are a number of *hims* that would fit logically into that sentence." Arisha makes a mark in a study schedule she's drafting, her wild brown hair uncharacteristically loose and brushing the parchment. We both know she doesn't need one and is simply using the busy work as an excuse to stay in the room with me all day. Keeping me company as I recover from last night or keeping me out of trouble. Probably both.

"Han. And not only because he shackled me to a wall. Granted, that's a pretty good reason too." I try to sound nonchalant, though the memories still send chills over my skin. The heavy dread that had wrapped around me after Coal left seemed to have lifted for a spell but returned with a vengeance a few hours ago. A low, rumbling oppression stalking me from the shadows.

I rub my face. The fight with Coal, that's what's eating me. Just when I thought the chain linking our fears would link our trust as well, Coal looked me in the eye and informed me that our connection mattered nothing. That he didn't want me in his heart, or soul, or life.

I glance at the darkness outside the window and light another lantern, my green silk pants and short-cropped top swaying comfortably. No gowns, no gray uniforms, not tonight. "Why is the man suddenly here?" I say, returning to the matter of Han. "Great Falls was never going to participate in the Trials—it's all the veil's doing to make a place for Tye."

"It isn't all that sudden, actually," says Arisha. "Tye came over a month ago. Once that happened, Sage suddenly had both the notion and the means to make Great Falls a real player in one of the continent's most important events. It makes sense that he'd start maneuvering to field a competitive—and royal—team. If princelings are competing, their throne-holding parents will come to watch. All because of Sage. The little worm is probably bathing in his future self-importance."

"Maybe. But Han still appeared right after I ran into the Night Guard." I rub my tightening chest.

"Word in the courtyard is that he's well known—has been in Prowess for a decade. The royals…"

Arisha's words blur. In the edges of my vision, the bedchamber flickers to a dungeon cell, to a forest, to whispering darkness all around me, night sounds making me flinch. My breath quickens, then catches, that shadow-stalking dread inside me uncoiling. Focusing. Getting ready to pounce.

"Lera? Leralynn." Arisha is on her feet and, by the sound of it, has repeated my name several times by now.

"I'm sorry." I blink my friend back into focus, her concerned blue eyes grounding me. "Sorry. I was just thinking… What is the veil going to do when Tye travels to the Trials? Is it going to be strong enough to convince a much larger group that he is—" I cut off, the wave of wrongness smashing into me strong enough to make my heart stutter with panic, a phantom scent of cayenne tickling my nose. Something is wrong. Very, very wrong.

I stuff my feet into my boots, barely seeing what I'm doing, and am at the window before I can form words from the onslaught of sensation. Not words—*word*. Just one.

"Coal," I tell Arisha, though I know nothing more than that. Only that something is wrong. That Coal is in the middle of it. That Coal is ready to die.

. . .

The darkened Academy is a blur as I shimmy out the window, climbing down the outer wall of the dormitory with practiced ease. Only lanterns in a few windows and torches on the ramparts light my way, casting deep shadows everywhere else. The familiar dark woods lining the inside of the Academy wall greet me with a rustle of leaves and a scent of pine that I mark only in the periphery. I run without knowing where I'm going, except toward the eye of the gathered dread. *What are you doing, Coal?* I demand in my head, as if the male might hear my question.

My foot snags on a root, and I stumble, momentarily pulled back into the now. Back to some common sense. *You can't just blindly run through the darkness, Lera.* Even if I'm right that the magic I share with Coal is guiding my direction now, rushing into an assault vicious enough to endanger Coal's life is more likely to make me a victim than rescuer.

With a curse, I realize my common sense returned too late for me to have grabbed any weapons. All I have on me is a boot knife Coal once gave me, and that just because it was sheathed in my shoe to begin with. A knife. That's all I brought.

I am considering returning for a sword when another wave of darkness slams into me, this one heralding a searing pain along my ribs. Leaning one hand on an oak, I force air into my lungs, breathing through the pain. *You aren't the one wounded, Lera. You are supposed to be the one doing the thinking.*

Right. Shoving down the panic, I force myself to survey the sounds, my thought finally coming to rest on the Academy wall. Not a surreptitious route by any means, but it does offer both a good view and an easy path around the Academy. With my immortal sight, I'll have a fighting chance of seeing something.

After a month of using the underground escape passage to get outside the Academy, it takes me a moment to locate a climbable approach. Hips flattened against the cold stone, I climb as quickly as I can find the scant grips and footholds. Rock scrapes my abdomen, my short top providing no protection against the stone. But even that is an advantage. A reminder of where my body is as Coal's darkness swirls dizzyingly in my mind. Of which body is mine.

Clearing the top of the wall, I straighten to my full height. The cool air billows my silk pants, the fabric crackling in the night. Below me, miles of wilderness and sheep farm and Academy grounds stretch in all directions, faintly silver in the moonlight. Nothing breaks the night's silence but wind and an owl's lonesome hooting. *Where are you, Coal? Where in stars' name are you?*

I turn to the Academy first. It is busier than usual for this time of night, the Ostera break relaxing the rules. A pair of cadets holding hands are sneaking into the reflection garden. A few more scurry across the courtyard. At the front gate, the guards argue about something among themselves. Nothing to suggest the death dance going on in the flashes of darkness in my mind.

Twisting around, I face the woods instead—quite aware that the last time I went out there, I nearly got myself dead. Could that be what's happening to Coal now? Did he run himself afoul of the Night Guard, not knowing what it is?

Even as I think it, I know that isn't true. Coal isn't battling for his life—he…he doesn't care. The bastard *doesn't care* one damn bit whether he lives or dies. *That* is why my heart pounds my ribs so hard, it's a miracle I've not cracked the bone.

I race along the top of the wide stone wall, letting the dread inside me act as a guiding light while my eyes seek any sign of disturbance.

Nothing.

Nothing.

There. My immortal sight catches on a small clearing along a side trail, two shapes moving too swiftly to be mortals circling each other in the darkness. My stomach clenches. Scrambling to the ground, I'm momentarily blinded by the trees around me, the bird's-eye view from the wall giving way to dense, rustling forest. But I know these woods by now, know how to get to the center of the darkness that pulls me like a leash. Wiping my sweaty palms on my pants, I break into a run.

I hear the fight before I see it, the soft grunts of males mixing with the snaps of dried branches cracking underfoot. Coal's metallic scent wraps around me, together with the sharp cayenne I'd smelled back in the room. And in the dungeon.

Han.

For some unfathomable reason, Coal is fighting with Han—and from what I saw on that wall, whatever the hell Han is, he isn't human. Can't be. I reach the edge of the clearing just as Han throws Coal in a great arc, my male landing hard on his back before rolling over his shoulder to escape the next blow. Coal's movements are as crisp as always, a blur of black leather against the tree branches, but I know him well enough to mark the slight hesitations. As if Coal battles his own mind as much as Han's limbs.

Which he very likely is. My hands tighten against the tree trunk I've stopped behind. Coal spent last night in a *dungeon cell*, the hours filled with terrors and ripped-open wounds. How many nights has it been since the male slept soundly, if the nightmares inside him roar fiercely enough to jump to me in the middle of a choke-hold demonstration with the whole class watching? With Coal keeping his distance from me, I've not realized how desperately the male's darkness was suffocating him. How deeply he's been spiraling down.

No wonder Coal welcomed a brawl—he needed the humans' greater numbers to create enough of an opponent to siphon off the violence inside him. Well, Coal is certainly getting a worthy enough foe with Han. Too much of one for Coal's present state, with his body, his mind, and his will to win all worn down to bare threads.

Crouching low, Coal sweeps Han's legs.

Han jumps over the sweep, closing the distance to Coal. The male's blue-gray eyes dim to obsidian, his smell spiking as he grabs Coal's wrist. A grapefruit-size stone that I missed seeing Han pick up off the ground now flashes in his free hand. Then he brings it down onto Coal's forearm.

The crack of bone as Coal's arm fractures seems louder than a crack of thunder. Coal screams, the arm dropping to his side like a piece of heavy rope. In all the time since I've met my males, it's the first time I've seen the warrior overpowered by a single foe. The first time I've seen him injured with no magic to mend the break. Coal takes a step forward, and stumbles. Falls to one knee.

Han grins, his muscles already coiling for the final blow, his eyes glazed with the feral gleam of a predator savoring the kill to come.

My thoughts stop. The world slows around me, each sight and smell reporting in full force. Tangs of pain and excitement scent the air, all wrapped in musky sweat. The too slowly moving leaves tremble in the breeze. Han's boot takes aim at Coal's head. One more heartbeat and Han will destroy my quint, shattering not just Coal but all five of our bonded souls.

Terror races through me. My magic bucks, throwing itself fiercely against its shackles with every ounce of my will. Once. Twice. On the third heave, one cord's tip breaks through the hold, slicing through the cracking defenses of the mortal world's wards. Like an invisible whip, the roaring orange fire cord—still pulsing with the recent strength of Tye's mating magic—flails uncontrollably before slamming into the ground.

The ground bucks, the power reverberating wildly through every stone and tree root. I grunt as I land hard on my knees, the world's speed returning to normal as the others lose balance as well. As Han sets his foot down to the ground, his gaze skids around the woods. Finding *me.*

"What—" Han starts to say.

But Coal is already up on his feet. Despite his limp arm, the male moves with more power than I'd yet seen tonight, placing his body between Han and me. "Osprey." Fear fills his voice. "Run. *Now.*"

As if. Even as Coal moves toward me, my hand is already on my boot knife, my fingers gripping the blade. The males may just have realized my presence, but I've known theirs all along. And I feel no hesitation as my eyes mark the broad target of Han's chest. See it expand with drawn breath, the deadly muscles shaping the cloth. Imagine a painted target and take aim.

The *lub-dub lub-dub* of my heart is like music, setting the stage for the cry of a startled hawk circling the sky.

Han's dark brows narrow at what seems a snail's speed, his handsome face confused. Then a smile tugs the corner of the bastard's mouth.

My arm whips forward, the knife soaring through the air.

Han's amusement shifts to wide-eyed surprise, my knife flying with the speed of an immortal's powerful muscles. The amulet heating around my neck might convince the bastard that he'd overestimated the knife's speed, but if I end him, it would save my veil the trouble.

With no time to move out of the blade's path, Han lifts his hand and…and snatches the dagger from the air. Blood pools around his palm, its coppery scent filling the clearing.

Stars. My eyes widen, my chest heaves, my muscles burning with energy. I grab desperately for the magic inside me, only to find the mortal shackles have recaptured the rogue cord of Tye's power. I tug at the binds anyway, beads of perspiration slipping down my temples.

"I seem to have underestimated the allure of your cock, Master Coal." Han takes my throwing knife into his good hand. "How fortunate you are to have comely young cadets throwing away their lives for you."

Despite his useless arm, Coal crouches into a fighting stance with a growl, blocking Han's path to me. Ready to fight for me in a way he hadn't for himself.

But we can't fight Han tonight. Not if we want to live. I swallow, my mind racing, groping for the experiences of the other males. *River. What would River do now?*

"You think you can kill both of us, Han?" I ask, pitching my voice across the battleground before either male can attack.

"Yes. Easily."

Coal growls. I grab his shoulder, a silent order to stay put that he, by the star's own miracle, heeds.

"I think you might be right," I tell Han, raising my chin. "But you won't. You came to the Academy for a reason, and you aren't going to throw it all away to scratch a midnight itch." I draw breath, the confidence I'm putting into my voice now seeping into my blood. Filling the very air around me. "The way I see it, Coal's body alone could be explained away. But the pair of us together? After you've already shackled me to a dungeon wall? You'll be answering so many questions, you'll have no time for anything else. Plus, you've no idea who else knows I'm out here."

Deep within the forest, a wolf's howl shatters the night.

Han looks between us, thought rushing behind his blue-gray gaze.

Beneath my grip, Coal's body is coiled and ready. If he is to leave this world, he will go out fighting for life. Which is already a victory, though not the one I'm going for.

Heartbeats pass in the night's darkness. One. Two. Five. Then, Han twists the knife in his hand and tucks it inside his coat.

"As satisfying as cleaning out the Academy's rubbish would be tonight," Han says, "it seems I'll need to wait a bit. Do me a boon and don't kill yourself before I can have the pleasure."

The relief washing over me is so fierce that I lean into my grip on Coal to keep from swaying.

Han's eerie moonlit gaze jerks to me, a gleam in his eyes saying he'd seen my near stumble just fine. "I will see you back at the Academy, Leralynn of Osprey." A smile that doesn't touch his eyes breaks the handsome lines of his face. "I would try not to get yourself stopped on the way back. I hear the headmaster is unkind to wayward students. If that sort of thing bothers you." Without waiting for my reply, he saunters off into the night.

14

LERA

I don't dare take my attention off Han until the sound of his retreating footsteps fades from my immortal hearing, the forest's creatures who went quiet during the quarrel reclaiming their domain.

In the distance, Shade's wolf howls again, his frustrated song soul-shatteringly familiar. An owl hoots. Beside me, Coal maintains his fighter's crouch, statue still but for the rapid rise and fall of his broad chest, his broken arm now tight against his ribs. Finally, seeming to mark the same change in sound I had, the male rises and has the audacity to glare at me.

"What the bloody hell do you think you are doing out here, Osprey?"

Blazing heat rushes along my spine. "Saving your life, you bastard. Since plainly, you can't be bothered with such minutia."

"What I do is none—"

I slap Coal's cheek as hard as I can. My nostrils flare, the fury and fear that have simmered too long erupting from my heart. "You think your damn life belongs to you alone? That no other soul would be shredded if you died?"

Coal flinches, rocking back from the strike. "Dying is a natural byproduct of battle. If you—"

I slap him again. "You weren't battling, you bastard. Battling is when you care whether you bloody win or lose." I go to strike Coal a third time, but the male catches my hand in an iron grip.

Blue eyes flashing, he straightens to his full height before me, his metallic scent filling my lungs. The lines of his beautiful face are etched with a soul-deep ache, his mouth but a step away. *Stars,* I can taste Coal from memory alone. My fingers long to run over his strong cheekbones and jaw, the hint of stubble there, to feel his warm skin beneath my touch.

The magic inside me rouses again, sensing its twin in Coal, making every sensation sharp enough to slice through flesh.

The terror of nearly losing him grips my throat again. I twist free of Coal's grip and spit on the ground. "Go ahead. Lie. Tell me I'm wrong, say there is no connection between us, that I've no way of knowing what you were doing." My teeth grind together, my eyes stinging. "Tell me to shut my mouth. Say I'm imagining things and you've no idea where I might have gotten my silly notions. Say that I'm just a cadet you rutted with once and that's all there was to it."

Coal swallows, his blue eyes turning so vulnerable for a moment that my anger hiccups.

"That is not all there was to it," he says, his voice quiet but clear. Covering the distance between us in one powerful step, the male grips the back of my head and presses his mouth over mine.

Heat flares through me as Coal's tongue brushes between my lips, parting them roughly. His metallic scent flares with a tang of desperation and need that stokes the blaze inside my soul, my magic, my sex.

Wrapping the strong fingers of his good hand in my hair, Coal pushes farther into my mouth. The deep leisurely strokes of his tongue make one turn before morphing to primal possessiveness. My scalp tingles where he grips my hair, the tiny twitches of pain waking my nerves to the full bouquet of his presence. When I try to move, to check whether his fractured arm might be caught in the press of our bodies, Coal only holds me tighter. Deepens his rough, claiming kiss. Gives himself over to it.

A wave of desperate relief rushes through me as I finally trust that Coal is not letting go. Not pretending he kisses me with anything less than the full force of his soul. I open myself to him, allowing him in more deeply.

Coal groans at my invitation, his tongue roaming my mouth,

staking a claim while his hardness presses into me. He makes no move to conceal that either, pressing his hips into mine, holding me against him until my body yields to the strength and comfort of his.

When we finally separate, our rough breathing the only sound in the still forest, Coal stares at me, dazed. He puts the palm of his good hand on my cheek, the calluses scraping my skin.

"I felt you in my cell," he says, never taking his gaze off my widening eyes. "That is how I knew you were still being held. I saw… images from your past. A stable. And I feared you might be seeing mine as well. Knowing my terrors might be hurting you was worse than feeling them myself. I tried to keep them controlled, but I couldn't make them stop." Coal touches the red marks on my wrist where I fought the shackle, the streaks a silent, undeniable proof of the truth.

I bite my lip, his words still ringing in my ears, stripping me naked.

Coal's jaw tightens, but he nods. "It's plainly a bit late to pretend otherwise. Or to pretend that staying away from you for a month didn't drive me insane, until the last shards of my control shattered." Shaking his head, he runs a finger down my cheek, across my lower lip.

I inhale, letting the words soak through me, a tight band around my chest releasing. He wanted me. This whole month that I thought Coal a stranger, he wanted me all along. I let my hands roam over his broad chest, the feel of the hard muscle beneath my palms slicking my thighs. Clearing my throat, I press my legs together tightly. Not to conceal my desire from Coal, but because we are too vulnerable out here already, without adding mating into the mix.

Except Coal is too damn Coal-like not to notice. His nostrils flare as he takes in my scent, and he presses closer to me, burying his face in my neck. Inhaling deeply.

It takes all my will to pull away from him. "We're not safe here." These forests are Night Guard hunting grounds now. And Han's. "What do you make of Han?"

Coal frowns. "Something about his movements… It makes me think he isn't human."

"I think he's as human as you and I," I mutter, the amulet around my neck turning scalding hot in warning to go no further in discussing our identities. Though Coal doesn't know it, he actually has a good point. If Han was like us—a veil-wearing fae—his amulet's magic would bend over backwards to convince Coal and me that his actions were normal and any oddness only imagined. Plus, when Autumn handed over the amulets, she said the set was unique—how would Han, whatever he is, have gotten hold of the rare relic to begin with? Marking the thoughts to discuss with Arisha later, I nod at Coal's arm. "How is it?"

"Broken in several places," he says flatly. Finding the open collar of his black shirt, the male tugs at the laces until I reach up to help, quickly realizing that taking it off the normal way would do more harm than good.

The well-worn fabric splits obediently when I rip it, the sound echoing eerily through the trees. My breath catches as I slide Coal's shirt off his chest, the squares of his abdomen plain even in moonlight. The male tenses in pain but lets me work as I guide his injured arm across his body, binding it in place until Shade can set the bone later. I try not to think about that procedure, but the realization of other things likely to still happen tonight triggers a whole new wave of anxiety.

Coal's nostrils flare delicately, his eyes sharpening. "What's wrong?"

I clear my throat, my face heating. After the violence we just escaped, the new problem seems miniscule. Except it isn't. Not to me. "What are you planning to tell River? I don't mean about *us*, but about what happened out here. With Han."

"I planned on the truth." He cocks his head, studying my face with an intensity that makes me want to shuffle my feet. "Han and I fought .You stopped it. Is that a problem?"

"I'm not supposed to be outside the Academy walls."

"This isn't your first time out here, Osprey. Or second. Or tenth, I think." With a snort, Coal pulls up my loose sleeve to expose the tail of the still-healing knife wound. "Also, I'm quite certain River either already knows we are out here or will discover it from Han shortly." Releasing my arm, he tucks a strand of hair behind my ear, his voice softening. "Keeping things from River is a piss-poor move."

"You're one to talk."

"Yes. From experience."

"It isn't the same," I snap, despite having meant to keep silent. Now that I'm talking, the words spill out beneath his attentive gaze. "You are his equal, and I'm nothing but a lowly cadet. River cares nothing for my reasons, my abilities, my knowledge. There is magic threatening the Academy—the whole continent—and I'm not going to hide under the bed while others do the fighting. But there's nothing I can say to him to make him take me seriously. He locked me up for a night because I disobeyed his orders to try to stop a fight."

"He did not." Coal's hand, already on my face, grips the base of my chin. "Leralynn. River did not order you held. He had no idea you were still in the dungeon. I've a bone to pick with him over that, but he never meant to hurt you. He's a good man." Coal's jaw—and grip on mine—tightens. "But yes, River does discipline cadets. And after last night, what I saw in your past… I've a notion of why that's a problem."

"He didn't know I was—" I stop, suddenly processing what Coal mentioned earlier and then again now. He saw my nightmares too. Saw Zake's beatings—my terror, my screaming. My shrinking away. The implications thud through me. It's a part of my life I wanted to keep locked away forever. And now I've never felt so exposed. My breath quickens, and I try to pull away.

Coal doesn't let me go. Doesn't laugh at me either. "Yes. We'll have to figure something out on that front. Meanwhile…" He frowns thoughtfully. "I see your point about wishing to keep River in ignorance of your secret world-saving schemes lest you have to fight him as well as magic. And since you plainly have *something* going on and will continue this something no matter what, I will make you an offer: anything you tell me in confidence stays between us. Anything you don't tell me and I discover on my own is fair game to share with River."

"That's…" I glare at Coal. "That's blackmail to ensure I tell you everything I'm doing."

A corner of his mouth twitches and despite pain-filled eyes, I see the first genuine smile the male has attempted in a long, long time. "I think I like the thought of knowing everything you're doing, Osprey." Leaning forward, he brushes his lips over mine. "Most likely, I like it too much."

My heart stutters, the sensations rushing from my lips all the way through my skin. Before I can savor him too deeply, however, Coal pulls away, his face serious again.

"But as for tonight, we *have to* go to River. He almost certainly knows already. And it is better if we both see him now than if he must seek us out later. Plus there is another matter I need to see him on." Coal runs his hand along my neck and shoulders and spine, finally settling his warm palm in the small of my back. "Come, Osprey. Let's get this over with."

15

LERA

"Coal. Leralynn." River rises from behind his desk. The light in his study window gave away his location despite the late hour. "I've been expecting the two of you."

I try to step back on instinct, but the feel of Coal's insistent hand on the small of my back keeps me moving forward. My pulse races. This isn't going to go well. There is no chance in all the bloody stars that it will. For either of us.

Striding up, River reaches over my shoulder to shut the door, his woodsy scent washing over me. "I understand you assaulted Han just outside the Academy," he says to Coal. With the ice in his voice, the crackling fire in the study's hearth gives no warmth to the room. "Is that accurate?"

"Yes," says Coal.

River's chin points to Coal's bound arm. "And you lost?"

"Yes," Coal repeats.

A muscle tics in River's jaw, though his chiseled face gives away nothing more of his thoughts.

When his stony gray gaze shifts to me, the flutter of anxiety spilling into my blood makes me dizzy. No matter how hard I try to see past the stern commander to the male who danced and studied with me, all I see is the male who left welts on Tye's back, who ordered me to a dungeon for disobedience, who sent *Coal* there despite knowing the male's past.

I see a male who would never accept a cadet as a peer.

"And what of you, Leralynn?" River asks. "How did you end up in the middle of that mess?"

"I…I saw Coal and Han fighting. From the top of the wall." I swallow, hating the slight hitch in my voice. No chance of River failing to notice—the male never misses so much as a blink, though he is too well controlled to show it. "Someone needed to stop it, and I was available."

River puts his hands behind his back, his shoulders spread wide as wings under his black silk shirt. The hard lines of his jaw and penetrating gaze make the air sing with tension. "And?" he asks.

"And?" I echo.

River's gaze slides over my shoulder, no doubt to brush Coal's face before returning. "You saw Coal fighting. For the second time in as many days. You had already been punished for joining in once. Why did you choose to do so again?"

My brows narrow, indignation kindling a slow flame inside me. "What do you mean why? Because it was the right thing to do, River." I feel Coal shift behind me in warning, but I can't make myself heed it. Of all the things that turn my knees soft beneath River's powerful stare, this one I will fight for. "Because that is what you do when you see a friend in trouble."

"I did not realize you considered Coal, your *instructor*, a friend," said River.

I hadn't either. Not *this* Coal. And maybe he isn't, but he is a part of my soul nonetheless. Raising my chin, I square off before River's might, my pulse racing. I know that keeping my mouth shut and head bent is the safer course, but I can't, so I won't. For all our sakes.

"You think broken rules were the greatest problem here in the past two days?" My voice rises, and I take a step toward the male. "That locking Coal up would cure *anything*? I ran to interfere in a fight because I saw mortal danger that you were either too blind to mark or too proper to bother with."

Silence settles over the room, punctuated by my too-fast breathing. I stepped over the line. *Stars,* I took a running leap over the line and peed on it in midflight. And I've no notion of what I'm going to do now.

River's unreadable eyes weigh me. "That is not how I would have phrased things," he says finally. "But you are not wrong." Walking toward Coal, he plants himself in front of the warrior, hands behind his back. "Per our earlier conversation, I've given it some thought, and I reject your proposal. Any objection?"

"No, sir," Coal says, offering no more explanation than that.

"Good."

All right, then. I shift my weight, my thoughts firmly on the door. Somehow, incredibly, it seems there's a chance that a dismissal rides in the wind. I'll worry about the why of it later. For now, I'm not going to look a gift horse in the mouth.

"We aren't done." River tells me, as if having read my intention to flee. "Come up to my desk, please, Leralynn."

I take one step before noticing the thin rattan rod River pulls from behind the heavy oak table. Not the leather belt as Zake favored, but similar enough in the ways that matter. At once, my whole body stiffens, my lungs too tight to draw breath. Curling my hands into fists, I let my nails pinch into my skin, focusing on the small sting to keep myself together.

"River," Coal says. His voice is hard and distant.

"I'm aware," River replies. Returning to my side of the desk, he removes the golden cuff link holding his silk shirt's cuffs together and rolls up the material to just above his right elbow. "I won't strike you, Leralynn," he says, his attention focused on his work.

A momentary wave of relief touches and flees. "Coal isn't—"

"Not Coal either." Sleeve secured, River finally shifts the whole weight of his attention to me. "I never intended for you to have been left overlooked in a dungeon cell, much less restrained to a wall. It was my duty to know what was happening to you, and you had every right in the world to expect as much from me. It was my breach of responsibility that led to a great many wrongs done today. Mine, and no one else's."

My eyes widen as River hands me the rattan rod, bracing his hip against his desk as he holds his bared forearm between us, the point of the elbow tucked against his ribs for stabilization. Perfectly corded muscle that a sculptor would envy tightens beneath taut skin, the sensitive flesh between the wrist and bend of the elbow dancing with shadows.

"Wait. What?" The hair on the back of my neck rises like hackles, a shiver shooting along my spine. "I don't understand."

"Yes, you do," River says, his heavy gaze lending his soul to the words. "There is nothing—nothing—more important for me than keeping you…" He falters. "Than keeping all my students safe. A duty at which I've failed spectacularly over the past two days. You've already paid for your transgression. I have not. One dozen, please, if you don't mind."

"Oh, bloody damned stars, you want to bet how much I damn well mind?" I sputter, jerking away from the rattan rod. I only realize that I've jumped across the floor when my shoulder catches River's bookshelf, stacks of journals, references, and ink bottles falling in a spectacular *whoosh*.

River blinks almost appreciatively at the mess but stays put otherwise.

Crossing my arms, I glare at Coal—who merely shrugs—and turn back to River. "Your strategy of adding more pain to that already collectively endured is… What's the word I'm looking for…? Ah, *stupid*."

With a short sigh, River braces his palms on his thighs before speaking again, his voice measured. "It isn't *my* strategy, Leralynn. It is the reality of where we are. Do you imagine I enjoy disciplining you? Watching you be terrified or exhausted or hurting? Wondering what the hell I'm going to have to do to you next when you defy the rules and teachers?" River's tone softens. "I need you to know that I understand the scope of my failure before you. That I am sorry. I need you to trust my word—" His voice catches, and he cuts himself off, trying to corral some emotion in his gaze. It seems he needs my trust on a level he can't fully understand himself, much less explain.

"Apology accepted," I say quickly. "I understand everything. I trust you. Can I go, please?"

River sighs, a muscle tensing in his jaw. "If you want other projects to continue between us, then you will do this now."

Other projects. The tutoring. The time with River I've grown to savor. Acid rises up my throat as River hands me the rattan again. I run my fingers along his bare sensitive belly of forearm, the skin lacking the thickness of the muscled side or calluses of his palms. River shivers lightly before he can suppress it, his eyes flickering.

"Leralynn," he prompts.

Bracing his arm against my left hand, I close my eyes and flick the switch, its tip landing just beneath the crease of River's elbow.

"It doesn't count unless it leaves a welt or draws blood," says River. "From a self-preservation perspective, I would prefer we achieved that point sooner rather than later."

The next minute is the longest of my life, the soft sound of River hissing at the sting driving into me as much as the raised welts that appear all too vividly along his skin. The male makes no effort to pretend he feels nothing, eyes closing, sweat breaking out on his temples as small flinches run through his body with each impact. And after a few strokes, I stop pretending either.

My stinging eyes spill tears onto my cheeks, washing out the hidden poison that was eating my soul. River didn't abandon me in that cell. Didn't relegate my existence to a secondary tier, to be addressed at his convenience. His maddening, frustrating ways are rooted in protectiveness, not apathy. Because that is who River is. A protector. And I don't know where that leaves the two of us.

The twelfth stroke has nowhere to land but on already hurt skin, and the sight of blood welling up at the welted intersection shoves me off the edge I've been riding. Sobs rake my chest, my breath hitching inside lungs that can't draw enough air. This is all wrong. Every horrid moment of it.

Not caring for the propriety of it, I bury my face in River's shoulder and, after a moment of stiffness, feel him smooth his hand over my hair. His woodsy scent fills my nose, mixing with a hint of lavender soap. "It's all right," he murmurs as if it were true. "We're done."

Behind me, I hear the sound of the door being pulled open.

River stiffens again. "Coal—"

"No. You broke it, you fix it." The door clicks shut, Coal's soft footsteps dissolving into the distance.

After a minute, River's hand settles on my shoulder, nudging me away gently.

I shake my head, my grip tightening even as I brace myself to be pushed away, for the bubble of intimacy to pop with a resounding snap of formality. It will happen, I know. It must, for without the magic's bond, that is what truly lies between us. River is a king, and I am a rogue.

River's hands on my shoulder tighten, the firm push a heartbeat away. I swallow only to realize that River has pulled me toward him instead when he sits on the edge of his desk, settling me on his lap and wrapping his arms tightly around me in one smooth motion that feels like a locked door giving way. His heart pounds under my ear, and with a soft sound in his chest that I feel rather than hear, he rests his cheek on top of my head. "Leralynn," he whispers, his breath ruffling my hair.

16

RIVER

River pressed Leralynn's small warm body against his chest, breathing in her lilac scent with a desperation that made his chest ache. The green silk of her top had ridden up her torso, and his hand itched to cup the soft curve of her waist, to rise higher to her luscious breast. It was madness, doing this to himself. In the part of his mind that still functioned, he knew that holding her was wrong. That he never should have let Coal leave, not when the pull Lera had on his soul overwhelmed all sense. Yet that voice of reason was as distant as the long-dimmed horizon, and all River's protective instincts demanded that he wrap himself around the girl, comfort her even as he took comfort from her in return.

How many in Lera's place would have savored the chance at vengeance? Would have been elated at the opportunity to even the score that the disparity in power always tallied between a commander and his charge? Especially after what River had done to her, leaving Lera abandoned and shackled when it was his duty more than anyone's to ensure her protection.

Was it her fast forgiveness that set the final noose around his heart, or her courage? When things turned hard, Lera stood up for others before herself, and that called to River as much as it terrified the living daylights out of him.

As he stroked Lera's silky hair and back, River had to concede that she was so like his beloved Diana that the images melded together. Or perhaps he was moving on. Falling in love, stars take him. With a student.

"I'm sorry," River whispered.

"You are a bastard." Lera raised her face to him, her brown eyes and pale cheeks glistening with tears. "For making me hurt you. I hated it."

"Me as well." River brushed his knuckles along her wet cheekbones, savoring the way she leaned into his touch. "But holding you makes it hurt less."

What the hell was he saying? River closed his eyes, trying to breathe in some common sense. Instead, he inhaled a lungful of tantalizing lilac. A heartbeat later, River felt the soft brush of lips against his and snapped his eyes open with the speed of a diving hawk.

The girl had moved so she was kneeling on his lap, her beautiful eyes only inches from his own.

"Leralynn." River cupped the back of her head, fully intending to pull her away. Gently but firmly. Then she bit her lip, and all his noble intentions sizzled away in a blaze of smoke. His cock tightened, his mouth demanding that it be him nipping Leralynn's lush mouth. Taking it so completely that she'd have breath for nothing but the moment. With him. Together.

This time when she leaned toward him, River covered her mouth with his, scraping his teeth along her bottom lip until he could plunge inside.

Leralynn gasped, driving him deeper. His tongue danced with hers until sparks showed against his closed eyelids. Without seeking her permission, River's hand slid to that maddening spot on Lera's waist, massaged it, slid firmly over each bump of her rib cage until it met the bottom swell of her breast.

Wrong.

But he couldn't stop. With Lera's gentle undulations against his lap driving the flames higher, River felt himself falling—a fall that started a month ago and took a dizzying turn the night of Ostera, heady jasmine blending with lilac as they spun under the full moon. Spiraling down to a place he might never be able to come back from.

And might never want to.

17

LERA

"I don't like it," Arisha says, swirling a spoon in a mug of the hot chocolate the Academy served with the midday meal.

"The part where Coal didn't die?"

"That too," Arisha says thoughtfully, stopping to watch the corner of the dining hall where a large wolf, a small boy, and a heaping platter of meat disappear behind one of the heavy window drapes. Shade. *Shade is back.* A moment later, Shade's wagging tail makes the curtain move obscenely. Arisha winces, then returns to the matter at hand before I can fully process my shifter's return. "But mostly all the other parts. Leaving Han aside for a moment, the little earthquake you caused without meaning to shook the whole school. And this strengthening connection with Coal? What happens if next time, he drags you into his nightmares instead of you pulling him out? Not only are the wards cracking, but the way the magic is spilling out is as controlled as an avalanche. Something is going to give, and sooner than we'd like."

I take a sip from my own mug, the rich chocolaty liquid coating my mouth in bliss. "The next time the universe asks me for how magic should leak, I'll be sure to lodge your complaint. Meanwhile, I want to bring Coal into the team."

The chocolate in Arisha's mouth flies out, raining onto the white tablecloth. "No no no no. That's... He... We don't like each other. The other day, he questioned how I manage to put on boots without falling on my face."

"You do fall when dressing half the time."

"That's not the point." She glowers at me. "We won't be able to speak freely if Coal is there."

"We can." I tap my finger against the tabletop. "I know we can't challenge Coal's amulet by telling him who *he* is, but with his arm broken, Coal will be staying put for a while anyway. And we should stay away from discussing my identity too, since Coal's veil will keep insisting that the fae and human versions of me are utterly different beings. But talking about the breaking wards, about Han, the sclices and Yocklols and the Night Guard? None of that is a problem." My words catch in my throat, another thought sweeping through me.

"What happens if we never beat the veils?" I ask Arisha softly. "If the wards shatter and the males' magic returns and they still think they're human? Or if the quint magic connecting us sweeps through and wages war against the amulets' veils? If just words make the males scream in pain, what happens when magic wages war on magic?"

Arisha winces. "I don't know. But we'll figure it out, Lera. Somehow. We have to."

"I want Coal with us." I sound petulant, but it's the truth. "I need him with me."

Sighing, Arisha raises her palm. "Fine, fine. You can keep him. But I'm wagering it's your backside he's going to bite first. And if he pees in the corners, you are cleaning it up... In fact, you should probably go practice the latter now."

Following Arisha's gaze to the corner of the room, I see a puddle spilling from beneath the drapes, while Shade and Rabbit make a run for the door.

~

"WHERE ARE WE GOING?" Coal asks, snorting as I press us into the shadows on the edge of the courtyard to avoid a pair of Academy guards.

"The library."

"In the middle of the night?"

"Do you want to know what I'm up to or not?" I ask. We've spent the last day recovering, but it's time to rally again, especially in light of

Han's presence. My fingers tap against my thigh, too many thoughts racing through my mind, tripping over each other. I despise lying to River, especially after last night, when he sent me on my way with a final chaste kiss and a desperation in his eyes that haunted my dreams —and left me wet until morning. But his colossal protectiveness leaves me no choice. As for Coal, the male's presence will be a new edge to walk. Fortunately, after Arisha agreed to it this afternoon, Gavriel gave his blessings as well. Now, we just need to explain the whole mess. "How is your arm?"

"Shade is an overprotective grandmother who I will smother with a pillow just as soon as I can move my elbow," Coal mutters, following me as I guide us through the now-familiar library door.

The small bell chimes its musical warning as we step into the grand central rotunda, where Arisha's and Gavriel's brown heads are already bent over a spread of drawings and theories while Shade's wolf inspects all the corners of furniture. My heart lifts at seeing him again, at having two of my males close once more.

A large board holds drawings of the main creatures we've run into thus far: mutated semi-visible sclices, Yocklol trees, the Night Guard. Arisha is pinning Han's picture to the board as we come in, the sheet dropping from nervous fingers at the sight of Coal.

Walking forward with a quick brow-rising glance at the enormous wolf scratching his shoulder on a table leg, Coal picks the drawing up off the floor and hands it to my friend. "You didn't know I was coming here?" He frowns. "Actually, I'm not really sure where I am."

"You're in the library," Arisha says helpfully.

Coal lifts a brow. "That explains the books."

"You are at a meeting of the Protector's Guild." Finally recovering herself, Arisha takes the sheet from him. "And yes, I knew you were coming. But knowing and seeing are two different things." Pushing up her glasses, she looks over at me with a small frown. "How are we going to do this?"

I lean down to rub Shade's gray fur, the wolf licking my face in greeting. "With introductions." Standing, I square my shoulders and turn to a dazed-looking Coal, who still can't seem to look away from Shade, perhaps recognizing him as the wolf who attacked him a month ago in Sage's office. "Welcome to the Protector's Guild, where we try to keep the mortal world safe from the dark forces eager to take advantage of the crumpling wards keeping magic at bay. You will work out the details as we go along, I'm sure. Meanwhile, I've been out of action for a few days. Where does that leave us, Gavriel?"

The librarian smiles at me, his brown eyes betraying only a hint of worry. "Basic patrol pattern tonight. Get your bearings back as you check on the remaining Yocklols and see if you can mark any signs of the Night Guard making themselves comfortable. I've your fighting leathers here."

Coal's eyes widen almost comically as I start pulling out weapons and my leather jerkin, the familiar feel of my tools already waking my senses. I'm ready to go back into the woods, to reach into the cords of magic that are waking, slowly but surely. Shade's healing mended my flesh the day the Night Guard attacked, and the connection with Coal's strange power has made itself clear as well. With Tye's fire magic escaping its shackles for a moment during the fight with Han, the pattern is too plain to ignore.

The wards are crumbling. But as my adversaries get stronger, so do I.

"Please tell me you are jesting, Osprey," says Coal, his voice echoing over the whisper of papers shuffling and tightening of leather stays. He twists to Gavriel when I fail to answer. "In that case, tell me you have more gear in there."

I feel a corner of my mouth lift as I sheath my sword down the length of my spine. "The Great Falls area is the zero point for the wards' weakness. Once your arm heals, there will be plenty to do. For tonight, it will be Ruffle and me." Shade yips softly and presses against my side, eyeing Coal warily.

Coal runs his good hand over his face, his head shaking. "Don't ever let River learn of this, Osprey," he mutters before turning to Gavriel. "Should I be taking notes?"

PART III: HIDE AND SEEK

PROLOGUE

I yank against the shackles, a searing pain shooting along my arm, lighting every nerve from fingertip to shoulder. I scream, shoving back against the assault. I can't see my prison guards, but I can smell them—rotten breath and the stench of old sweat.

A whip cracks, and my shoulder explodes in agony. Beyond it, the smell of a heating iron is already drifting from the brazier, mixing with the scent of singed cotton and—

"Lera!" Arisha's voice pierces the nightmare haze a moment before a bucket of cold water drenches my head and shoulders.

I curse, sitting up in bed, the equally wet wolf beside me growling his displeasure. I wipe the water from my face and massage my left arm, the phantom pain still lingering in the bone. "Next time, go douse Coal. It's his bloody broken arm that's setting off the latest nighttime pleasantries."

Arisha fumbles for her glasses, her blue eyes round and owllike in the moonlit room. "Does Coal have fire magic?"

"No." I start stripping the bed of wet linen, muttering beneath my breath. Arisha did *not* need to go this far just to wake me up. She knows I'm barely sleeping now, with Coal's nightmares—amplified by his frustration with the limitations of having a broken bone—reaching a fever pitch.

The girl's hand closes over my upper arm, forcing my sleepy

attention to her. "Then you really can't blame him for setting your pillow on fire now, can you?"

Following the direction of her finger, I find a fingernail-sized charcoal mark on the corner of my pillowcase and feel my heart stutter.

The wards are crumbling faster than I imagined. And sometime soon, they will break altogether.

1

LERA

"I'm unclear on what you think I can do about this, Coal. Both bones are broken, one of them in two places." Dressed in dark gray pants and a thin gray cashmere sweater that hugs his muscled chest, Shade runs probing fingers along Coal's forearm, then flicks an uncomfortable golden glance in my direction.

Our gazes meet for but a moment, but it's enough to send a wave of heat through me. With the week of Ostera's liberty coming to an end, Shade has returned to the Academy to resume his responsibilities —and the predatory gleam in his eyes has returned with him. The male is still hunting for his mate, and I think his wolf knows it's me.

Shade himself, however, does not.

"Leralynn..." Shade sighs, which makes his beautifully angled face even more devastating. "I am also not quite clear as to your presence in my treatment room. Lieutenant Coal hardly requires a chaperone."

Sitting atop one of the countertops in Shade's infirmary, I give the shifter a smile. Truth is, despite savoring the chance to see him after our forest coupling, I am actually here because Coal is driving himself—and everyone else—insane. And I don't just mean the memories leaking through our bond. "Wait for Lieutenant Coal to answer your question, and then tell me whether you still think so."

Coal growls softly, pulling his arm back from Shade. His blond hair is in its usual tight bun, but in every other way, he looks a dire mess.

There are deep shadows under his eyes from the same nightmares that are waking me up each night, his skin is blanched with pain, his fingers twitch with unspent energy. "I've been in a sling for almost a *week*, Shade, and the muscle is already melting like butter near a stove. Come up with a better plan than turning me into an invalid. Strength training. Potions. Something. Otherwise, this sling is going into the next fire I see."

I raise a brow at Shade. *See what I mean?*

Shade pinches the bridge of his nose. "You are upset because you've been in a sling for one bloody week? Coal. Listen to me. You have a *shattered arm.* That means there are sharp little shards of bone that aren't connected, which—if you take off the splint—will grind against each other every bloody time you move. You can't force it to mend faster by ignoring it, straining it, or drinking brews. It needs rest. Immobilized rest. Unless you think I've some magic I'm unaware of, your only option is a splint and sling."

My hands curl around the edge of the counter, the sharp scents of camphor and cajuput, clove and mint, filling my lungs. Without meaning to, Shade just outlined the crux of the problem exactly: in Lunos, without the mortal world's shackles, Shade's magic mends bones well enough that Coal little hesitates bruising my ribs in training. Which means that for the past three hundred years, all the quints warriors have learned to fight like there were no limits on their bodies, relying on Shade's healing magic to make fractured bones whole. A dangerous instinct in the mortal world.

Coal's veil-fogged mind doesn't remember this, but his body does. And it's straining his soul as badly as the injury itself, letting the darkness wrap itself tighter and tighter around him. Coal is a warrior at his core, one who can't live with himself if he can't fight—and now his own body is another set of shackles. A problem that his shared nightmares make clear enough.

"Listen to him, Coal," I say quietly. "Please."

He turns piercing blue eyes on me, making me instantly regret saying anything. "Go to hell."

"I visit it every night," I snap back. "A bloody repetitive place, if you ask me."

Coal's eyes darken for a moment, a swirl of some unreadable emotion in them making me wish I'd kept my mouth shut—again. Then he faces Shade, turning his back to me with the subtlety of a three-year-old. "Find a better option." Sliding off the exam table, he storms out of the treatment room with a rush of black leather and male musk, slamming the door hard enough to make the medicine vials tremble.

Shade and I both reach to steady the fragile glass before it shatters, the male's scent enveloping me as his arm stretches across my lap. Damp earth, the air fresh from rain mixed with a bit of wolf, all drowning out the pungent smell of herbs and salves that give the infirmary's air a confusingly sharp tang.

Shade freezes, his yellow eyes dilating slightly as his nostrils flare. Taking in my scent like I take in his. That quickly, I'm back in the moonlit woods on Ostera, Shade's body moving over mine, my desire and magic flaring up like a blaze as he enters me. My thighs clench at the memory of his cock raking across the ridges in my channel, the pain of my closing wounds turning into molten heat that enveloped my apex. Of my name, loud and clear on Shade's lips, ringing across the dark forest as he found his release. As he remembered me.

That feeling of being recognized by one of my males, even for just an instant, still makes my chest clench with longing. I'd give anything to have that feeling again—anything short of messing with their veils. Arisha is right to be worried about Coal's and my bond. There's no telling what the shared nightmares could do to his mind if the amulet deems them too dangerous. No telling what they could do to us both if things continue as they are either.

"I..." Shade steps away from me so quickly that the very bottle he was trying to save topples onto its side. With his black hair hanging loose at his shoulders, his strong jaw and tanned skin give him the exotic feel of a predator in civilized clothing—the very thing, I'm pretty sure, that makes the Academy's entire female population go weak on sight. He clears his throat. "I beg your pardon. And I'm sorry I was not able to give Coal better news. Was there anything else you needed?"

Warmth fills my cheeks. I try not to flinch at Shade's cool, professional words, the echo of his touch on that mossy stream bank still tingling across my skin. Frowning at the closed door, I force my mind to anchor itself back in the here and now.

The here and now being one unreasonably angry fae warrior. "I realize you can do little for a fracture, but can't you give Coal something for pain? He said nothing about that, but..."

"But broken bones hurt. A lot." Shade's voice regains its casual cadence, his golden eyes kind and professional once again. "And yes, I could—but I'm not going to." He holds out his palm, warding off my objections before I can voice them. "Right now, pain is the only thing keeping Coal from doing himself greater harm. It's the body's protective mechanism hollering to cut the stupidity. If he won't mind me, perhaps he'll mind it."

Fair point, even if I don't like it. Sighing, I go to hop off the counter—only to halt midmotion, my eyes caught on an extinguished overturned candle. Beneath the dripped wax, a small singed spot in the cloth scratches at my thoughts.

Since inadvertently lashing out with Tye's fire magic in the midst of last night's nightmare, I've tried—unsuccessfully—to reengage the power trapped by the mortal world's shackles. Whether my failure signals the wards' resilience or simply my own lack of magical experience and power, is an unfortunate unknown.

Yet while purposeful manipulation of magic remains out of my reach, the number of accidental discharges is growing by the day—each instance tied to an intense connection between the males and me. Which, unfortunately, supports the inexperienced-Lera theory—the wards little care whether I *mean* to use magic, so if mine leaks sometimes, then so does the Night Guards', except they no doubt have better control than I. They certainly can't have worse. Which all means I should do better than I am. That the wards allow any magic through is a very bad thing, but if the magic is leaking regardless, I should be making better use of the scraps.

I rub my thigh, the once-harsh wound there from my battle with the Night Guard now nothing more than a thin pink stripe. Why? Because Shade's magic awoke during our coupling, his healing power flowing through the connection to heal my injuries. My heart quickens, the possibilities opening before me.

Shade can't heal Coal. But could I?

Although I lack Shade's skill, I do have healing magic. A cord of power that mirrors Shade's, just as the other strands of my magic mirror River's and Tye's and Coal's. As a human weaver, I could only echo the males' abilities, but as fae, the magic belongs to me outright. And it grows stronger when connected with the males.

I bite my lip, my thoughts racing. My *second* coupling with Tye made my fire magic strong enough to escape its mortal binds during the fight with Han, and then again last night. Could coupling with

Shade again strengthen the healing magic inside me enough to make it usable? To let me heal Coal's fracture?

"Leralynn?" Shade frowns at me. "Is everything all right?"

Sliding down to the floor, I cover the few paces between us with slow, deliberate steps, suddenly grateful that I've already changed into a low-cut gown for dinner. A shimmering moss green that glows in the early evening light slanting through Shade's window. Even at a distance, Shade's desire for me is evident in bulging clarity, my own thighs moistening at the sight. His fresh, earthy scent surrounds me as I get closer, and I have to stop myself from inhaling deeply like a starved animal approaching supper. Stopping beside Shade, I lay my palm on his chest, my fingers splayed over the soft wool of his sweater. The rock-hard muscle beneath.

Shade's nostrils flare delicately, the wolf inside him no doubt scenting my arousal. The male's breaths come too fast, his fingers opening and closing at his side as if unable to contain the tension.

I lick my lips, unable to keep from imagining something very long and velvety and delicious between them. "Shade—"

Shade's throat bobs, his attention narrowing on my mouth as a small shiver runs along his broad chest and shoulders. When his hand closes on my wrist, the large strong fingers wrapping around me easily, I can already taste him along my tongue.

He pushes my hand away. Kindly, but firmly enough to make his point. "If I recall the schedule correctly, liberty ended this afternoon." His voice is low. Raspy. "The Academy intends to welcome us back with a formal feast. I should go get ready."

Heat fills my cheeks as the rejection registers. "Shade—"

"You are a beautiful cadet, Leralynn," Shade says softly. "But you are a cadet." Without waiting for my reply, he bows to me and walks out of the infirmary, the door swinging in his wake.

2

LERA

"Tye." I keep my voice low as we all flow into the Great Hall, knowing the immortal male a few paces away is perfectly capable of hearing me over the swell of violin music and murmuring voices. The hall is a dazzling vision, tables draped in the finest linens, candlelight glinting off crystal chandeliers above and sterling-silver serving platters below. Formal gowns in every color of the rainbow and sharply tailored suits swirl together as cadets find their seats.

Tye frowns at something across the room and keeps walking, his broad back perfectly straight and red hair unaccountably tidy, nothing about him suggesting that he marked my voice. The act is so effective that I'd believe it—if he'd not been avoiding me all week. Hadn't so much as made eye contact with me since the night Han walked him out of the dungeon cell, leaving me behind. I know we'd gone further than we'd intended that night, but Tye's the one who started us in that direction to begin with. And now he's acting like…like I stole his favorite toy and stomped on it.

Giving me an *I don't know what to say* headshake, Arisha leads us to one of the empty tables in the front of the room. The gilded porcelain plates and matching soup bowls are already on the tables, the savory spice of roasted lamb drifting in from the kitchens. The meat at the Academy is cooked a bit more than my fae taste would usually prefer, but the chefs do wicked things with the apples and cranberries they add to the roast.

Scowling at Tye's back, I survey the rest of the room, including a long instructors' table at the front of the hall. My face heats again when I mark Shade, achingly handsome in a fine white tunic and black pants, his rejection suddenly coming back to me with all too much clarity. Coal's refusal to deviate from his signature solid black—along with his deeply etched scowl—sets him apart from the rest. River and Sage sit together in the middle of the table, the Academy's other instructors extending to the right and left of the pair. Han, damn the man, is there at Sage's left elbow, the headmaster leaning so close to Han that he almost sits in his lap.

I study him closely, as I've done automatically every time I've seen him since our encounter in the woods. Groomed black hair, piercing blue-gray eyes, sharply handsome face—and completely normal ears and canines. My eyes aren't compelled away from them like they are with my males. Not a veiled fae. *Human.*

But no matter how many times I come to this conclusion, my instincts still scream that something is off. He fought like a fae male, from his preternatural speed to his impossible strength.

I grind my teeth. "Maybe he has some other kind of veil," I murmur beneath my breath to Arisha.

"Maybe." She sounds unconvinced, her freckled cheeks tightening as she studies him from under her curtain of unruly curls.

"You have a better theory?"

"I think it's wise to be careful about how many conclusions we draw solely from the fact that he broke Coal's arm, especially when it was *Coal* who went after *him.*" Arisha sneezes into a handkerchief, throwing a withering glance at the elaborate bouquet of lupines and peonies on our table. Sadly for her, spring is still in full, spectacular bloom. "The incident probably speaks more to Coal's state than Han's. Do you think the Prowess team is under orders not to speak with anyone, or did they conjure that on their own?"

Following Arisha's gaze, I note the one table covered with satin linens in the Academy's red and gold hues, in contrast to the white and gold of the other settings. There, standing behind their chairs as they wait for Sage's introduction, Han's Prowess athletes are in their rich red parade uniforms instead of court dress. Tye's lithe and proud silhouette draws the eyes of every female in the room, just as Princess Katita's golden hair and perfect curves draw the males'. Beside each other, they look like a stunning royal tapestry.

Delightful.

"They must be under—" I shut my mouth. Tye hasn't met a rule he didn't break on principle, so the choice to ignore me might well be his. Which stings even more.

Before I can say anything more, Headmaster Sage stands up and taps a fork against his crystal goblet, the melodic chime bringing the violins and voices to a sudden halt.

With his small frame and hunched shoulders, the standing Sage is little taller than the sitting River—who I catch moving his chair back slightly to try to keep from upstaging the headmaster. Sometimes I wish River's courtesy was just a little more selective.

As if feeling my gaze on him, River glances over, the gray eyes I've not seen since that day in his study piercing right into my soul. One bloody glance and my insides melt. I'm just starting to wonder what exactly this will do to our study sessions, which will resume with the normal schedule, when Sage interrupts my thoughts.

"My lords and ladies of the Great Falls Academy. It is my pleasure to welcome you back from the Ostera holidays to the final stretch of this academic year," Sage announces, the hall's acoustics amplifying his croaking voice.

I try to distract myself from sudden thoughts of the coming intimate tutoring sessions by taking a slow sip of wine.

"Before I release you to your dinner," continues Sage, "allow me to be the first to share the Academy's proud news. With the assistance of Master Han—the new Prowess coach whom some of you may have already met—and our distinguished athletes, the Academy has petitioned the Prowess commission to hold this year's Trials competition right here at Great Falls itself."

My hand freezes halfway back down to the table, tightening dangerously around the crystal goblet.

Sage pauses, the previously silent room suddenly abuzz with excited scents and darting whispers. Cadets shift about, grabbing each other's shoulders and near knocking down plates in their enthusiasm, their lives suddenly a hundred times more exciting than they were only a second ago. All but the actual Prowess athletes, who stand at attention at their places.

Against the room's sudden spike of energy, the deafening silence in my head is that much starker, a cold panic seeping into my veins. Despite both Arisha's and Gavriel's untiring efforts, we've made zero progress in halting the wards' deterioration, much less in coming up with a way to rebuild what was already broken. My killing off Mors's vile creatures seeping into Great Falls' woods was never meant as a solution, only some stitching to buy time until we conjure a fix or else Lunos sends aid.

And now the Prowess Trials, the single event gathering the continent's rulers in one place, is coming to Great Falls. The very heart of the cracking wards' spreading web and the Night Guards' hunting ground. *Bloody ever-loving stars.*

The initial weakness in the wards may be natural deterioration, but I've no doubt the Night Guard has been picking at the cut. Widening it for their plans, which all center *here.* And now Sage wants to host a convention of mice in the middle of a snake pit.

My heart quickens, the smell of food suddenly turning nauseating. If the Trials come here, people are going to die. I can barely keep the occasional aberrations at bay, let alone hold off a full and inevitable Night Guard assault. And even if I stood a chance, I can't be everywhere at once. *Stars,* the very Academy might be compromised already. My eyes flicker to Han, whose pale eyes look calmly satisfied.

The very worst part is that this whole mess is our fault. I have to bite back a scream of frustration. The Academy was never even supposed to have a Trials athlete. Not until the veil spun the story for Tye—

Whap!

A small rap of pain bites my shin, cutting off my spiraling thoughts midstream. Turning, I find Arisha forcing a smile though her clenched teeth. "You are happy about this," she mutters. "You aren't thinking what I know you are. We are all *normal and happy.*"

Right. Taking a deep breath, I force a smile onto my face just as Sage raises his arms to call for silence once more.

"I appreciate your enthusiasm and support as we show the continent the true glory of our prestigious Academy." The self-satisfaction in Sage's voice thick enough to spread on bread, his bald head gleaming brighter than ever under the vast chandeliers. "While the Prowess Committee has not yet confirmed our request, I have full confidence that we will be victorious—both in the hosting of the trial and the subsequent unquestionable victory." Despite calling for silence a moment earlier, Sage pauses again for the cheers and applause, speaking only when the last of the voices has died down. "To this end, we are changing the end-of-year exams."

This time, the general fidgeting has a more cautious tone.

"Our royal visitors, understandably, will expect to see more than just the athletes. They will wish to inspect the quality of instruction Great Falls offers." A new streak of ice enters Sage's voice. "The final exams will thus be held orally, during the Prowess Trials' opening, allowing our esteemed guests to observe the students in action. I expect each of you to bring honor to the Academy and yourselves with your performance. Anyone unable or unwilling to pledge that should withdraw from our rolls now."

River's gaze flickers to me for a moment before returning to Sage, and my already churning stomach sinks like lead. Instead of keeping a low profile with the humans, I will now be humiliating myself in front of the mortals' greatest leaders—and taking the Academy's reputation down along with it.

Sage raises his glass, his eyes alight with satisfaction. "The next two months will be grueling for both our athletes and nonathletes alike. Yet, I am certain we are all of one mind— Great Falls is the premier Academy on the continent, and we welcome the chance to remind the world as to why. With that, let me wish you a good meal and a good night's sleep before classes resume in the morning."

The Great Hall explodes in applause, the walls magnifying each clap as obediently as they did Sage's voice. Beneath the noise, I sink into my chair, my mouth bone-dry.

"I imagine there will be a few people packing up shortly. It is the responsible thing to do." The high voice from across the table hits me so squarely between the eyes that I can't very well pretend I don't hear it. Vivian—one of Katita's beautiful hangers-on until the princess joined Han's team and became sequestered with the rest of them—cuts her gaze to her companions before returning her attention to me. "Is that how you interpreted Master Sage's words as well, Lady Leralynn?"

I give Vivian an icy smile. "Don't be so hard on yourself. I'm sure the headmaster didn't mean you."

The girl's cheeks color, but I turn to my food without waiting for a response. I've greater problems to worry about than Viv—such as how in the hell to stop the Prowess Trials from happening.

3

LERA

"We are not going to stop the Prowess Trials from happening," Arisha says from behind a stack of books as she strides out from the bowels of the library, her muffled voice echoing softly against the high-domed ceiling.

Peeling away from the wall, Coal uses his good arm to grab the volumes from her. Gavriel doesn't look up from his study of a text on ancient fae magics. Without having to discuss it, the four of us found our way here at quarter past curfew, the meeting time having become habitual over the past week. Even Coal's presence is no longer a surprise, though we've not quite worked out how much of the truth we can discuss around him without setting off the veil he wears.

"I was fine with them, sir." Arisha frowns at her departing treasure. So long as she doesn't look at Coal, my friend is not shy about challenging him at these meetings—and I've a notion that keeping from spooking Arisha is one of the reasons the male never invites himself to the table. "Nothing was falling."

"Yet." Coal sets the books down, the pain tightening his jaw so subtle that I'm certain no one but me noticed. "Nothing was falling, *yet.*"

"I—"Arisha's foot catches the carpet, and she hops about to regain her balance. Coal watches her with a raised brow. Ignoring him, she sits down and pulls the manuscripts toward her. For the past week, our guild meetings have focused on narrowing down the zero point of the wards' weakness—which, based on the travel pattern of Mors's rodents and my Ostera mishap, Arisha and Gavriel now believe lies in the Gloom beneath the Great Falls mountain range. Today, however, the whole conversation is shifting to the new looming disaster.

"I've gone through the headmaster's journals for the past decade, and Sage has been maneuvering for the Academy to host the Prowess Trials all that time. Which also explains why the amu—" Arisha clears her throat and gives me a meaningful look. "Why Sage recruited Tyelor. We are seeing a manifestation of what the headmaster has been trying to achieve for a long time, not a brand-new reality that just came to mind from nowhere. Which makes sense."

The veil dresses up reality; it doesn't actually change it. *Yes, I got it, Arisha.*

"All right, so Sage has always been hell-bent on the Trials happening here." I tap the table. "That doesn't change the fact that inviting every mortal royal to an area infested with magical human-mauling beasts could be tantamount to inviting them to death. At the very least, any extra outside scrutiny to the Great Falls area could expose the extent of the magical threat building right outside these walls. Why would Sage risk that?"

"Because the headmaster doesn't believe there *is* a real magical threat, remember?" Arisha says. "Or if he does, he won't admit it. The Academy's reputation is too important to him. The moment he whispers about a problem, his precious royal students will be flooding back to their palaces faster than he can say, 'Don't slam the door on your way out.'"

I feel my jaw crack under the strain of my clenching. If I'm not careful, I'm going to lose a tooth. *More time.* I need more time to both figure out what's going on here and bring back my males' memories so we can defeat it together. All the world's royals in one place will be a great temptation indeed, and we're not ready to defend the Academy from whoever—or whatever—takes the bait. I spin to Coal. "What does River have to say about all this?"

Having retreated from Arisha, Coal is back to leaning against the wall, his good arm crossed over the injured limb. If his dark mood were visible, the male would have wisps of blackness trailing about him. Or maybe that's my own. I've not had a decent night's sleep since before the dungeon, and it's hard not to feel all those sleepless hours every time I look at the scowling male.

"He doesn't like it, but again, his only grounds for argument is the threat of magic," says Coal. "Which Sage already shut down a month ago, when River wanted to send the royal students home. And, your brew of secrets here aside, to the outside world, things have the appearance of getting better."

"In other words, my putting downs sclices is actually working against us now." I shake my head. "Brilliant."

"What about the Night Guard's presence?" says Arisha, blue eyes trained on me as if she can pretend Coal doesn't exist. "That is new."

"I discussed the dark fae with the deputy headmaster after Leralynn ran into them," Gavriel says, looking up for the first time. In his worn olive-green robes, he practically sinks into the shadows. "Commander River and I have an understanding that my sources of information are not to be asked after, but my exemplary track record in providing facts has earned me a certain—"

"Uncle Gavriel," Arisha says gently. "What did River say?"

"The deputy headmaster is already taking every safety precaution he is able to. There is nothing more to be done without proof."

"Fine." Standing, I head for the large wooden chest where we keep my spare set of leather armor and weapons. "If River and Sage need proof that the Academy is under imminent bloody threat, I'm going to get proof."

Coal's scent spikes dangerously before I'm halfway across the room. "How?" he says. "By wandering the woods by yourself in hopes a Night Guard fae tries to kill you?"

"If I have to."

Coal snorts with no hint of humor. "So long as the proof you are after is your own dead body, it's as solid a plan as I've ever heard."

I twist toward him, my blood starting to simmer. A week ago, Coal didn't know the Protector's Guild even existed—now he wants to stop me from the outings I've been taking for weeks. "You have a better idea?"

"We start by you not getting dead and go from there." Coal's muscles shift sinuously as he rises to his full height and steps away from the wall and toward the wooden chest, as if he could physically bar me from opening it. "Wait a few days, and we will go together. There is little to be lost by holding off that long."

"What bloody world do you live in, Coal? You won't be capable of so much as wiping your arse with that arm in a few days. And you are the one who got yourself into that mess to begin with."

"Lera—" Arisha starts to say.

"No. Coal can keep his votes of no confidence to himself." My gaze snaps back to the male. "I was patrolling by myself for a month before you came along. And I *will* keep doing it."

Coal's eyes darken as I speak, and now his lips pull back, showing the sharp canines my amulet tries to tell me aren't there. "Like hell you will."

"Exactly. Like hell I *will*." My words escape through clenched teeth, the flame of frustration that started with sleepless nights and fed on Sage's death-trapping stupidity shifting into a full-on bonfire. I step toward Coal until we're nose to nose. "You were invited to the guild to help, not to order me about. As for what you are actually capable of just now—that would be an extra dead body at best and a liability at worst."

Coal's furious body heat washes over me. I don't know who's he angrier at: me for pointing out the obvious, or himself for still being injured. In the corner of my narrowing vision, Arisha throws her arms protectively around her precious manuscripts, while Gavriel inconspicuously gathers up his china teapot.

"Get out of my way," I say simply.

"Master Coal—" Gavriel starts, probably feeling the brittleness of every single thousand-year-old book page surrounding us. One breath could blow them to dust, let alone two raging immortals. "Tempers seem to be—"

Coal slams the heel of his palm on the tabletop. "Go out alone tonight, Cadet, and I'll ensure you regret it." His eyes are blue lightning, and I have no doubt he means every word.

Unfortunately, so do I.

~

NOTHING.

I've patrolled every inch of the forest around Great Falls, north to the great thundering waterfall itself and south to the borders of the village, and all I've found is a big fat nothing.

Normally, I'd have stumbled upon a herd of Yocklols at least, maybe a few slobbering sclices, or a rippling shadow that speaks to something lurking in the forbidding gloom. Normally, I'd have had a perfectly reasonable shot at stunning or killing something to drag back and drop at River's feet.

But not tonight. Just silent woods, soft leaves underfoot, and the warm weight of Shade's wolf at my side.

It's almost as if they knew I was coming.

As dark night lightens to a silvery gray, the huge wall of the Academy comes into view. I curse softly, scaring an owl from its roost. I don't resent the night of missed sleep—I needed a break from Coal's dark, bloodstained memories anyway—but I do resent what I just risked for this big fat nothing.

Fortunately, I don't think Coal spotted me going out—which I judge mostly by the fact that no blond bastard tried to tackle me as I left. Much as it grates me to appear to have appeased the overbearing male, I've enough wits to know that a physical confrontation with Coal wouldn't end well for either of us. So I was beyond careful when I snuck out my window and across the grounds, keeping to only the deepest shadows, grateful for the slim crescent moon as I climbed the stone wall. And I'll take the same precautions now. I know how to remain hidden. For all the good it did me tonight.

Shade pants lightly and presses against my leg—a warning. A guardsman paces across the top of the wall in front of us with torch in hand, silhouetted against the lightening sky. The tunnel it is.

And then a long day of acting completely normal around Coal—and plotting my next move to get River the proof he needs. To do *something.*

4

LERA

"What in the name of all the stars is this nonsense?" Stopping a few paces short of the training corral for the morning class, Arisha watches Coal spin-kick a post, each blow shaking the wood. The male's left arm is bound tightly to his shirtless body, the other up in defense. If I didn't know better, I'd think the warrior had simply taken one arm out of action for training purposes. Certainly, Coal gives no evidence of feeling the agony that must shoot down his bones with every vibration.

His muscles dance under his damp skin, sculpted to perfection. I'd enjoy the view if I didn't see fury in every twitch. If I didn't know the idiot was doing greater damage each time he struck.

"That's Coal being Coal," I murmur, dread starting to sink into me in cold waves. Something has changed between last night and this morning.

"Do you think he is trying to prove his arm isn't actually broken? Or that broken bones don't matter?" Arisha winces, a long whistle-like sound coming from her lips. "Ow, ow, *ow*. Stars. Who does he imagine is daft enough to believe either anyway?"

Watching moisture bead on Coal's temples, I shake my head. With the morning chill, the sweat is from pain alone. "He's proving himself to himself," I say very quietly. The other gray-clad students now crowd the fence, taking in Coal with wide eyes. "Coal doesn't tolerate any kind of shackles well."

"You don't think he knows you…" Arisha makes a running motion with her fingers.

"No. Of course not. I mean, I don't see how he could." Not even Arisha knew I'd left last night until I was back. Is it possible that, somehow, in spite of evading my own *roommate's* notice, I still didn't manage to evade Coal's?

"I heard Lieutenant Coal started a b-b-brawl with the guards," says one of the male cadets, a lean red-haired boy named Kirill who rarely speaks when the royals are around. With Katita, Puckler, and Rik all now training with Han, the cadet seems to have found his courage. "No one could stop it, until River himself came on *horseback*."

"I've always known Coal isn't fully sane," Vivian confides in a whisper loud enough to be heard across the continent. "You can see it in his eyes."

"I didn't realize you'd ever looked up enough from Coal's britches to notice that the man had eyes," another boy calls from behind us, inciting a ripple of laughter that strikes my hearing distantly.

The more I take in Coal's taut tendons, the harsh lines of his face, and the glistening beads of pain-spurred sweat, the louder a cold ringing in my ears becomes. One thing I'm certain of is that whatever is happening, it will get no better with time.

Might as well get this over with.

Without waiting to see how Vivian's conversation continues, I vault over the railing, landing softly on the sand beside Coal. The *thump, swat, thump* of his strikes fill the metallic-scented air between us, the sound appearing to be the only greeting I'm going to get.

Fine. We'll do this on his time. Tugging down on my gray uniform shirt, I take a step to the side of the corral.

"Osprey, pick a sword," Coal orders, never slowing his assault on the post. "Everyone else, circle up."

Arisha raises a questioning brow at me, but I can only shrug in reply.

Gritting my teeth, I walk over to the weapons rack and run my hands over the offerings, looking for the balanced practice blade with a small chip on the handle that I've come to favor. With it in hand, I turn to find the rest of the class—now slightly more active without the royals present—already formed up in a large circle around the perimeter of the corral.

Vivian gives me a suspicious look as I brush past her to get into the middle, the other fifteen sets of eyes staring at me with similar uncertainty.

Coal spins a final time, knocking the training post clear off the ground, the thick rope-wrapped wood dropping with a thunk to the sand. Kicking the log out of the way, Coal grabs an hourglass from the top of the weapons rack. He still hasn't so much as looked at me, and his cold inattention is far worse than shouting would be. "Everyone will have up to three minutes to land a killing blow on Osprey. Anyone failing to do so will run a lap around the Academy. Two laps if you allow her to kill or disarm you before the time is up. Osprey will likewise owe me two laps for each killing blow she receives—though I will wait to collect on that until after the rounds."

My jaw tightens. There are sixteen cadets standing around me. *Sixteen.*

"What the bloody hell did she do?" Vivian murmurs to Kerill, who gives her a bewildered shrug.

"Osprey." Coal strides to stand in front of me, finally meeting my gaze with so much force that I almost take a step back. His devastatingly beautiful face is as coolly unreadable as the first time I saw him on the Academy's training pitch. At least in that instance, his battle of wills hadn't been personal. "I recommend you end your matches quickly, or our time together will get long quickly."

Before I can tell him that *our time together* is already too long, Coal jerks his chin to Vivian. "First in. Grab a weapon and go."

5

LERA

Giving Coal one final glance, which I infuse with all the ice I can, I focus on the obstacle at hand. Though trained in a similar style to Princess Katita, Vivian is a weaker fighter than the princess—one that I could finish swiftly.

Could. But should?

Whatever happens, I don't intend to give Coal even the vaguest notion that any of this is anything but a welcome workout. He might think this a lesson to show me the error of my ways, but it isn't. The bloody real lesson is one I'm about to teach him: I'm strong enough to handle myself, no matter what comes my way. *You can take your broken arm out on me all you want, Coal. It's not changing the fact that I'm a warrior in my own right. And I deserve to be treated that way.*

Unless Coal fully understands this now, our time working together is only going to get worse.

So I will ensure he understands, will own every moment of this challenge, and turn Coal's intended punishment into a favor.

I nod to myself. Coal has just granted me a whole morning of personalized training, and I'm going to be *happy* about it. In this light, my classmates are here for my sword-swinging pleasure, and Vivian—she is warm-up fodder.

As if sensing she's just become prey, Vivian tightens her grip on the blade, her olive skin blanched and pretty almond-shaped eyes narrowed in concentration. Deliciously nervous. My nostrils flare, taking in the scent.

"Go," Coal calls.

I fall into a defensive stance, allowing Vivian to come at me with the high attacks she favors. Left, right, down the middle.

Tap. Tap. Tap. My arm stretches lazily through the parries, the predictable pattern warming my muscles while the grains of the hourglass fall through the chambers. Vivian isn't bad, exactly, but she is slow. Uncreative. Perfect for my current purpose. *Tap. Tap. Tap.*

With a few seconds of the match left, I finally hook the blade in Vivian's hand and pop it free of her grip. The airborne sword makes a wide arc in the air, landing with a soft plop beside Coal's downed training post. Fitting. Behind me, a slow, tentative clapping skitters around the ring of watching cadets. A corner of my mouth twitches toward a smile while Vivian braces her hands on her thighs and pants, sweat running into her eyes.

I almost feel bad for her. It's a long way around the Academy—longer still when your lungs and pride hurt.

"One lap, both of you," Coal calls, quieting the applauding cadets.

"But—" The question is out before I can stop it, the sting of changing rules spurring my pulse the way the match with Vivian failed to.

Coal's blue gaze is unapologetically level. "You plainly want a warm-up, Osprey. I'm offering you one. Go."

Bastard.

Swallowing a curse, I fight the urge to launch at him with every nerve in my body, and offer a small bow instead. "That is very considerate of you, sir." Flashing Coal a smile before he can answer, I jog off to take my lap around the Academy, returning to find the others busy with basic strength training. Trembling arms and sweat-spotted gray uniforms speak of time well spent.

Reclaiming my practice blade to a chorus of poorly hidden sighs of relief from the rest of the group, I settle into a fighting stance, my mind focused. Ready to dance. At Coal's mark, I let loose my blade, the circle of cadets growing quiet as my ruthless cuts take out one, two, five of their number in under a minute's time each. Warm blood courses through my veins, my heart keeping beat with the swinging blades. *Tap. Tap. Tap.* The world beyond the practice pitch falls away, no sound but the thumping blades, my beating heart, and Coal's curt commands penetrating the bubble.

Tap. Tap. Tap.

Through the haze of straining muscles and stinging lungs, the challenge of each new well-rested opponent reaches further. Simple parries that bored me at first morph into precious moments of respite. The short reprieve Coal grants me between rounds turns from a battle of wills to unabashed gasps for breath.

I refuse to look at him. In part, to keep my mind in the here and now, no matter what protests my muscles lodge. In part, to keep from learning whether my growing weakness satisfies the male's intentions or disappoints him. Either way, any flagging on my part will undoubtedly fuel Coal's fire, offering proof that I can't handle myself out in the woods alone. And that isn't acceptable. Not when the Night Guard may have a shot at turning the mortal world into a magic-filled hell.

I may be swinging my blade against cadets, but I know I'm truly battling Coal. And I can't let him win.

I'm on the tenth fight when the first truly painful blow rushes past my weakening defenses, the tip of Kirill's practice blade jabbing into the left side of my groin, where my hip bends. My leg goes numb for a heartbeat, Kirill grinning in triumph as I grunt. Inhaling Kirill's celebration, I gather enough energy to drop my level into a deep squat and lunge in so quickly that the cadet is flat on his back before his premature victory call is finished sounding.

By the eleventh match, I've no more strength for such things. The pleasant spring sun has become an oppressive torch as it climbs to its zenith, the hilltop breeze a maddening joke. Each movement costs me breath I don't have, my muscles now trembling beneath the strain. The *thump thump thump* of wood against my flesh becomes a new, distant normal, the sting failing to ignite the anger that might give me an extra boost.

"Time," Coal calls, ending the match before either of us score a killing blow. I brace my hands on my thighs, my breath coming in desperate pants. Sweat running along my face comes to the point of my chin and drips to the ground. When the cadet I face holds out his hand for me to shake, I stare at the offered palm without comprehension until—

Stars.

Rushing to the side of the training fence, I empty my stomach outside the ring, my shoulders still heaving when Coal's cold voice calls, "Next."

I don't look at Coal as I trudge back to my place. The world sways slightly. In the back of my mind, I'm certain that if I ask for a reprieve, Coal will allow it at once. That I'll do no such thing is the only thing I'm certain of just now. Everything else—including how to hang on to my sword through another round—is a hazy consideration.

For a moment, I entertain the notion of letting myself be disarmed quickly, but that would be surrender—and the tiny part of my mind that can still think knows it's not an option. So be it.

I can barely stand by the time the last cadet of the circle steps out onto the pitch. Arisha. She holds her practice blade with all the delicacy of a club, but given that my own sword shakes so hard that even I can't predict where it's going next, her grip will unlikely matter.

"Lera?" she says softly, making me blink at my name. Her eyes are blue and soft, her freckled face pinched with worry.

"You aren't here for tea, Tallie," Coal snaps, his body a towering bare-chested presence in the corner of my vision. "Ready guard."

The world sways as I bring my blade into position, and I fall to one knee. There's a pregnant pause, a collective held breath as I force myself back to my feet. At this point, I don't know if the other cadets want me to fail or succeed. The sword in my sweaty hands weighs as much as an anvil, my battered body throbbing with bruises and welts.

Raising her own blade into position, Arisha closes her eyes.

"Tallie." Coal's voice rumbles with warning.

Arisha shudders. Then, just as Coal opens his mouth for the next order, my friend tosses her weapon down on the sand. Twisting toward him with a defiant glare and an impressive amount of grace, the girl shakes her head. "No. Sir."

My chest squeezes, my heart hammering my ribs. If Coal raises a hand to Arisha, I will kill him, whether I can move or not.

Cocking his head, Coal takes stock of the corral. Arisha, trembling but standing her ground. Me, my eyes flashing with thunder despite my shaking legs. The cadets, tense and silent lest they bring Coal's ire on themselves.

Striding across the pitch, he wordlessly reaches down to retrieve Arisha's discarded blade. The chiseled muscles of his abdomen ripple as he straightens, weighing the weapon in his good hand. With controlled slowness, he stares down at Arisha, then me, from his much greater height. "I see," he says finally, his low voice prickling along my skin. "In that case, I'll take Tallie's turn for her. The rest of you are dismissed for the day."

Fight Coal? *Now?* The overwhelming notion presses so hard on me that it's an effort to force air into my lungs. But I still too. Even as I watch my dripping sweat leave wet clumps in the sand, as the others hasten to make themselves scarce before Coal changes his mind, I keep breathing. Keep my chin lifted to hold Coal's intense scrutiny.

"Still think it's a wise idea to go battle sclices, yocklols, the Night Guard, and anything else in those woods all by yourself?" Coal asks quietly, his blue eyes riveted on my face. Beneath his fury and frustration, I mark another emotion—fear. Desperate fear of a mate that I'll do something he can't save me from. Coal swallows, his emotions buckled down deep once more. "Do you imagine they will care more than I do whether you are tired or not?"

I flash Coal a smile that doesn't touch my eyes. "I imagine they will at least talk less than you do. Can we get started? I've some running to do yet."

6

LERA

"Unification of the c-c-continental kingdoms is both symbolized and furthered by G-G-Great—" Standing at the front of Master Erik's *Understanding Islanders' Goals and Strategies class,* Kerill speaks over the tops of all our heads as if addressing a phantom listener in the ceiling.

"G-G-Get on with it," Puckler calls from his seat.

Kerill's freckled face darkens.

Or maybe that's my eyes closing. My whole body aches. From bruises and strain to an odd knifelike pain that pierces my shin when I step. Despite having inhaled everything in sight for lunch, I was hungry again by the time I walked out of the dining hall—Coal watching my every step with a gaze caught somewhere between righteous and haunted.

And then, then the bastard caught Arisha and bid her to watch me. As if two hours of harsh work had rendered me a cripple.

That last burns the most. Conscripting my own friend in the campaign to patronize me. It would have been different if Coal had forced me into the stream as he once did, or let the unfiltered power of his blows tear me to shreds. But he did none of that. He just pitted me against one human after another after another. Because if I can't keep up with a few cadets, what chance *do I* have against immortals?

My jaw tightens. We clearly still have a long way to go before Coal trusts me to defend myself—let alone get myself safely from dining hall to dorm without wasting away. But if he imagines he can make me surrender to self-pity just by throwing a few more runs and sparring matches my way in the meantime, he has another thing coming. *I never claimed I was perfect, Coal. Only that I'm the best option we have just now.*

At the front of the room, Kerill shifts from foot to foot before starting his sentence again. This time, the stuttering starts on the first word, and Puckler snorts loudly.

I wait for Master Erik to call the royal down, but he just looks on with impassive eyes. Either the impending arrival of the royals' parents makes disciplining Puckler less attractive, or else Erik wants Kerill to self-select himself out of the Academy. Either way, the master says nothing. Doesn't even look twice at the Prowess Trials team, all sitting together in their red dress uniforms in the middle of the class. A perfect, colorful island.

Teachers already turning a blind eye to open cruelty—which bodes poorly for the next two months.

"And so it starts," I mutter beneath my breath as I glare at the back of Tye's tousled red head, the male's broad back and shoulders standing out in the crowd no matter what he wears. With his long legs extended in front of him, Tye has an aura of indulgent boredom, equally indifferent to his teammates' rudeness as he is to the simpering glances of all the female cadets in the place. *What's happening to you, Tye?*

The only person Tye actively refuses to make eye contact with is me—which, at this point, I'm ready to take as a compliment. Avoidance has to be better than apathy, doesn't it? Our coupling in the dungeon now feels like it happened between two entirely different people. I don't see that Tye anywhere in this one—and that scares me almost as much as Sage's announcement.

I shift in my seat, my face blanching at sudden knife-deep pain ripping through my left shin. Taking a deep breath, I wait for the blaze to settle down, staring at nothing for several heartbeats. When I rotate my ankle, the muscles along my lower leg seem to creak like a rusty door hinge, and I know I'd feel more crackling if I was to run my hand along my flesh. The thought sparks a wave of nausea to creep up my throat, and I swallow quickly.

Are you all right? Arisha's note lands on my desk just as I recover.

Fine. My pen hangs in the air a moment too long, a drop of ink fluttering from the tip. When I jerk to save my dress, another knife blade jabs into my shin. Biting my lip, I add two more quick lines. *I'm just one big aching bruise. Feel free to leave your unholy alliance with Coal any time now.*

The bell rings before Arisha can reply, and I gather my things quickly, aiming to intercept Tye at the exit. As if marking my trajectory, Tye lingers by his seat until I'm too far to change course, then heads for the other door that heads deeper into the keep instead of straight onto the central courtyard.

"Just because I think that watching you for injury is a reasonable idea doesn't mean I'm in alliance with Coal," Arisha says with an angry swish of her brown braids as we head toward the dormitories. "After the horseshit he pulled this morning, I hope his arm blazes with infernal flame and Yocklols wither his balls."

"I'm not injured." *I'm hurting. That's different.* I quicken my step to demonstrate my perfect walking ability, the stabbing pain in my shin making me stumble only once. "Stop looking at me as if you are waiting for a piece to fall off."

"Fine, you aren't injured. But you are in pain," she says, frowning fiercely, her dress a splotch of yellow against the green-walled hedges of the reflection garden. "Tell me how bad it is."

Right. So she can report it all back to Coal and Gavriel under some *Lera's own good* umbrella. My fingers curl over the fabric of my dress. I know Arisha means well, but she doesn't understand Coal—not like I do. Doesn't realize that whining about a bit of discomfort would undo everything I'd won by meeting Coal's morning challenge.

Frankly, the ongoing insistence I lay out my shortcomings for general scrutiny is wearing my nerves down. Five minutes. I want five minutes to lick my wounds without someone pointing out that I have them.

Arisha huffs. "Stop being silly. We need to tell Coal that—"

Heat floods my blood, and I stop short, stepping in front of her. "That what? One morning of a hard workout and I'm ready to whimper and cry? The point isn't to have him lighten up on me, it's to gain his respect as a warrior so we can work together to protect the whole damn mortal world. Sniveling isn't going to get me there." I take a breath, the corner of my vision marking the one being I want to see even less than Arisha or Coal just now—Shade. The healer's trained eyes will ask questions that will drain every last drop of my energy to withstand scrutiny. "Listen… I'll see you in a bit."

Without waiting for Arisha's reply, I duck into the tall hedges of the reflection garden, hurrying to make myself scarce before the male might spot me.

7

SHADE

As he crossed the central courtyard toward his infirmary, Shade's muscles woke, a movement beside the reflection garden catching his full attention in that primal way a scurrying rabbit or errant squirrel often did nowadays. Instantaneous and so rousing that if things continued in the same trajectory, he'd be chasing mice for fun soon. Unfortunately, this target of his body's full attention was not a small animal but a small cadet, her lush curves and lilac scent carried on the breeze driving Shade insane.

Literally.

Because there was nothing normal about the way Shade's whole attention zeroed in on Leralynn, the way he marked all her movements, from the swinging of auburn hair to the brush of fabric skimming her ankles. To the fact that Leralynn was limping, her usually graceful body rigid as she put on a fake smile for her friend Arisha's benefit.

Yes, Lera was hurt and trying to hide it. Which made her his professional problem.

Unfortunately.

After how hard Shade's cock had throbbed yesterday when Lera splayed her hand—her *hand, for stars' sake*—on his chest, he little trusted himself. Especially if she was hurt. As if he were a predator sensing blood, Lera's vulnerability made some primal part of Shade rear up with the need to chase her down. To cradle her against him.

After spending most of Ostera liberty unsuccessfully hunting the woods for an elusive fae female—whom Shade was no longer certain he hadn't imagined—he at least expected his body's frustrating fascination with Lera to finally melt away. He'd found his mate, and it wasn't the cadet. But instead, his fascination had grown, tugging Shade's soul so hard that he could barely stand being in the same room with Lera without dragging her to his bed. Or the floor. Or the ground.

Or against the infirmary wall, cadet or not.

Watching the last of Leralynn's red dress disappear into the reflection garden, Shade shook himself. He was a professional. An instructor. And he should act as such instead of devolving into a horny dog unable to keep from mounting a bitch in heat.

Plus, if he didn't see to Lera, someone else would. With the thought of another healer's hands roaming Lera's naked body making the hackles stir along his neck, Shade raised his voice. "Leralynn."

The girl's steps quickened, the quick flashes of her dress showing through the occasional break in the reflection garden's greenery.

Shade's muscles tensed, his nostrils flaring as he sniffed the breeze for her scent. Difficult as it was to control himself around the cadet when she was standing still, it was near impossible when she ran from him, the drive to chase and hunt and conquer making his blood roar.

"Leralynn, stop." Shade dropped his voice to a low, commanding timbre that usually brought wayward soldiers and patients in line. Usually. But not today.

With a soft growl rumbling through his chest, he prowled toward the reflection garden, the serene world of tall green stems and flapping butterflies closing around him. Striding through the labyrinth of blooming rhododendrons and tall bamboo shoot walls, Shade isolated Lera's lilac scent with an ease that frightened him. As he turned a final corner into an isolated alcove, he found her sitting at the foot of a picturesque stone archway, the burbling fountain and bird feeder behind it providing a rain-like backdrop against the Academy's sounds. With her red skirt spread casually over her legs, the girl held her beautiful face up toward the sun in a feigned bliss that only added to his straining temper. Her rich auburn hair was pinned up off her neck, showcasing the tempting curve of her jaw and creamy skin.

"Leralynn." It came out rougher than he'd intended, and he cleared his throat.

Opening her eyes, Lera blinked with an innocence that utterly mismatched the scent of pain and anxiety drifting from her. In fact, Shade would wager that after realizing he'd spotted her, she'd moved deeper into the reflection garden solely to find a place to sit. Because she couldn't stand very well.

Bracing his arm on one of the archway columns, he glared down at her. "This would be a good time to apologize for ignoring me calling you," he said evenly despite his speeding pulse. "You can follow that up with an explanation of your limp."

Lera braced her hands on either side of her stone seat, her face impressively calm. "I apologize. I—I didn't hear. I've a stone in my shoe and was searching for a place to get rid of it."

Three lies in as many sentences. Shade felt his face harden, knowing he was losing the fight but not sure what winning would look like. "Would you like to try that answer again? You might be surprised to learn that I'm not nearly as stupid or blind as you seem to imagine."

Lera's chin rose in a stubborn gesture that looked too familiar by half. "What exactly would you like me to tell you? I trained with Coal this morning, and I'm sore. The same as half the Academy most days. Are you demanding answers from a hundred cadets this morning?"

"No. Only ones I don't trust." At least she was done lying about the shoe pebble. "And ones whose instructors ask me to watch them." Not that Shade had needed Coal's encouragement to pay attention.

"Not you too," Lera muttered. Color filled her cheeks, her eyes narrowing as anger seeped into her scent. "I didn't know spying was part of a healer's duties these days."

She was mad at *him*? Heat simmered through Shade's blood. He considered himself easy-going most of the time, but not when it came to lies and utter insolence. Few pushed Shade far enough to learn his limits the hard way, and Leralynn had just signed herself up for that list. "Get up."

"Why?" Lera's face twitched with weary suspicion.

"Get up," Shade repeated icily. "We are going to the infirmary."

"But—"

"Unlike even Headmaster Sage himself, as an Academy healer, I've the power to remove you from all physical training with a single stroke of my pen." Pushing away from the column, Shade put his hands in his pockets. "Continue this dance of lies and evasions, and I'll put an end to the whole thing so efficiently, it will leave your head spinning."

8

SHADE

As they made their way across the Academy grounds, the occasional student casting them a curious look, Shade felt like a warden escorting a prisoner to an execution block. The effort Lera put into *not* limping was enough to make him swallow another growl. Did the cadet not understand how her every evasion only fed Shade's drive to hunt, straining his self-control until it trembled?

No. Of course she didn't. Neither did he.

"Last chance to speak truthfully before I stop wasting my breath on questions." Shade closed the infirmary door behind them, the thick scent of salves and tonics overwhelming after the fresh outdoor air. With her shoulders bare and gown clinging to a supple waist before billowing in a cascade of red skirts, Lera was making him hard just by standing near him. Leaning a hip against a countertop, he crossed his arms and waited.

Leralynn scowled at him and remained silent.

Shade sighed. "Very well. Strip."

A muscle ticked in the girl's jaw. For a second, Shade thought—hoped—she would break, talk to him. Stop this absurd battle of wills.

Instead of melting, Lera reached back to take off her gown, the fabric spilling onto the floor as she released each hook with a soft *snap, snap, snap.* Heartbeats later, instead of a pliable cadet, Shade had Lera standing before him in her underclothes, looking even more tempting

—and more hurt. The girl's thighs and hips were shifted to take weight off the left leg, her creamy skin marred with dark bruises that disappeared under her chest wrap and thin white undershorts. An especially wince-worthy mark, likely originating at one of the many vessels on the side of the groin, spilled from beneath the remaining cloth. Not that Lera gave any indication she was even aware of her injuries' existence.

Stars. The combination of stubbornness and vulnerability wafting off the girl prodded at the leashed predator inside Shade. Remaining where he stood, towering over her, Shade nodded to Lera's remaining covering. "Keep going."

His last play.

The spots of color flooding Lera's cheeks were too delicious by half, and Shade swallowed a sigh of relief. He truly preferred the role of a kind healer to that of interrogator and once Lera asked him for something—a blanket, an averted gaze, a moment to herself—the dynamic would shift. The girl would acknowledge she was a patient in Shade's infirmary and cooperate as such.

Lera's lips parted. Closed. And, with no further hesitation, she pulled at the end of her chest wrap.

Shade froze.

Lera did not.

A mix of hunger and horror washed over Shade as he watched Leralynn unwind the cloth. Everything Shade's body screamed at him was the very opposite of good bedside manner, yet he could do nothing to banish the thought. As she slipped out of her briefs, taking extra care to fold them as if her nakedness little bothered her, Shade forgot to breathe.

He'd been a fool. He should have known the girl—*this* girl—would wage their stubborn war to its bitter end. Which now left him with a very naked cadet, a very throbbing cock, and a deafeningly roaring conscience.

Lera's perfect, lush breasts rose into pink tips that begged to be suckled. Lower down, the smoothly flared hips opened to a perfect width to wrap around a man. And her mound, covered in damp auburn curls… *Stars.*

Shade closed his eyes for a brief moment that he knew Lera wouldn't miss. Lilac filling his senses, Shade gathered every bit of strength inside himself. When he opened his eyes once more, he was a healer.

Ribs to toes, splotches of bruises covered Lera's satin skin. The particularly large one Shade had noted earlier indeed started at the crease on the left of her groin, where someone had landed a lucky blow. Coal had said he was pushing Lera hard, but hearing and seeing weren't the same. Especially when it came to the girl before him.

Without waiting for instruction, Leralynn hoisted herself up onto the exam table, her auburn hair falling freely over bare shoulders. Stretching herself flat, she curled her hands around the table's edges, her knuckles blanching in the first true echo of her vulnerability. Beneath her bruised skin, Lera's chest rose and fell with too quick breaths, the pulse in the hollow of her neck fast and thready.

Shade's gut twisted. Lera was stubborn and insolent and incorrigible. And caring and nervous and frightened. Of *him.* Which Shade was quickly discovering he had no appetite for. Leralynn had had a hell of a morning, and Shade had thus far succeeded only in making her afternoon worse.

"You know, most people feel better after seeing me." Shade softened his voice to a healer's trained cadence. As he spoke, his hands were already roaming along Lera's head and ribs, his eyes watching for any sign of pain the bruises couldn't account for. "It is what the Academy thinks it's paying me for."

Lera's brows tightened for a moment before she schooled her face to the same false flatness she'd had since the reflection garden.

"You don't believe me?" Shade asked, surprised by how much the implication bothered him.

"I think you believe it."

Making a noncommittal sound, Shade palpated the slightly swollen shin he'd been eyeing since the girl undressed. Unsurprisingly, the tissue crackled beneath his touch, as if a hundred tiny bubbles took up residence in the muscle. Seeing Lera's body go rigid, he lightened his touch—though he'd pressed lightly to begin with. "Is that what hurts the most?"

"No." She swallowed, frustration leaking through her placid facade—finally. "It doesn't hurt. Nothing hurts. I want to go back to training, please."

"I never said you couldn't—" Shade stopped himself. Of course he had—he downright threatened to take her out of action in the reflection garden. And he brought up Coal, who Lera was probably trying to prove something to, hence her resistance to Shade's medical attention. With the puzzle pieces now in place, he saw too clearly the crossroads he stood at with the girl—and he wanted to curse at himself for not seeing it sooner.

He could have her trust or her obedience. Be a friend or an instructor. But he couldn't be both. Everything in his head said the choice was clear. Unfortunately, his soul said the same. And the two didn't agree one bit.

Releasing Lera's shin, Shade walked around to crouch beside her face. His heart pounded, his brain calling him ten times an idiot. But he couldn't help it any more than he could hold his breath forever. "I'm sorry I threatened you, cub. I won't stop you from leaving. Or blame you for it. I've been a great deal more of a bastard than I needed to be."

His hand twitched toward her cheek, and it was harder than it should have been to halt the motion. When her gaze swept to the door, the fear that she would turn away from him seized Shade's chest.

"Please stay," he whispered. "Coal isn't stupid. He'll notice your limp just as I did, and whatever message you're trying to send him, it won't work. However much it…*doesn't* hurt now, it will start to interfere with your running eventually. I can help. If you let me."

Sitting up, she bit her lip. "What will you tell Coal?"

Shade hesitated for only a moment. "If he asks me directly—and only if he asks—I will say that I ordered you here over your protests and cleared you for training." This time, Shade didn't stop himself when he placed his hand on Lera's cheek, savoring the way she leaned into his touch. Tracing his thumb along Lera's cheekbone, he let the full protective rawness of his need seep into his voice. "Trust me, cub. Please."

For a heartbeat, nothing happened, Lera's body staying stoically rigid as a muscle at the side of her jaw twitched. Once. Twice. And then, finally, Lera drew a shuddering breath that seized Shade's heart.

"I hurt," Lera whispered, her brave facade shattering so quickly that Shade barely had time to put his arms around her before she began shaking. "I'm tired and I hurt, and I know I should be better than I am. I *need* to be better."

Pulling her against his chest, Shade rocked her small bruised body. "Of course you hurt," he whispered into her hair, his fingers tracing the curve of her shoulder blades. "It makes you no less a fighter, cub. I promise."

She snorted softly. "Fighter. Right. Just look at me."

Shade knew she meant the phrase rhetorically, but he pulled the girl away from him anyway. "I am looking at you." Reaching to his counter, he scanned the medicines before selecting a small tin that smelled of mint and cumin. When he opened it, the balm's hot and cold sensations tingled his skin at once. Resting Lera back on the table, he ran his hand along her skin. "I'm looking at an overused leg that never stopped running. At arms that didn't let go of a sword, no matter how many parries they missed." Shade's gaze gripped Lera's eyes. "I'm looking at someone who is going to face down Coal tomorrow come hell or high water. And if I can do something to make it easier, I'd hold it as a privilege."

Not waiting for a reply, Shade focused on his work, his salve-coated fingers slipping to soothe the bruises along Lera's ribs, nudging aside the lush bare breasts, sprawled lazily over the ribs he needed to check. Try as he might to avoid looking at the plump nipples, he could do nothing to stop his body's tightness.

When his hand reached the crest of Lera's hip, Shade suddenly felt as awkward as a schoolboy. The large dark bruise covered a good portion of her left groin, spilling to the top of her auburn mound and between her thighs. Places he wanted to touch so badly, it hurt. His heart quickened, the room suddenly too hot for comfort.

"This tin is empty," he mumbled, turning to his counter to grab a new tin. Buying himself a few moments of composure that were doing nothing for his bulging needs. Worse yet, as he turned back, the slight glistening on Lera's bare thighs shot a wave of predatory desire through him.

A professional. He was a professional. As if to prove as much to them both, Shade scooped a thick swath of balm and slid it without hesitation over Lera's sensitive skin.

A small sound escaped her, her tightening thighs making Shade wonder if she too was imagining how the balm might feel on her other parts. Judging from the sweet tinge of arousal mingling with her lilac scent, it was quite likely.

Lera reached for Shade's face, the feel of her hands brushing his skin filling him with cock-throbbing warmth. The tip of her tongue flicked over her lush lips, touching a tiny scar. The white speck was so cleanly placed that Shade had an uncomfortable feeling it'd been done on purpose.

His throat closed, a memory on the edge of his consciousness pounding to be let out.

He blinked, forcing his mind from the phantom scents of forest and stream to focus on Lera's face. On how she leaned toward his mouth, her hand tangling in his loose hair. Shade knew Lera was saying something about keeping secrets, but it didn't matter. He understood the intent well enough and was powerless to stop it. Powerless to listen to any of the hundreds of alarm bells ringing in his head, telling him this was wrong.

With a groan, Shade covered her mouth with his. Gently at first, savoring her sweet lilac scent, the way her soft lips seemed to fit perfectly with his—and then with a possessiveness that had him cradling the girl's head lest he slam it into the table.

A wave of need pummeled Shade with animalistic fury, his tongue plunging deeper, pillaging for every bit of taste and warmth. His body pressed against her, Lera moaning and pulling him closer yet, dragging one of his hands up to cover her heavy breast and arching into it.

It was a cadet's nipple between his fingers, a cadet's mound rubbing hungrily against him. Somehow, that fact only drove his flames higher.

His cock throbbed painfully. His body ached with the need for more. His mind hovered on the edge of—

"Master Shade?"

Lera gasped.

The knock at the door sounded persistent enough that it finally penetrated Shade's hazed mind. "Master Shade?" The voice was female and vaguely familiar.

Reluctantly pulling away from Lera, who was scrambling to sit up, her eyes wide, Shade raised his voice. "I'm unavailable just now. Please come see me tomorrow."

"But it's an emergency," the voice whined. "I desperately need your aid."

Shade rubbed his eyes. Sliding to the edge of the table, Lera mouthed the girl's name. *Vivian.*

"No," he whispered. He put a hand on her stomach to stop her. He wasn't willing for this to be over. He needed one more moment—was so desperate for it, it scared him. Despite himself, Shade traced his index finger along the inside of Lera's moist thigh even as he raised his voice toward the door. "Please see one of the other healers, Vivian," he called. "I'm very busy just now."

Beneath his hand, Lera's hips were undulating slightly despite her clear attempt to focus her gaze on the chaste ceiling, Lera's desire slamming a very untimely avalanche of need into Shade. He drew a quiet but very full breath, begging the stars not to let him lose control into his too tight britches.

Beyond the door, the voice grew louder. "But it will only take a bit of your time, sir. I won't keep you long at all. Here, let me just show you."

The sound of the turning handle sent a shiver through Shade before he could even see the door start to creep open. He never locked it. Why would he? *Stars.*

Leaping over the exam table and a very naked Lera, Shade managed to wedge his foot against the door before it could open more than a hand's width. "What's the emergency, Vivian?" he asked, corralling his heavy breaths. Behind him, he could hear Lera quietly slipping off the table to collect her clothes, his heart pounding with disappointment.

"I think I pulled a muscle in training today, Master Shade. Won't you please have a look?" Vivian pushed against the door, her green eyes widened in concern. "Can I come in?"

Hearing the door to his small attached study open and close, Shade sighed and motioned Vivian inside, reminding himself that any visions of ripping the girl's throat out with his teeth were firmly misplaced.

9

LERA

By the time classes end for the day, I'm so exhausted, I decide to skip dinner and the Protector's Guild meeting and go straight to bed. Coal will just seethe silently anyway, and I've not the stamina to argue. More to the point, I'm in no shape to tie my shoelaces much less patrol tonight.

I'm already crossing the courtyard toward the dorms when the problem with my plan strikes me like an anvil. Tutoring with River.

He's expecting me, and knowing River, if I don't go, he'll let Coal know with concern that I skipped one of our "clerk" sessions because I wasn't feeling well. Back to square one.

Shade's balm has diminished the worst of my muscle aches, and a tight shin wrap now keeps my leg from feeling like someone is jamming a hot rod between my muscles—but that's a long way from actual comfort. The first step up to River's tower office makes me flinch, and by the first landing, sweat has broken out on my temples. I grip the railing, using so much arm strength to get up that my biceps start to ache.

By the second landing, I want to throw River and his tutoring off the tallest parapet on the keep.

No. Tutoring is good, I chant to myself. *Climbing stairs is good.* Even without the extra nuisance my failing the exams would create, the tutoring is the one touch point of trust between River and me. I'd never realized the intimacy sharing knowledge could have, River's genuine pride twines with mine each time we conquer a new equation or text. Strange as it sounds, failing the exams feels like failing River.

"Leralynn." The door to River's study opens as I'm still climbing the last set of stairs, and the male's impossibly broad shoulders and beautiful face fill the entryway. In his tucked-in white shirt with a golden sash and matching cuff links, he looks his usual controlled self, so handsome and polished that I feel like a sweaty rag doll next to him. Only the intensity in his gray eyes as he watches my approach gives away his inner tension.

I swallow. With the male's busy schedule and my own avoidance tactics, this is the first time I've returned to his study since the night he made me whip him. I didn't have time to worry about that while I was dragging myself up the stairs, and it hits me now. The memories of that encounter still rake my chest, not even drowned out by the leg-trembling kiss that followed it. My cheeks flame. Unable to help myself, I glance at River's forearm, his shirt's snow-white linen concealing whatever bruises may still linger.

"I'm a bit sore." River answers the unspoken question, his voice too understanding. Too perceptive. A tiny corner of his mouth twitches up. "I hear you might be as well. Do I want to know what it was you did to antagonize Coal?"

Stars, has anyone not yet heard of my morning? I brush down my dress's crinkly fabric, grateful that it will conceal any new wrinkles from being dumped onto the floor of Shade's clinic. "Coal and I are in the midst of a discussion. A difference in opinions on a philosophical matter."

"How very…civilized of you." Reaching around me with a brush of warm, woodsy-scented air, River shuts the door, his face shifting to soul-piercing worry when I flinch at the sound of the clicking latch.

After spending the night in the dungeon, I'm not sure I'll ever get used to the sound.

Stepping in front of me, River touches my shoulder for a heartbeat before thinking better and drawing his hand away. "Lera, look at me," River says with commanding confidence, as if he can pour his strength into my soul if he tries hard enough. "You are all right. You are safe. The door is unlocked. And if you would rather not be alone in a room with me—"

"I'm happy to be in a room alone with you," I say firmly. At least I think I am. My notion of who River truly is has shifted so many times in the past weeks that my head and heart are both still spinning. Drawing a breath, I grip his muscled arm, my small hand barely able to cup his sculpted triceps. This close to him, his dominating height and breadth consume me, making me feel more delicate than I know I am—or want to be.

A wary look crosses River's gaze, and he makes no move to touch me in return—but he doesn't pull away either.

I bite my lip, unprepared for the sudden need to share my thoughts and worries with the brilliant male beside me. "Can we speak as friends for a few minutes? Before we start?" The words tumble from me, futile or not. "I want—I need—to say something, and if you tell me off for it, I will likely kick you. Which would not end well."

The male glances at the door, then out the window of his study, as if a key to his decision might stride across the courtyard. In the ensuing silence, my heart strikes my ribs in a steady, too-loud beat. Then River finally sighs and, stepping away from me, leans his muscled backside against his desk. "I'm afraid to ask, but what's on your mind, Leralynn?"

Everything. I draw a deep breath, forcing my shoulders to settle. Despite River's agreement to hear me out, he is still the Academy's commander, whose instinct—for better or worse—is to keep me safe. And that very well may include telling me to mind my place as a cadet and leave the worrying to the administration. Only one way to find out. "Having the Prowess Trials at the Academy is a mistake."

River's fingers drum a slow rhythm against the oak desk. "I don't disagree."

"Can you just—" I cut off, his words registering. "Wait. What did you say?"

"I dislike the notion of gathering the continent's leaders at Great Falls when I can't confirm that the magic blight that mauled several people earlier this year won't rear its head again. That said, I don't believe there is anything to be done for the decision except to fortify the Academy. That last, you will be pleased to know, I am actively doing."

Exactly as Coal said River felt.

I bite my lip, searching for a new tack. "What about Han? Don't you have the sense of something being *off* about him? He broke Coal's arm. How many humans do you know who are capable of that?"

River swears under his breath, his face tightening with sudden intensity. "Please never—ever—make a similar statement again, Lera."

"Because—"

"Because you just more or less accused someone at the Academy of fae craft. I recall *you* being accused of the same, and your very words cast Coal under similar suspicion. What if someone hears you—or worse, believes you? Just imagine a fae hunt on Academy grounds, with rival royals making accusations against each other. It would be a greater threat to the continent than any magic." River runs one hand through his hair so the dark strands stand up adorably, defying their usual pin-straight neatness. "As for Han and Coal… I see no more mythical force behind Han's skills than I observe in Coal himself—or in Shade, Tye, and myself. And you too, Leralynn." A hint of a smile brushes River's face for a heartbeat. "My refusal to allow a cadet into the front lines doesn't make me blind to your own skills. And with the darkness we both know Coal swims in now, I can't help wonder if a part of him allowed himself to get hurt."

"I know," I whisper, so quietly that I'm not sure whether I mean the words for River or myself.

With a sigh, the male braces the heels of his hands on his thighs and leans closer to me. "I share your concern with the Trials, but there is no evidence of an actionable threat from magic, while there is a known danger from the islanders. Gut feelings aside, the Academy is a fortress, and likely the only place on the continent that can gather the kingdoms without political bickering. In that light, there is no better place to hold the Prowess Trials." River shakes his head. "Unfortunately, having the heads of ten kingdoms in one place is dangerous no matter what."

"So there is truly nothing we can do about this?" I ask.

"So long as Sage and Han have a competitive team to field—and with Tye here, they've that, even if the others are barely able to qualify—the trial will happen here. And to that end, I will bring in so many guards that even an invisible foe won't get through their line." River's voice has the confident timbre of someone who has already worked through the problem. Of course he has. It's River. "The Academy is a defensive fortress, and I'd be a poor commander indeed if I couldn't figure out how to use it as such."

"Sometimes I wish you weren't so bloody logical."

"Indeed." A corner of his mouth twitches toward a smile again before his beautiful face schools itself to its usual piercing attentiveness. "Now, if I've passed your evaluation of my defensive operations plan, I recommend we return to studying. We've worked too hard to waver now." River cocks his head, watching me as he pushes away from his desk. "Leralynn. Did you hear what I just said?"

I nod absently, his reference to exams and studying suddenly a distant buzz against his earlier words. Sage can field a Prowess team—and thus bring the whole of the continent into the jaws of crumpling wards—for one reason only.

Tye.

And that is what—who—I need to stop.

10

LERA

For three nights following the revelation River doesn't even know he made, I wake up in a cold sweat, fending off Coal's worsening terrors with my arms and legs and sometimes Tye's fire magic. And for three days, I stalk Tye.

The affair reveals itself to be a great deal more time consuming than I could have imagined. With Tye downright avoiding me during the day and never appearing without the Prowess team around him—who are often surrounded in turn by a sea of buzzing, excited cadets—lying in wait at the bathhouse is my final option. River's words, spoken so casually and accurately, continue sounding in my head.

The whole Prowess Trials fiasco hangs on the one male who shouldn't be competing in human games to begin with—Tye. If he withdraws, the whole thing just might collapse like the house of cards that it is, making my life—and the Protector's Guild's job—a whole lot easier.

And that makes getting him alone my number one priority.

Now, wedged between the thick branches of a shadowed oak, I rub my eyes and squint at the dark horizon. Crickets sing in the grass of the training yard, and down in the valley of Great Falls, a lone dog barks. No first rays of dawn to be seen, meaning I might finally be here early enough to catch Tye as he finds his way to the bathhouse before anyone sane is up. Unless the male has given up bathing at all, this is the only time of the day I've narrowed down the possibilities to.

Dong dong dong.

I jerk as the Academy bell calls four in the morning, cursing myself for having nearly dozed off at my post. The last thing I need is to actually have one of Coal's nightmares while I'm up here and fall off a tree branch. Stifling a yawn, I focus on the outline of a male figure finally striding down the path to the baths. Tye's large body and lithe muscles move with a feline coordination that send a wave of heart-squeezing familiarity through me. The slight slump of his shoulders and heavy gait, on the other hand, are nothing like the male I know. He looks exhausted—defeated. *So this is what you're like when you think no one is watching.*

Stopping before the bathhouse door, Tye takes a deep breath and turns the handle, sticking his head inside before finally walking in. Ensuring that the place is empty? That's my only explanation for his choosing this hellish hour to bathe at in the first place, but Tye has never been shy before.

Feeling only slightly guilty, I wait until my prey is well inside the door—and has likely had time to get himself undressed—before sliding down from the tree. Whatever slight guilt I feel over the intrusion pales beside the rising excitement of finally, *finally* having cornered the elusive rogue.

As a human, the capture might have felt entertaining. As a fae, the sensation of hunting and trapping is magnified manyfold, making my heart speed and muscles tingle with addictive energy.

Brazenly opening the door to the male baths, I breathe in the immediate moist heat of the pools, hear the gentle bubbling of natural springs, my memory unable to stop from brushing over the things Tye and I have done on their stone lips. Even as I stride forward, my thighs clench at the phantom feel of Tye's hands brushing my skin with sinful lightness, his callused thumb parting my sex.

There is no sign of that male now, however, not in the muscled figure hunched at the edge of a large heated pool across the room.

"Tye?"

Despite having surely heard me coming, Tye doesn't look up. Doesn't even answer.

My nostrils flare delicately as I stalk closer, his pine-and-citrus scent mixing with the lavender soap and the slight sulfur tinge of the water.

And copper. Blood. Tye's blood. The irony of Shade catching me hurt only a few days ago isn't lost on me as I stride to where Tye sits on a pool's edge, a small tower of healer's supplies laid out at his side.

"Stalking me?" Tye asks when I'm a few steps away. His normally lilting voice is even, emotionless except for the slightest tinge of annoyance.

"Avoiding me?" Walking around to see his face, I gasp. Deep rope burns cover the insides of his calves, thighs, and arms, and the small toe on his left foot is so discolored, I'm certain it's broken. The injuries look even more lurid in the dim room, the torchlight turning his muscles and bruises into a deep contrasting field of shadows. On his upper body, the male's right elbow looks larger than his left, more swelling around his shoulder hinting at recent dislocations. Beneath his mane of red hair, his usually bright face is tight, his green eyes dull, his freckles standing out against blanched skin. His silver earring is missing, and this, for some reason, is the thing that makes tears lodge in my throat.

Stars. In the week since Han arrived, he's already shattered Coal's arm and is well on his way to destroying Tye too.

Sitting next to him, I reach out to touch a bruised knee. Guilty as it makes me feel, perhaps the injuries will make urging Tye to step away from the Prowess team easier than I expected. Surely this isn't what the male imagined when he started down this path.

Tye catches my wrist before I can touch his skin, the grip tighter than his usual playful tugs. "Don't."

"What happened?" I ask, staring unabashedly at his naked body.

"You wouldn't understand." He releases my wrist. "It's not personal, Lera. There is a certain amount of pain and strain that comes with training for top-level athletics—things that look brutal to outsiders but are a normal part of elite training. To be blunt, I don't have the energy to explain that to everyone who wants to gasp and criticize every scratch. Hence my preference to bathe outside other's company." He raises a brow at me, just in case I may have missed the implication that *other's company* very much includes me.

I raise my chin. "I'm not others," I say, refusing to grant Tye any distance. "I'm—"

"You are gawking," he says flatly.

Yes, I am. I frown but don't look away. Slipping off the edge, Tye lowers himself into the water. A few more moments and he will walk out of my reach unless I hop fully clothed into the bath as well and trail behind like a simpering admirer.

Crouching with my forearms on my knees, I drill my gaze into Tye's back. "Wait."

To my relief, the male pauses, though his coiled body says his patience is wearing thin. If I want to talk, I need to do it fast. And I'm not above bringing mating into the mix. Not if it brings Tye back to me and away from Han. "In the dungeon, we—"

"We played." Tye's emerald eyes flash, for a moment filled with the life energy I'm used to—even if it's rooted in annoyance. "That was what we agreed to, lass. A distraction. I was honest with you then, and I am honest with you now. I need to go. Han doesn't want us… He wants us focused on training. Nothing else."

"Han is a sadistic ass who I wouldn't trust to wipe dung off my boots."

Tye's sharp face tightens, a muscle ticking in his jaw. "No one is asking you to trust him. Or to like him. After Han refused to release you from the dungeon, I don't blame you for despising the man. But he's the one person who understands that *I* need to win the title. I've sacrificed too much—" He cuts off raggedly. "The Prowess Trials title is why I'm in the Academy in the first place. I don't expect you to understand, *Lady* Leralynn of Osprey. Or approve. I do expect you to stay out of my way."

I bite my lip, the seconds ticking. Then, in a moment of reckless abandon, I throw down my cards. "Pull out of the Prowess Trials, Tye. Please."

Tye freezes in utter bewilderment, the warm water lapping his washboard abdomen and circling smoothly around his hips. For a moment, the only sounds are the bubbling springs and softly spitting torches. "Why in all the sky's stars would I do that?"

I take a breath and straighten my spine, having only one last move to play. The truth. Or as much of it as I can manage without setting off Tye's veil amulet. "Because you know there are things—magical, evil things—that prowl the Great Falls woods. You've fought them. Because keeping the ten kingdoms' kings and queens out of the Academy—out of the blight's reach—is the responsible thing to do. And you are the only one with the power to make it happen. Pull out of the Trials, and, without you, there is no Great Falls Academy team and no Trials on Academy grounds."

Tye's face darkens with an ire I've not seen before, his lively emerald gaze closing off to me with the finality of an iron grate snapping closed. With slow, deliberate steps, he walks toward the edge of the pool and looks me right in the eye, his heady pine-and-citrus scent now taunting me. He's not mine—he may never be again. "Did you just ask me to throw away my life's destiny to head off some wildly unlikely threat that's fluttering in your imagination?"

"I asked you to use your power for someone beyond yourself," I shoot back.

"Because I'm the only one who can stop the Trials?"

"Yes," I breathe.

"Not Sage, the headmaster of Great Falls Academy, who is actually in charge? Not Han, who is training the team. Not the Prowess committee, which is making the final decision on venue. Not any of the royals, who are the only reason the Academy even cares about the competition? No, not any of them." Tye braces both hands on the pool's edge, looming over me, his glistening muscles vibrating with fury. "What you meant to say, Leralynn, is that I'm the only one you think can be manipulated to do your bidding."

"I'm not manipulating you. I'm…" My words fumble, the last of my hopes crumbling to dust. I take one last wild stab at reasoning with him. "What do you think Han and Sage are up to exactly? Why bring the Trials here to the edge of the continent when there are far grander cities and bigger arenas elsewhere?"

Tye snorts without humor. "I think the pair of them are using the fruits of my lifetime of training to parley a bunch of snot-nose royals onto a competition pitch. And I think I'm going to swallow it all with a smile for the chance to win. To break out of common poverty into a life that matters. A title. Land. The things that noble-born ladies like you take for bloody granted. Now, if you would kindly take your presumptuous arse out of here, I'd be much obliged."

Without waiting for my response, Tye turns away—nearly falling into the water as his knee wavers for a moment before his body regains control of itself.

My throat tightens, my plans and hopes all drowning beneath the blood-tinged water. I rise to my feet—then pause, my eyes glued to Tye's swollen shoulder.

Not *all* of them.

One last option suddenly looms before me, so terrible it steals my breath. An option that Shade taught me only three days ago. For a moment, with bile crawling up my throat, I consider walking out without the courtesy of telling Tye the horrid move I'm about to make. But at least I've enough shame to own my words.

The walls of the bathhouse close around me, the thick humid air we once shared with such pleasure now suffocating me. "I'm going to report you."

Tye pauses, but remains with his back to me. "For what—bathing before dawn?" Despite the derisive snort that accompanies the words, the tension vibrating beneath them is as clear as a violin chord. "Do you imagine another set of bruises from River will make any difference?"

"Not to River." My mouth is dry, my gut twisting with each word. *I'm doing the right thing.* For the mortal realm. For the quint. For Tye himself. I have to be, because otherwise, I'm as reprehensible as Tye is about to think me. "I will report you to Shade as an injured cadet."

Tye turns, water running down the grooves of his muscles, the storm in his eyes darkening as he works through the implications of the words. The greatest threat from River may be a thrashing, but Shade can do the one thing Tye truly fears—bench him from training and competition altogether.

When Tye finally speaks, there is nothing of the male I love lingering in his voice. "You wanted to make yourself an enemy, Leralynn of Osprey? You have succeeded."

11

LERA

I bolt upright in my bed, the deafening clank of shackles and the stench of pain still lingering about me. Air catches in my lungs, making breathing an effort of will. Beyond the window, sharply glittering stars fill the night sky, offering desperately needed proof of my being aboveground.

Swinging my legs off the bed, I brace my elbows on my thighs and cradle my head. My night shirt, a short slip of red silk that Autumn packed for me before I left Lunos, is damp with patches of sweat.

"You wanted to make yourself an enemy, Leralynn of Osprey? You have succeeded." Tye's voice pierces my newly freed mind, the loathing in the male's face cutting as deeply as the whips from Coal's night terrors.

I shudder. In my mind's eye, Tye's ire-filled face is replaced by Shade's impassive one. He listened silently as I said the words that could end Tye's imagined career, his gaze growing harder with each sentence. When I was done, he just told me he would look into it. And did not follow me as I ran toward the closest patch of trees to empty my stomach, my fear over what's coming overpowered only by my grief at betraying one of my own quint-bonded males.

A small, pain-stricken growl escapes my chest. I'm out of ideas. Of options. Of hope.

"Lera?" Sitting up in bed, Arisha pats her table in search of her glasses. "Are you all right?"

Instead of answering her, I stuff my feet into my boots, knocking them against the floor to seat my heels.

"What are you doing?"

"What does it look like I'm doing?" I stand up. "I'm exhausted. I want to sleep. And Coal's bloody nightmares are not letting me. So I'm going over to Coal's damn bedchamber and waking him up."

I need to fix *something*, or I think I'll go insane.

Though a smaller voice inside me says I need to strike something, and Coal is the only available target.

Arisha pushes her glasses higher on her nose. "Are you certain that's wise?"

It's such an understatement that I almost snort. "Of course it's not. But I'm certain that it is the only bloody thing I can do something about. And if all I get out of the mess is one night's sleep, I'm ready to take it. Why are you looking at me like that?"

"The logic of blaming Coal for his nightmares aside, in what world do you imagine it would be a good idea for a cadet to sneak into the instructors' wing of the keep in the middle of the night? Much less dressed—undressed—like that?" Arisha waves at my bright red slip.

I frown. "I'm not done dressing yet."

"So…you put on your boots for the sake of walking two feet to your clothing chest to get pants?" She coughs and points to her ears. "Also…"

Right. The amulet. I would have forgotten to put it on.

Giving Arisha a glare that she in no way deserves, I remove my boots and pull on a gray training uniform over my night shirt. Not glamorous, but practical, as is the pinned bun I wrangle my sleep-tangled hair into before clicking the amulet into place. The heaviness settling over me is suffocating.

Finally dressed, this time appropriately, I stalk to the door only to stop with a hand braced on the doorframe as my common sense—or at least Arisha's—finally registers. "There will be hell to pay if I'm caught in the instructors' wing, won't there?"

Arisha cocks her head in serious consideration, a move that's so classically her, I almost want to laugh—though it would make me seem even more insane. "At the very least, River is going to pull you from Coal's class. And I wouldn't be surprised if you were back on stable duty until the end of the millennium."

I tip my face back, weighing the situation in my fatigue-ridden mind, then turn and scramble out the window instead of using the door. Being careful with my paths, I can do—continuing the sleepless nights, I can't. It's not sustainable. Not for me. Maybe not for Coal either.

I stay to the trees for as long as I can, the fresh scents of pine and damp grass bringing me fully awake. Then I cut into the keep and let myself into the library with one of the keys Gavriel made for our group. Walking between the stacks of books is eerie without the others here, the words and knowledge seeming to watch me as I head to the back door and out into the sleeping corridor beyond.

Trailing my fingers along the stone walls, I work my way through the dark keep, the occasional scurry of a castle cat and *all is well* calls from guards the only sounds to break up the night. I rush through the pools of torchlight and linger in the shadows. It isn't until I'm into the instructors' wing that the full weight of what I'm doing settles on me. There is no explaining my way out of this if caught now.

And if I'm not caught? I'm not sure how I'm going to explain myself to Coal either. Whatever happens, it can't be any worse than the disaster with Tye. Or maybe it can. I'm too tired to think. To truly contemplate that quiet voice that says I'm provoking a fight just to have something other than reality to focus on.

The wide, tapestry-lined corridor looming before me is intimidating for its openness. For having no alcove or deep shadow to hide in. Identical oak doors line both sides of the hall, intricately worked candleholders above each entrance casting overlapping shadows onto the elaborate red-and-gold carpet. At the very end of the corridor, the largest door belongs to River's sleeping chambers, Headmaster Sage having apartments elsewhere in the keep. Despite River's tendency to work late into the night, there is no light escaping from beneath the door. The male is either already asleep or in his study at the top of the tower.

I run my fingers along the engraved nameplates, making my way deeper into the forbidden den. *Master Erik, history. Master Briar, mathematics.* Coal is close. I can feel the male's turmoil agitating my own. *Master…* My throat tightens. *Master Han, Prowess Trials.* I recoil from the sign, ending up on the other side of the hallway. Mercifully, Coal's name catches my eye a heartbeat later.

Stopping before the door, I take a deep breath, trying to slow my racing heart enough to think. To give my sanity the benefit of one last chance before stepping forward. The scent of polished wood and melted candle wax fills my lungs, but brings no clarity with it.

Somewhere close, a cat trots along on soft feet—but otherwise, the hall is quiet as a crypt, the thick walls muffling the room's sounds.

This is it. Now or never.

Turning the knob, I push on Coal's door.

Nothing happens. Locked. Of course Coal would lock his door. Knocking it is—softly at first, then as loud as I dare in the hall. Although the surrounding stone entombs the rooms in silence, the sound still makes me jump.

Nothing.

A shiver runs through me, but I didn't come here to turn away now. With a quick mental thank-you to Tye—who spent many evenings in Lunos trying to impart to me whatever skills River was least likely to approve of—I pull the pins out of my hair and get to work on the lock.

I *will* resolve something tonight, if it's the last thing I do—and it very well may be.

Against the silence of my held breath, the soft click of the lock's metal teeth is wonderfully crisp to my immortal hearing. Pin one of four gives obediently. Pin two. Pin—

The door swings open, Coal's knife pressing into my throat before I even register his presence.

12

LERA

I don't dare move, not even to rise from the crouch I was in to work the lock.

Pulling the knife back, Coal jerks me into his room with a hot brush of metallic-scented air. His face is a storm as he closes the door behind me, and I stumble to reclaim my balance.

Beyond his half-dressed body, the room is an odd mix of heavy Academy splendor and the male's personal attempt to turn every chamber he occupies into a makeshift armory. The carved mahogany four-poster bed has nothing but a rumpled blue sheet on it, the down cover and pillows having fallen—or been tossed—to the stone floor. A lit lantern in the corner wards off the worst of the dark, though Coal's immortal eyes don't require the extra light to see by. The top of the clothing chest is lined with sharpening stones and leather cleaner—and a bucket with hoof pick and curry comb, which still smell of the stable.

The strangest part—or perhaps not, given the room's occupant—is the furniture arrangement. Everything, from the bed to the washstand, has been shifted over to create a patch of empty space. The rack of weaponry standing beside it offers all the explanation needed.

I rub my throat, my chest still too tight around my lungs. "You couldn't hear me knocking, but you heard the lock being picked?"

"I heard you knocking," says Coal. With his feet bare and a loose pair of cotton trousers hanging on his hips, the male looks deadly and beautiful enough to make any female damp—sling or no sling. His sculpted chest and torso gleam in the lantern light, his blond hair hanging loose around his shoulders. "I chose to ignore it."

"Good to know you are a bastard at all hours of the day."

Coal braces his good hand on the wall and looms over me, his chiseled face harshly beautiful. "If you are still upset because I opposed your suicide mission, whine to someone else. Shade is good for soothing whimpering. Tye may give you some sport for distraction as well."

The last hits my chest and ripples outward. It takes me a few breaths to regain my equilibrium—to remember that I came here to call Coal out on his demons, not let him conjure up any of my own. "Your bloody nightmares are keeping me awake."

Coal blinks.

Seizing the advantage of having the male off-balance, I step into his space, so close that the loose rabbit ears of his sling brush up against my tunic. "Chains, shackles, an evil being coming up behind you to do bad things. *Those* nightmares. I'm tired of them keeping me awake half the night while you do nothing about them but brood in your room and get into fights."

The flash of lightning in Coal's blue eyes is at utter odds with the ice in his voice. "You want to talk about facing nightmares, Osprey? I'd be very careful what you wish for."

The reasonable part of me hollers to heed Coal's warning and get the hell away. Unfortunately, I'm too tired and upset and bloody overwhelmed to mind better reason. "Your threats and marching about like a feisty cock are getting old, Coal." The truth, coiled and festering inside my chest, spills in an unfiltered torrent. Jabbing my finger into Coal's injured arm, I snort when he gasps in pain. "If your head was where it belongs, Han would never have been able to break your arm. He's good. But you are better. At least when your damn head is not so far up your ass that it would take three healers to extract it. And now, because of your stupidity, you can't so much as have my back on patrols."

I know I should stop, but I can't. My breath quickens with every word, heat simmering in my blood. Even Coal's metallic scent, tinged with a dangerous ire, isn't enough to stop my words. "Everybody else might tiptoe around you, let you work through your past in your own damn time—but everybody else isn't having to see the images of your torment night after night. I am. And I'm done with it. Done with the memories, done with the panic of knowing—*knowing*—you are ready to throw your life away. So you are going to talk, or meditate, or stare at a pair of shackles—I don't care what you do, so long as you keep doing it until something works."

I don't see Coal move until his hand is already gripping the back of my neck, twisting me into the wall. I gasp, my cheek pressing against the hard plaster. Jabbing a knee into the back of my thighs, Coal efficiently pins me to the wall while he reaches for something on top of his clothing chest.

A moment later, the snap of a leather weapons belt in the air stops my heart.

"Remember this dream, Osprey?" Coal breathes the words against the back of my neck, his breath tickling my skin. "You think walking into my nightmares was a one-way passage? Let's talk about facing this one first, shall we?"

13

COAL

Coal's heart pounded against his ribs so hard that his bound arm throbbed with the beats, his muscles tight with a mix of fury and determination. Leaning into Lera, he brought his lips close to her soft neck, letting her feel his breath along her skin as he loomed over her. Larger and stronger and fully aware of the very thing that scared her spitless.

The fear leaking from her spiked as vividly as it had when Coal had cracked the belt in the air moments earlier, shamelessly recruiting her own terrors to his cause. *Good.* She needed to be terrified—needed to stop thinking of Coal as a friend and remember he was a too-experienced warrior who knew exactly how bad a routine patrol could turn. He'd kept his word to keep from disclosing Lera's Protector's Guild machinations to River, but that sure as hell didn't mean Coal had any intention of standing by while Lera toyed with the suicide she was too brave and stubborn and inexperienced to see.

Worse, Coal had been making her more vulnerable these past weeks. In letting the strange misguided connection between them thrive unchecked, he'd opened the girl further to the assaults of his mind, cost her sleep and focus, and roused her own inner demons. That connection needed to end. Now. Tonight.

Still pressed against the wall, Lera flinched as a tremor ran the length of her spine. Her intoxicating scent filled Coal's lungs as surely as the heat rolling off her body wrapped around his soul. Her silky auburn hair had started coming loose from its pins, loose tendrils falling against her neck, and he wanted to wrap them around his fingers, to bury his hands in her hair and release more of that heady lilac. *Yes, damn the stars.* He wanted her. Despite knowing the damage he was causing, Coal wanted the beautiful cadet anyway, and not just with his cock. The more time he spent in her presence, the richer the world around him felt. Around her, colors and tastes and sounds vibrated so vividly that sometimes Coal felt as though he stood on the edge of a greater world. One where he was whole.

The thought of something happening to Lera was so unbearable, Coal swore he felt it like spikes set against his soul.

Unfortunately for him, it all coalesced to one conclusion—Coal could protect Lera's budding friendship or protect her life. Not both. Put that way, the course was clear. The best thing Coal could do was build up the cadet's skills while slamming a healthy dose of reality into her. He'd already started on it the morning after she threw all caution and advice to the wind and went patrolling alone. And he would continue. Would wring her in training for every ounce of energy she had, lest that one unpracticed parry let through a foe's sword.

Except that wasn't enough, was it? Coal had been so busy demanding Lera respect the foes in the Academy's forest, he'd overlooked the danger lurking right before her nose. *Himself.*

But he knew it now. Just as he knew that he could not stay away from Lera if she kept injecting herself into his life.

Which meant the girl had to stay away from him. Whatever pain Coal caused her now was nothing compared to what might happen if she continued the connection. If the darkness encroaching on Coal infected her any deeper.

"I'm not who you think I am, Leralynn," Coal said into her ear, his voice a low rumble. "I'm not kind. Or nice. I'm a damaged unpredictable bastard you want to steer clear from." Angling his body, Coal left an open path to the door, as clear an invite to get the hell out of his chamber as he could conjure. "Now would be a good time to start."

Lera didn't move. Too brave and stubborn for her own good, damn her.

Coal's hand tightened on the leather, then he slapped it against his thigh hard enough to make the horrid sound of leather striking flesh, straight from Lera's nightmares. Knowing what the bastard in Lera's past had done to her, Coal wasn't certain he could bring himself to hit the girl even once, which was the problem with peddling in threats and fear. He begged the stars he wouldn't need to go further.

"Go," Coal growled at her through clenched teeth and slapped his thigh again, each *whap whap whap* sounding through the room making Lera gasp. "I won't give you another warning."

Nothing.

"Go!"

Stars-damned nothing.

Fine. Coal swung, watching the belt sail through the air, the arc wide and slow enough that Lera could easily escape the blow with a single step.

Except she didn't—she didn't move at all.

Ice gripped Coal's throat, his nostrils flaring to take in her scent—and the acrid, paralyzing terror spilling into it. It wasn't just fear—Leralynn had a deadly chink in her armor the size of the Academy's keep, a chink that sounded exactly like a cracking whip. The girl trembling against the wall wasn't being stubborn and brave, wasn't choosing to take a blow to make her point. She was…*stars damn it,* Leralynn was surrendering. Giving up.

The world slowed, reality slamming into Coal, wrapping everything that came before this point in cotton irrelevance.

He pulled the blow so hard, the leather flew across the room and wrapped around one of the bed's four pillars. Grabbing Lera's shoulder, he spun her around to face him, his broken arm screaming.

"You don't stop fighting, Leralynn," Coal hissed into her face, her glazed chocolate eyes and racing breaths spurring his own bounding pulse. Panic surged through Coal's veins, bubbling from the same primal place inside him that drove him to stop Lera's lone patrols and push her so hard in the ring. "You took on sixteen trained cadets and *me* back to back. You are not going to let one crack of the belt turn you into a frozen rabbit. Do something. Anything. Just not this. Do you understand me?"

The trembling nod she gave Coal did nothing to convince him. Lera was a horrible liar.

He cursed. "This can get you killed, Lera. Dead."

The glazed look in Lera's eyes said she no longer heard him. And that frightened Coal as much as anything.

Running his hand along her face, he gripped her chin, the gesture feeling more intimate than he was prepared for. "You are at Great Falls Academy. In my bloody room. And I am much more of a threat than that fat lord doling out lashings. You don't back down from me, and you sure as hell don't bend the knee for him. You fight. And I will keep you here until you do."

Twisting Leralynn back to face the wall, Coal put his forearm across her back. "Escape, Leralynn. Duck, hit me, use the wall. Do something."

A weak, ineffectual elbow came his way, as if she were afraid of retaliation. Of course she was.

Coal poked Lera's ribs. "I have a broken arm." He growled into her ear. "Use it to your advantage. Use everything." He poked her again and again until the girl finally, finally was fed up with him enough to twist and take a swing at his jaw.

Coal let it land for both their sakes, the impact echoing through him with welcome relief. She was fighting again. Badly, but making an effort. He could work with that. He could work with anything but surrender.

Reaching for Lera's shoulder to put her in another bind, Coal paused when the girl grabbed his wrist instead. The feel of her small strong hand on his bare skin sent a rush of energy through him, the jolts echoing through his chest and thighs and cock. Lera's large brown eyes, no longer glassy, flashed, her skin blanched with fear and anger.

"Are you back with me?" Coal asked.

"No. I'm back without you," Lera answered. "Play your games with someone else, Coal. I'm done." Throwing down the wrist she'd captured as if it were a diseased rodent, Lera held Coal's gaze long enough to ensure he knew the message was genuine. Her words hung in the air with a finality that silenced the world. Then, shoving past him, she finally did what Coal had been after all along—she stalked for the door.

Except things had changed since he'd told her to go. Everything had changed. Coal had thought he needed to stay away to keep Lera safe, but it seemed he needed to get into her soul instead. Get in and stay in, until he pried open the jaws of the paralyzing terror that could hold her life hostage. If an enemy triggered Lera to freeze as she had with him, it would cost her her life. Coal couldn't let that happen, no matter what it cost either of them.

Snatching Lera's waist, Coal swung her right back to the wall. "No, you're not done," he told her, inhaling her scent of fury. Fury, *stars be thanked*, not fear. "Do it again."

14

LERA

A blaze of fury explodes through me, filling my muscles with uncontainable force. My vision narrows, my face so hot, I can feel the beads of steaming sweat. I'm done. Done with Coal and his games. I was insane to think I could come here and reason with him, get him to address his memories once and for all so I could get a good night's sleep—it sounds laughable now. I'm done being in this room, with having the terror of Zake's beating used as a plaything.

But the only way out is through him.

Bracing both my hands against the wall, I shove away from the hard surface and slam the back of my head into Coal's chin. The impact feels as distant as the sound it makes. Twisting around, I hook Coal's ankle with my leg and shove him backward onto the hard floor, angling the fall toward his broken arm.

Coal tucks as he takes the fall, shifting fluidly to absorb the impact on his good side and avoid the bed's footboard. Even with that, a grunt of pain escapes as he lands. With his hair loose for once, it falls around him in a wild blond mane, his lithe muscles contracting just enough to control every fiber of his beautifully dangerous body.

The metallic scent coming off him mixes with an intoxicating tang of violence that turns his stormy eyes into clear blazing flames. My pulse spurs into a gallop as the magic inside me wakens, strikes the mortal shackles and finds them wanting.

Heart pounding, I follow Coal down to the floor and straddle his bare chest. His heat rises through my pants, up my thighs, and straight into my sex. I feel the rise and fall of his powerful body trapped between my muscled thighs, the hot velvet of his skin under my hands. Magic flares inside me, rousing more desperately to the call of battle—just as the primal predator in me does. Thoughts narrow. Simplify. The drive to hunt, to fight, to mate filling my world.

My breaths come quick and hard, Coal's solid muscle beneath me focusing all my sensation on the here and now, our two bodies connected. Cocking my fist as far as it will go, I slam it down toward the bastard's perfectly chiseled face.

Coal takes the blow, a small trickle of blood beading where his lip catches on his teeth. His chin rises defiantly, his heart hammering so hard that I can feel it between my thighs, just as I feel his hardness pressing against my backside.

His lips pull back in a snarl, and for a second, I'm certain I see his glistening canines despite the heating amulet. I know his arm is hurting him, and I know he doesn't care. Our gazes meet, our chests heaving with mirrored breaths.

Yes, the magic inside me breathes, recognizing its mate. *Yes. Play.*

He grabs my wrist, then traps the same-side ankle and bucks his hips, rolling us over. One heartbeat, I'm straddling him, and the next, it's me on the bottom, the uneven stone pressing into my shoulder blades.

His eyes are blue flames above me, his damp chest heaving.

I arch my hips to buck Coal off, the power inside my core too great to be mine alone. As his balance wavers, he grabs the front of my tunic and yanks me up to my feet along with him, spinning the pair of us in a circle that ends abruptly when my back slams into one of the four posts of his bed.

The scent of wood polish mixes with Coal's metallic musk, which taunts me with every heave of his hard chest.

His hand still tangled in my tunic, Coal's nostrils flare as he leans down, his face close enough to share breath. And then closer still until my whole body shakes with the need for him, my sex clenching around unbearable emptiness. A small moan escapes my throat.

Coal's pupils dilate. "Lera—"

I capture his open mouth with my own, our tongues tangling

viciously. Coal lets out a low rumbling growl, and I capture the sound greedily just as he plunges his tongue deep into my mouth.

The magic inside me flares, twining with the power pulsating from Coal. As I reach for the bulge inside his pants, Coal rips my tunic right down the middle. I gasp against his mouth. Continuing down, Coal yanks the waistline of my pants until they pool at my feet. The bottom of my silk nightshirt spills between us, red and damp with my arousal.

With a feral snarl, I rake my fingernails along Coal's hot, naked shoulders.

The male kicks my legs apart in answer. Sealing his mouth over mine again, he plunges his hand ruthlessly between my slick folds. Heat races through me at once, my legs and back and soul vibrating with energy as pressure builds between my thighs. My sex throbs. I grind against his hand hungrily. Blindly. The void inside aches, howling for Coal's cock, for the last link in the chain of power connecting us. Each heartbeat when my channel tightens around nothing drives me closer to madness until I care about nothing but my need.

With our mouths still locked, I sink my canines into Coal's lip.

He sheathes his cock deep inside me with a groan, the single brutal stroke bringing me up onto my toes.

Pleasure surges along my spine, my muscles coiling as jolts of sensation explode through me. My toes curl. Gripping Coal's hair, I pull back his head as he starts thrusting without mercy, the bed creaking behind us. He hooks my backside with his good arm and holds me still, thrusting deeper and faster until our mouths break apart with frantic breaths. I grip his shoulders and ride him, his cock finding every ridge inside my blazing channel and shoving us closer to the release that our fight started.

Toward *more.*

Coal's blue eyes fill with specks of purple, his memories flooding me, along with the strange magic connecting us. With nothing to hold on to, my mind is swept into the nightmare storm of Coal's making until I'm looking through his eyes. Short, horrid images flash through me. Chains holding wrists. The tapping feet of tormentors approaching from behind. The stench of burned flesh and copper blood and the decaying scent of the qoru themselves—the Mors creatures that truly held Coal a slave for centuries.

My hands tighten on Coal's hair, my gaze holding his. His thrusts never slow, his grip on my bottom so tight, I know it will leave a bruise.

Stay with me, Coal. I open my mouth, groping for words to pull him back into the now, but someone beats me to it. A familiar female voice, echoing through the bridge between Coal and me. The magic inside me flashes and slips from my control, pulling me so deeply into Coal's soul that I watch the nightmare through his eyes. Think his thoughts, hear his blood coursing through my veins, and feel his muscles trembling in my arms and legs.

"You are not alone," says the phantom woman who held my soul together in that prison—until she disappeared, leaving me shattered. Pain explodes through me, though whether it comes from my broken bone or the woman's inevitable fading, I can't tell. It doesn't matter, I cannot stop either one. I've seen this too many times.

But this time, it's different. This time, I look right at her, spearing her chocolate eyes with my gaze. "You left. Why did you leave?"

Outside the nightmare, Lera's hands tighten in my hair, forcing my head down to meet her eyes. Achingly familiar chocolate eyes. The same woman. I inhale a lung full of lilac. "I didn't," the woman says in Lera's soul-gripping voice. "You wouldn't see me."

15

LERA

"You wouldn't see me," I shout along with Coal's phantom, only realizing how much the words hurt after they leave my mouth. How deeply I blame Coal for failing to force his way past the illusion of me that the magic's veil spun in his mind. And now, with him inside me, each thrust of his cock sending a zing of sensation right to my swelling apex, the truth of that admission pounds against my soul.

Pain bubbles inside me, along with images of Coal denying the bond between us. Coal on the training pitch, his dismissive gaze skittering over me as I step onto the sands. Coal telling me to quit. Coal ignoring me for a month. My eyes sting. "You were supposed to recognize me. You were supposed to fight harder."

Coal grips my face, his cock stilling in my channel. Blue-purple eyes filled with devastation stare into mine, a mix of confusion and guilt lining his beautiful face. Inside me, the spidering silver cord of his magic pulses to the rhythm of our hearts.

"Tell me who you are," Coal says.

The amulet around my neck goes so hot, I fear it will melt my flesh. "You have to work it out yourself," I whisper.

"Tell me how," he growls, his breath harsh in the silent bedchamber, his cock pumping into me again once, deep and hard.

"You know how," I gasp. "It's in your memories."

Grabbing Coal's wrist, I pin it to the post above my head. The wave of panic rushing through our bond makes me whimper. But Coal lets me do it. Lets me hold his wrist captive as his mind puts him back into shackles, fills his nose with the stench of blood and fear, his ears picking up the menacing footsteps approaching from behind. Tormentors that Coal thinks are just islanders holding him captive—but I know to be creatures far worse than any human.

For a heartbeat, I feel Coal balking from the unfolding darkness. Then he draws a shuddering breath, braces himself, and plunges into the torrent with predatory intent, my own mind descending with him. Coal's hips undulate, his cock filling my channel again and again as the dark cell comes into focus around us.

This time, instead of looking through Coal's eyes, I'm watching the scene from just in front of him—from the same place my real body occupies. Coal's face and the thick dank stone walls around us are beaded with moisture, the *drip drip drip* of something just out of sight both rhythmic and horrifying. Over Coal's shoulder, I can see the gray qoru come closer to Coal's back. Gray-skinned creatures of Mors, with lidless milky pink eyes and webbed hind legs. The first one stretches a round mouth of razor-sharp teeth into a horrid grin, ready to feed on Coal's pain as it's done for centuries.

Coal swallows, his muscles trembling. He can't see the qoru, but he can feel them—even if the amulet's magic keeps insisting that they are *islanders.*

I suddenly know the answer to Coal's question. He has to turn. To look at the qoru. When I open my mouth to say as much, the tattoo marks on Coal's skin, the footprint left when his body absorbed the amulet, glow a bloody red.

Coal's body is rigid now, every fiber inside him doubtlessly screaming not to look back. Never look.

"Coal," I call.

His glazed gaze shifts to me, his eyes filling with longing. Yet I know it's not the real Lera he sees when he looks at me, but the woman from his magic-spun dreams.

I call his name again.

Behind Coal, the milky-eyed qoru jerks its attention away from Coal, its ire suddenly aimed at me. Terror pours into my blood, and I scream despite myself.

Coal roars, twisting against his own fear, as if his instinct to protect me over himself exists even in his nightmares. His breath stills the moment he sees the qoru, then returns with a vengeance.

"Don't. Touch. My mate." Coal tries to put himself between the qoru and me, yanking so hard on his chains that his arm breaks. He seems to care little about the arm, though. Care little about the pain or fear or anything—except me.

In the bedroom, the bedpost behind me cracks in two, a blaze of phantom pain shooting through Coal's fractured bone as we spin to land on the bed. The mattress cradles my back, Coal's blue-purple eyes fixed on mine. Our chests heave.

Coal's gaze breaks away from mine and roves over me feverishly. My hair, face, breasts, shoulders, his eyes take me in thirstily, his pupils dilated with desperate wonder.

"Leralynn," he says hoarsely.

"Coal?" I whisper, though I can barely breathe. Can barely fight against the rising hope.

He grips my face with his good hand. "Leralynn," he repeats, his blue eyes glittering with specks of purple. With recognition. "Mortal."

With gasping breaths, Coal pulls me until my backside is at the edge of the bed. As the tension-charged air cools my exposed sex and backside, he hoists my legs onto his shoulders and buries himself inside me so swiftly that I have to muffle a scream with my arm.

My swollen, sensitive channel throbs, stretching to accommodate the male's great size and power. I bite back moan after moan as Coal—my Coal—thrusts harder still, the thick head of his cock hammering against a spot deep inside me, his motions driving me up the bed. He follows on his knees and pounds into me until the bed shudders against the wall, the slap of sweaty skin against my damp backside echoing through the room.

His face hides nothing from me, need and love and grief crossing it in lightning-quick succession. I reach up and pull him toward me until his bound arm brushes my breasts, our foreheads pressed together. His breath hitches, but he never lets me separate from him. Never backs away just because holding me hurts him.

"I didn't know who you were, Lera," Coal rasps, the hurt carried on his words' wings so intense that it chokes me. "But I fought for you long after I stopped fighting for myself."

Gasping for air, I inhale his metallic musk, not yet ready to answer, craving something, anything, to drown out the tearing in my soul.

As if sensing my need, Coal's callused fingers invade my slick folds, tracing my inflamed bud. With the fullness and stretching from his cock already holding my every nerve hostage, the extra sensation shoots through my body so fiercely that gripping the sheet with my hands is all I can do to keep from screaming.

That's when Coal brushes his thumb right over my apex.

My body spasms around him, my focus narrowing to nothing but the eruption of searing, agonizing pleasure exploding from my sex. The rising wave of sensation just begins to calm when Coal's cock gives its own final spasm, spilling his warmth into me. My channel clenches all over again, milking the emptying cock inside it for every drop. Coal buries his face in my neck and whispers my name, nipping my neck as my second release shudders through me. Then his mouth is on mine, and nothing exists but our lips and breath and racing hearts.

16

LERA

I tremble against Coal's bare chest, tracing each ridge of his abdomen with my fingers, the arm he has wrapped around me an iron band of reassurance. The amulet's tattoo-like runes on Coal's skin are a pale version of themselves, and I can almost swear I feel the conquered magic grumbling in disapproval.

My own amulet lies on the floor amidst the wreckage of the room. With the enhanced strength of magic that surged when we mated, Coal's native healing gifts went to work on his broken arm, searing the shards together enough to let him remove the sling despite still wincing at the movements.

My mind is still stunned, disbelieving, not quite knowing where to start. I've been on the outside of my males' lives for so many weeks now that I've forgotten how to be a bonded quint mate.

Trust still hasn't settled into my bones—trust that this is real. That it will last.

Coal squeezes me tighter as if reading my thoughts, leaning down to search my gaze with piercing blue eyes before taking a deep kiss that plunders my mouth. Part reassurance, part fae's primal possession.

"You don't like hugging," I remind him stupidly, my mind and soul still spinning wildly to process what's happened to bring us to this moment.

Coal flashes his canines. "I'm not hugging you, mortal. I'm ensuring you don't race off to save the world before I get my full fill of your presence."

"What do you remember exactly?" I whisper.

"I remember a reckless mortal being too brave for her own good." Coal's callused thumb traces the pointed top of my ear, which is nearly as sensitive as my sex. "Everything that I did and knew in my veiled human form is just as clear in my memory as what came before it, though I'm now aware that parts of it are fiction. When I think of my role as instructor here, I feel the amulet's footprint around my neck grow warm and insist that I believe its tale."

"That's what I feel like when I wear the amulet." I burrow myself deeper into his hard chest, the magnitude of the night's consequences falling onto my shoulders like drops of rain that quickly morph to a downpour. Did Coal's conquering of his amulet's magic break the veil? Or will the humans continue to see him as one of them? Will the effects last? Without the mental connection that Coal and I share, will the other males ever come back? What should I—

"Stop it, mortal." Leaving off caressing my ear, Coal grabs it instead, pulling my head back to find my eyes. "Whatever you are thinking, you no longer get to think it alone. Understand?"

Heat fills my blood, though I'm not sure whether I want to kiss the bastard or kick him. I settle for sticking my tongue out at him.

Coal snorts, then glances out the window. "First things first, you can't stay here in the instructors' wing and I can't go out there until we know whether my veil is still effective on humans. I presume that the walking disaster you call Arisha is in your rooms?"

I nodded, chewing my lip. "You want me to try to bring her here?" The thought of separating from Coal just when I've gotten him back is ridiculously difficult, but the male is right. I can't stay in his bed—or what's left of it with the post broken—forever. "Now that I know where your room is, I think we can use the window and avoid the corridors."

"Good stars, no," he mutters. "I don't trust that girl to walk across clean raked sand in broad daylight without tripping over her own feet, much less prance to the instructors' wing in the middle of the night. Nor can we use the Gloom… I can feel the curtain between the Light and Gloom being thinner than it should be, but it's still there."

I frown, somewhat stunned. All these weeks of trying to figure out what's happening with the wards, where their weakness is originating from and what's causing it, and Coal can *feel* what's happening with his body. Like a bloody divining rod. "I didn't notice that," I say dumbly.

"That's because you are about as good at stepping into the Gloom as Arisha is at negotiating stairs," says Coal with no hint of exaggeration. *Yes.* The bloody bastard is certainly himself again. He rubs his face, then studies me critically, his beautiful, chiseled face heartbreakingly precious even when it's annoyed. "Find one of my shirts to call a dress, and let's move. You follow my steps exactly."

Coal proves to be right on both counts. Not only does he successfully guide us through campus without getting caught, but the moment we enter my bedchamber through the open window, Arisha starts walking toward us and trips, falling face-first to the floor. As soon as he's settled my friend into her chair with a rag to catch the blood seeping from the nose she hit, Coal recaptures me against his solid body, his large hand splayed possessively along my ribs.

"Well?" Coal asks Arisha. "What do you see?"

"I see an instructor pawing my friend," she tells him, before turning to me with a protective slant to her freckled face. "Do we approve of him doing that?"

"We very much do. Especially since he remembers who he is now."

"Interesting. He still looks human to me." Arisha shrugs, characteristically unimpressed, and glares at Coal, her frizzled hair and bleeding nose somewhat diminishing the intended scolding look. "This means you are finally going to start being nice to her?"

Coal runs a warm hand over my hair, brushing it behind my ears and off my neck so slowly and steadily that I have to fight to keep my eyes from fluttering closed. I know he needs the reassurance of physical contact just as much as I do. "Of course not. If you think I'm a bastard under the veil's magic, you won't likely enjoy getting to know the real me." Coal looks down at me. "Morning practice continues, mortal. We'll have to keep our disguises until we accomplish what we came here for. But I'm a little worried about that." His face changes. "You've done well keeping everything together, Leralynn—both on the mission front and in keeping our thick heads alive. And you've done it all on your own." Coal grins when Arisha clears her throat loudly. "*Mostly* on your own. Do you have it in you to keep going?"

"Yes," I say. "Of course."

"How, specifically?" Arisha says over me.

Turning me around to face him, Coal lays his callused palm along my cheek, his blue eyes sparking as they scan mine. "I've a few ideas."

17

OWALIN

"You realize it doesn't actually matter who wins the little Prowess Trials game, right?" Owalin asked, walking up to where Han was working up training schedules with the meticulousness of a general attending battle plans.

"Who wins the Trials competition matters to me." Han looked up long enough to accept a stein of ale from one of the human serving girls that Zake had sent their way to make the Night Guard's mountain range base camp more comfortable, then returned to his scribbling.

Settling in the chair opposite him, Owalin relieved the girl of the second stein and sent her on her way with a smack on her backside. He regretted it a moment later—the handprint would likely linger for days on the too-fragile thing, making the serving staff sullen—and it was difficult getting a steady stream of replacements.

It would have been a great deal more pleasant if the native weakness in the wards had started somewhere more hospitable, but what the mountain caves lacked in luxury, they made up for in security. Most of Owalin's guard could step in and out of the Gloom easily here—and, depending on the moon's position, in patches of the surrounding forest as well.

Taking a swig of ale, Owalin shook his head and returned his attention to Han. All the Night Guard contingent that had come to the mortal lands with Owalin were shifters, but of all the wolves and birds and other common creatures, the lithe male sitting before him was the only one who shifted into a human. Which had made him terribly useful over the decades.

And more than a little eccentric.

"All right, Han. I give up." Owalin put down his mug. "The Prowess Trials are just a lure for bigger fish. I agree that you were brilliant to foresee such an opportunity years ago and applaud your placement in the Prowess circuit in general and now the Academy in particular. But…at this point, exactly why does it matter how your little rats actually perform?"

"Call it nostalgia," Han said, finally looking up, his eerily intense blue-gray eyes giving Owalin the shivers. "I used to race horses."

"And now you race humans."

"I like sport. You might enjoy trying a hand at it yourself once this is all said and done. It has a different flavor from the usual beasts. But it's no less an art."

"I'll take your word for it."

Han snorted, then pulled himself together, probably remembering the time. Being out too long was not good for an Academy instructor. "I've not found any fae on the grounds, though several of the mortals are feistier than I've marked in the past."

"Or more of your ilk?"

Han frowned. "Possible, I suppose, though I'm unaware of other human shifters in Lunos. I don't like it."

Neither did Owalin, but at day's end, he had near a hundred warriors. Even if a fae or two stepped where they didn't belong, it would make little difference to his plans. Shaking his head, Owalin waved a hand at Han's human features. "Are you going to stay that way all night?"

"I am," Han said, putting down his stein. "Shifting isn't the instinct I need my body to reach for too easily just now. I imagine your true intention is to show off Krum's latest efforts in filing down the wards? I will take your word that he's making progress and that I'll find shifting easier when the time comes."

"Am I that predictable?" Owalin smiled, then let the mirth drop from his eyes. "It won't be just shifting you will find easier, Han. When the time comes, I recommend you have full control of your civilized faculties lest the magic sweeps you up right along with your pets."

~

FINISH the adventure with GREAT FALLS PROTECTOR, Power of Five Book 7. If you are reading this in ebook format, continue on for a FREE preview.

~

ALSO BY ALEX LIDELL

New Adult Fantasy Romance

POWER OF FIVE (Reverse Harem Fantasy)

POWER OF FIVE (Audiobook available)

MISTAKE OF MAGIC (Audiobook available)

TRIAL OF THREE (Audiobook available)

LERA OF LUNOS (Audiobook available)

GREAT FALLS CADET (Audiobook available)

GREAT FALLS ROGUE

GREAT FALLS PROTECTOR

IMMORTALS OF TALONSWOOD (Reverse Harem Paranormal Romance)

LAST CHANCE ACADEMY

Young Adult Fantasy Novels

TIDES

FIRST COMMAND (Audiobook available)

AIR AND ASH (Audiobook available)

WAR AND WIND (Audiobook available)

SEA AND SAND (Audiobook available)

SCOUT

TRACING SHADOWS (Audiobook available)

UNRAVELING DARKNESS (Audiobook available)

TILDOR

THE CADET OF TILDOR

~

SIGN UP FOR NEW RELEASE NOTIFICATIONS at https://links.alexlidell.com/News

ABOUT THE AUTHOR

Alex Lidell is an Amazon KU All Star Top 50 Author Awards winner (July, 2018). Her debut novel, THE CADET OF TILDOR (Penguin, 2013) was an Amazon Breakout Novel Awards finalist. Her Reverse Harem romances, POWER OF FIVE and MISTAKE OF MAGIC, both received Amazon KU Top 100 awards for individual titles.

Alex is an avid horseback rider, a (bad) hockey player, and an ice-cream addict. Born in Russia, Alex learned English in elementary school, where a thoughtful librarian placed a copy of Tamora Pierce's ALANNA in Alex's hands. In addition to becoming the first English book Alex read for fun, ALANNA started Alex's life long love for fantasy books. Alex lives in Washington, DC.

Join Alex's newsletter for news, special offers and sneak peeks: https://links.alexlidell.com/News

Find out more on Alex's website: www.alexlidell.com

SIGN UP FOR NEWS AND RELEASE NOTIFICATIONS

Connect with Alex!
www.alexlidell.com
alex@alexlidell.com

www.ingramcontent.com/pod-product-compliance
Lightning Source LLC
Chambersburg PA
CBHW030356310726
48979CB00001B/333

* 9 7 8 1 9 4 9 3 4 7 1 1 1 *